STORM TIDE

Withdrawn

MEL KEEGAN

STORM TIDE

THE GAY MEN'S PRESS

First published 1996 by GMP Publishers Ltd,
P O Box 247, Swaffham, Norfolk PE37 8PA, England

World Copyright © 1996 Mel Keegan

British Library Cataloguing in Publication Data

Keegan, Mel
Storm tide
1.Australian fiction — 20th century
I.Title
823[F]

ISBN 0 85449 227 5

Distributed in Europe by Central Books,
99 Wallis Rd, London E9 5LN

Distributed in North America by InBook/LPC Group,
1436 West Randolph Street, Chicago, IL 60607

Distributed in Australia by Bulldog Books,
P O Box 300, Beaconsfield, NSW 2014

Printed and bound in the EU by The Cromwell Press,
Melksham, Wilts, England

Acknowledgements

I owe a deep debt of gratitude to several people, whom I would like to thank here. First, to my good friend, librarian Lane E. Ingram, whose ideas and shrewd observations put the first draft of this story on track – very different from the novel it became, but full of promise. Lane also played devil's advocate as the plot developed, and I'm grateful. Lane, I owe you. Also, I must convey my most sincere thanks to Bill Charles, now-retired seaman, who told me about old merchant marine ships, their crews and routines, and gave me access to such first-hand sea stories that I feel I know these old break-bulk freighters myself. In fact, I never set foot on one, but I checked and re-checked the details with Bill, who was the soul of patience. Any errors I have made with regard to these old ships are all my own. Thanks, 'Skipper', I owe you one, also. Lastly, thanks to Beth and Joyce in Texas, who read the last draft specifically to check for any incongruities in 'Americanisms' directly relating to the character of Sean. They helped me get it right, and once again, I'm grateful.

One

IN THE last forty minutes the wind had begun to rise sharply and rain slashed the grey horizon. Since midnight the radio had been broadcasting warnings of the incoming storm, and every coastal town down the entire length of the Gulf Saint Vincent was making ready to meet the violent weather. High winds, thunder and torrential rain were forecast. The lowlands would flood, property damage would be immense, lives would be lost. What boat owner in his right mind would be five miles offshore, staring into the teeth of the rising storm?

Rob Markham hit the ignition a third time and swore as the twin Evinrude 400s coughed, stuttered, and stalled out. The wind whipped the surface off the waves and flung an icy, salt spray into his face as he hoisted himself out of the red vinyl seat. His blue jeans and grey jersey were already soaked and his skin prickled in the mid-August chill.

The *Fancy Dancer* had begun to toss like a cork, and Rob had just started to worry. In the well of the boat behind him, Sean Brodie had stowed the rods, bait and the box holding their catch. The bream, mullet and trevally had been biting quite well. According to local lore, the fishing was always outstanding in the last hours before a storm hit. The trick was to get one's boat and oneself back home before the wind and white water began to ravage the coast.

Sean turned his back on the wind and shrugged into his electric blue anorak. The gusts ruffled his short cropped dark hair. He braced his denim-clad legs against the pitch of the deck as he got to his feet in the stern, and gestured at the outboards.

"What's wrong this time?" That Californian accent cut across the rising wind like a knife.

"I wish I knew." Rob made his way aft, struggling for balance as the boat heaved. She was an eighteen-foot pleasure craft with a brilliant yellow fibreglass hull, powerful motors — and a completely open cockpit. Not exactly the kind of boat in which one would choose to ride out a storm. Rob glanced over his shoulder at the south-west sky. "You can always count on the bloody weather to louse things up!"

"Could be we got a couple of damp plugs," Sean suggested as he zipped the anorak.

"How would I ever have thought of that?" Rob demanded fatuously. He was already unlatching the lid of the toolbox, and lobbed an aerosol can of dewatering fluid into Sean's waiting hands. "Give me a hand here."

They crushed in together between the outboards, warm body against warm body. The press of Sean against him brought the smile back to Rob's face. It was too difficult to hold onto his annoyance when Sean was so close — which was the whole reason they had taken this vacation.

For months they had been drifting apart. They were beginning to lose one another, and if they wanted to save a relationship that had been so good, it was time to invest some hard work in it.

In the last six months a dozen factors had conspired to drive them apart. Sean was working late, sometimes entire nights, if his project was on a deadline. In the previous year, Rob had been moving from job to job, finding it impossible to settle, but not until he secured permanent employment did the trouble begin at home. He had a wealth of experience on the shop floor, and motorbikes were his lifetime fascination. But Rob never made friends easily, and working with hostile colleagues always inspired him to seek another job; and then another. After years of hunting, he literally stumbled into employment with good working conditions and congenial company... and soon wished he had passed by. Work and travelling forcibly separated him from Sean. When they could find time to be together at last they were too often tired, preoccupied.

And then, there was Peter. Rob had not even known about the young tennis player until the affair was history, and Sean confessed that he had been seduced. He swore the flirtation had never been emotionally profound. It was just a means to release the tension that had begun to build up explosively.

Still, Rob was deeply disturbed. It was the first time he had consciously realised he could lose Sean. He could wake up one morning and find himself alone. After thirty years of being more or less alone, he had no wish to return to those days of deprivation. He had always believed that finding Sean was the best moment of his life. Losing him again would be the worst. And if it happened, Rob would have no one to blame but himself.

The Peter Kramer affair had shocked Sean too. Rob never demanded the facts about his relationship with the blond, petite and impishly alluring Peter, but a pale-faced Sean haltingly volunteered his confession. With Rob away one time too often, he had been alone and miserable, and he went to the gym, thinking he could sweat the bleak mood out of himself with an hour's hard physical effort. Peter was using the weights. His body was velvet smooth, gleaming with a healthy sweat; his long hair was roped back in a damp pony tail while he worked at the weights. He had seen Sean the instant he walked into the gym. Sean noticed him moments later. He stripped to his shorts and began to punish his muscles, but his eyes were on Peter. Two hours later they were in bed, and the scene was repeated several times a week for the next month.

When Sean could bear the deception no longer, the confession rushed out of him as if he was determined to force either a confrontation or a resolution. Pain assaulted Rob, but he forced himself to listen, and to understand. Sean had been in Australia for only a few months when they met. Most of his friends and all his old lovers were at home — he would always think of Santa Monica as home. He was in Australia to do a job, on a two-year working visa.

What happened when his visa expired was largely up to Rob. He could be on the next flight back to the US. Or he could take the boss's offer of an extended contract, apply for permanent resident status, and stay in Australia. Adelaide was not exactly a Mecca for either tourists or gays, but it had clean air and good beaches. Aids was still almost unknown, the state of South Australia boasted a Mediterranean climate... and good company, Rob thought. No. *Great* company.

The night following Sean's confession was stormy, but by morning had made their peace. Peter Kramer was twenty-two, ten years Sean's junior, and he was racing from bed to bed with the reckless delight of youth. Just a year ago, Sean had been in LA, where the kid's careless, promiscuous antics would have raised more than a few eyebrows. Here, in this untroubled state, literally on the edge of the world — the embarkation point for Antarctica — Peter was in surprisingly little danger. Aids was something that happened to other people, or was occasionally mentioned on television. Many moving obituaries were published in *The Sydney Star-Observer*, but Sydney seemed a world away. Adelaide was like a cocoon, as if it belonged in another decade. Someone once called it a graveyard with lights.

Years later, the quip was that even the lights had been switched off. Sean regarded Adelaide as a country town. It had many of the advantages of a city, and few of the disadvantages: no real pollution, and no omnipresent, haunting shadow of Aids. But the gay community was quiet and quite small. It could be difficult for a young man to find his own kind of companionship.

Rob had begun to think he would spend his whole life alone if he did not get himself into the hub and heart of Australia's gay life. Sydney and Melbourne beckoned like beacons on a stormy night, and he was on the point of quitting his job, packing and leaving when, like a bolt out of the blue, Sean arrived.

The handsome, dark-haired and blue-eyed stranger was an engineer on contract to Aurora Petroleum. When he saw the job advertised in a Los Angeles paper, Sean could not even have found the city of Adelaide on a map. Three months later, he lived in a small apartment block overlooking the South Parklands, worked in an executive suite ten storeys above Grenfell Street, and spent Friday and Saturday night trawling Hindley Street, searching for *someone*.

That winter, Sean was thirty-one. *Anyone* would not do. The novelty had worn off Peter Kramer's brand of blissful promiscuity. Sean Brodie wanted to know that he would wake up to the same smile, the same kiss, that he had gone to bed with. He was looking for someone about his own age, well built but not enslaved by the gym, someone who laughed easily, dressed casually, liked the same kind of food and music, so there would be a patch of common ground to share.

Propping up the bar in the noisy, smoky, overcrowded pub that cold June winter's night was a man two years Sean's junior. He was just a few inches shorter, with deeply wavy hair the colour of a ripe chestnut, which he wore long on his collar. He dressed in crisp blue denim, a designer tee-shirt, tan leather jacket and Reeboks. Robert Markham was gazing into his Fosters as if he could read the future in the depths of the almost empty schooner glass. He was totally ignoring the antics of the boys around him. Most of them were of the pimple-chinned matriculation-year brigade, barely old enough to be getting plastered on the low end of Hindley Street at half past ten on a Friday night. Some still wore their school trousers. Sean ignored them as resolutely as Rob disregarded them. They might not have been there at all. Sheena Easton launched into something vivacious, filling the bar with well-intended noise. A dozen boys began to dance, but Sean raised his voice to cut over the din of overloaded speakers, and without a moment's hesitation, he deliberately propositioned Rob.

For eight months, right through summer, it was superb. The 'graveyard with lights' had at last come alive for Rob, and Sean was settled in the job that had begun to bore him. Rob moved into the apartment by the parklands, which suited Sean fine. Rob was a naturally early riser — Sean was not — so breakfast was always on the table when the six-thirty alarm rang.

And then, after months in a dole queue, Rob moved cautiously into a new job at the Honda agency on Pirie Street. The money was good and the company was pleasant. But the hours clashed badly with Sean's, and the scene was set for disaster. The personal drift began slowly, insidiously.

World-weary veterans swore it happened to every couple, gay and straight alike. Marriages steered onto the rocks. Relationships ended on the scrap heap. Peter Kramer happened along at the worst, or best, possible moment. Rob could never recall the boy without a shiver, yet if anyone was responsible for single-handedly patching up a relationship that was starting to split wide open, it was that young, irresistible damned kid.

It was June again, the night when Sean had laid his cards out in plain sight, made his apologies and mutely pleaded to be understood. They were deep into winter. The wind was cold as ice on the street and the rain had been lashing without a break for a week. Sean was miserable, and so was Rob. Winter blues made their mood even worse. But that night was a second beginning. They were better in bed than they had been since summer, and Sean's relief at having the truth in the open made him putty in Rob's eager hands.

That night was almost a return to their first exhilarating weeks together, and they both rose willingly to the bait. They talked almost through till dawn. The following morning, smudged and hungover, they both called in sick at work, and spent the whole day at the apartment, until nothing remained unsaid. They must spend more time together before they became strangers who occasionally managed to find their way into the same bed, almost coincidentally. They must regain the closeness they had treasured, before it was too late.

That day was still sharp and painful in Rob's memory. This unseasonal vacation — two weeks almost completely alone, with the opportunity to share a friend's holiday shack on the coast between Goolwa and Victor Harbour — had sounded like sheer heaven. Not even the threat of stormy weather was enough to dampen their spirits. They would make it. Rob clung determinedly to that belief.

The shack was a timber-frame holiday home, standing above the tidal zone, up the coast from the tourist destination of Victor Harbour. It had not been opened since summer. The air inside was stale and the phone turned off, but the power was on, the building was sound and dry. And the bed was enormous.

The *Fancy Dancer* was one of the three things of any real value Rob owned. He ran a battered Toyota Landcruiser, and garaged at home, jealously guarded, was his bike, the big 1100RC Honda. Most of the previous week, the boat had been tied up at the water's edge, while he and Sean divided their time between the single-minded pursuit of sensual pleasure and the more innocent diversion of fishing. Sean had always liked fishing, since the boyhood afternoons shared with his uncle, as far from the smoke and noise of Santa Monica as they could drive for a weekend.

For Rob, angling was an exquisitely painful penance. He never caught a thing, but the quiet and solitude compelled him to grapple with the problems which were tangling his life into a Gordian knot.

For a week, he and Sean had shared the sea, the shack and each other, and Rob was content. They were closer now than they had ever been, closer than most families could claim. The feelings Rob nursed for Sean was strong and enduring, a foundation on which they would build. The most ironic aspect of this interlude was that it was all the handiwork of a blond, leggy, carefree little tennis player. Peter had a lot to answer for, not all of it bad.

As the wind began to lash in earnest, the *Fancy Dancer* pitched and yawed underfoot and the deck was slick, treacherous. Still, a sudden boyish grin stripped years from Sean's face. His blue eyes crinkled at the corners. Drops of water clung to his short cropped hair, though it was not raining yet. He slipped his arm tight around Rob's waist as they pressed together between the obstinate outboards.

"Not wishing you'd stayed home, are you? It was you who insisted we come out this morning!"

"Ask me again in about an hour," Rob said drily. "When I'm up to my shoulders in a tub of scalding water, with a double scotch in one hand... and you in the other."

Sean licked his lips salaciously. "I'll take that as an invitation." He swiped the cap off the dewatering fluid and gave Rob enough space to lift the big, scarlet head covers off the Evinrudes.

The interiors of both were wet, and Rob whistled. An hour before, the *Dancer* had caught a wave broadside. A solid wall of water slapped the outboards hard, and they were not new. The casings would be waterproof in most conditions, but they were well worn. Immersion proof, they were not.

The fine oil misted everything, and then Rob lunged back to the control panel and hit the starter. The battery sounded sick, but this time the Evinrudes coughed, spluttered and settled into a steady, ear-splitting V8 growl. Sean gave an exuberant whoop and slapped the covers back into place.

"For my next trick," Rob said brashly as he bowled the DWF aerosol back into the tool kit and slammed the lid, "I shall attempt to saw my assistant in half while whistling excerpts from *The Valkyrie.*"

The levity made Sean chuckle. He slid in under the wheel, revved the motors and turned on the radio. A dense sheet of static white noise blanketed the local commercial station. "Damn, this interference is getting thick."

"Who the hell needs a weather report?" Rob demanded as he settled in the seat beside Sean. "You can *see* that bitch of a storm."

The south-western sky was dark as a funeral shroud now, and lightning had begun to flicker. Far away, thunder pealed like a drum roll over enormous loudspeakers. The weathermen were describing a vast low-pressure cell which had built up over the Southern Ocean. Meteorology was a mystery to Rob. He only needed to know that he was cold, wet, and he had seen the first licks of lightning.

The *Fancy Dancer* came around smartly. The coastline was a grey-green smudge, low down in the east, a craggy vista of hills, valleys and creeks running down to the boulder-strewn, eucalypt-forested edge of the sea. The radio cleared, but the station was just repeating the same broad spectrum warnings as had been issued since midnight.

The storm had already ravaged the south-west of the state. The tuna-fishing town of Port Lincoln had suffered major damage, and to make matters worse, the coming evening threatened the highest tide of the decade. When that king tide came up the creeks after a day of torrential rains, the valleys and lowland paddocks would be six feet under.

Most small boats would be tied up in port, while larger vessels would have moved out beyond the hundred fathom line, where they would turn their bows to the gale and set sea anchors. The last thing Rob had expected to see as the *Dancer* came around toward the headland where their shack stood, was another boat sharing this stretch of water.

It was a rich man's dream toy, an ocean-going cabin cruiser, with acres of plate glass and chromium, a dove-grey hull that was almost invisible against the sea from a distance. Her radio masts whipped overhead in the wind, and across the transom was her name, in fancy lettering. She was the *Minuette.*

A moment after Rob spotted her, Sean saw her too. He whistled through his teeth. "Will you just take a look at that."

"I am," Rob said drily. "Avariciously."

"They're not manoeuvring." Sean nodded at the stern, which showed no wake of prop froth. He shut back the *Dancer's* throttles and the powerboat cruised down. He angled a glance at Rob. "They may be in trouble."

"Are you kidding? That thing must be worth five million bucks!"

"And the storm that's coming in will still chop her to driftwood," Sean added. He switched on the shortwave and lifted the mic. "*Fancy Dancer* to *Minuette*, are you receiving?"

He repeated the call four times but the radio remained dead. Rob leaned over and fiddled with the tuner. "We could be blanketed with interference," he muttered under the whine of the rising wind. Thunder rumbled, uncomfortably closer at hand, and he shivered. "Try them again."

"*Fancy Dancer* to *Minuette*," Sean called, and then dropped the mic in disgust. "This is useless. Why sit here calling when they're only two hundred yards away? Their shortwave could be on the fritz."

It was possible. Wealthy owners or no, they could be in real trouble, and one of the laws of the open water was that any vessel would stand by another in a situation like this. Still, some animal nerve made Rob's hackles rise, though he could not have said why.

He straightened in his seat and held onto the surround of the low windshield as Sean put the wheel over and opened the throttles a little. The outboards had just begun to gargle when they saw the flash of orange-yellow flame, a puff of silver-grey smoke, from a window in the side of the cruiser.

"Damn, they *are* in trouble. The buggers are on fire!" Sean opened the throttles full, closing the distance between them in a matter of seconds.

The chop was already three feet high, and Rob was seriously considering the wisdom of putting on a life jacket. The sea was nearer grey than green or blue as he struggled aft. He threw a line over the transom, onto the deck of the cruiser, and perched on the side while Sean brought the powerboat in close enough for him to hop over. She tied on to a chrome steel cleat, bobbing wildly, and Rob extended his hand to help Sean up onto the polished redwood deck.

No passenger or crewman was in evidence. The wind whipped Sean's hair into his face. He raked it back and cupped a hand to his mouth. "Hello! Is anyone there?"

The boat seemed deserted. The engines were shut down, the deck was unattended, and they saw no figures in the glassed-in wheelhouse. Sean nudged Rob's arm and pointed at a doorway to the right side of the ladder which climbed to the flying bridge. Inside were steps leading down a few feet into the compartment.

"You reckon we're trespassing?" Rob murmured, one hand on Sean's arm to hold him back as he made to move inside.

"Standing by a vessel in distress can hardly be called trespassing," Sean argued. "We both saw the smoke. You want to go back to the *Dancer* and try the shortwave? With this storm coming in, we'll be lucky to raise anybody."

He was right, Rob admitted, and bit back his words of caution as Sean stepped through into a plushly appointed lounge. The carpets were wine red, the fittings were all polished pine and brass, highlighted by framed art prints of famous yachts and China Sea clippers. Behind glass was an enviable collection of silver trophies. But the air reeked of burning plastic, and there was no time or breath to waste on cynical comments about the privileges of rank.

Rob coughed a little on the chemical stink. "Smells like it's this way. The galley, maybe," he guessed. Sean was a pace ahead of him when he saw the bright red cylinder of a CO_2 extinguisher in a bracket by the door. He plucked it out of the clasps, checked it and hurried after Sean, who had moved through one of two inner doorways into the next compartment.

There, the smell of burning was almost suffocating, and they saw the first wisps of smoke. Rob's heart beat a tattoo at his ribs. "Can you see what's burning? Where's the fire?"

Sean was trained in emergency procedures. His work sometimes took him aboard oil rigs, as far afield as the Bass Strait, where safety regulations were stringent and even day visitors were given rudimentary instruction. Rob would trust his judgement here without hesitation.

But Sean was not listening to him. He was frozen just inside the doorway, his broad shoulders blocking Rob's line of sight. Although they both knew they had a duty to assist in an incident at sea, Sean took a step back, as if he was now intent only on getting off this boat, the fastest way he could find.

"Sean?" Some raw instinct warned Rob to keep his voice down. "Sean, what's the matter? I don't see the fire." Sean stepped back, almost colliding with him, and as Rob caught him by the arms he felt the sudden tension in the larger, stronger frame.

Like a cat on hot bricks, Sean moved aside a little, allowing Rob to glimpse into the compartment, and a pulse began to beat in Rob's temple.

"Is that what I think it is?" Rob swallowed on a throat grown suddenly hoarse. "Oh, Christ."

On the long, low table between the plush furniture were a large number of plastic packets, each filled with white powder, and tightly taped. Beside them was a laptop computer with a blue-green LCD screen displaying columns of figures. On the couch beside the table lay a wooden crate, painted some indeterminate shade of khaki. The top was off, and Rob glimpsed the gunmetal shapes within. Other weapons were stacked around it. He saw the unmistakable shapes of M-16s, a Fabrique National assault rifle, and something that might have been an AK-47. Russian hardware.

"What the hell have we blundered into?" Sean whispered.

For a moment they stood rooted to the spot, feeling the roll and yaw of the deck, nostrils filled with the toxic stench of burning plastic, and then Rob's fingers closed like talons on Sean's arm.

"Get out, while we've got the chance," he said soundlessly. "They may be on fire, but they can work this out by themselves."

He turned, keeping a grip on Sean's sleeve to physically drag him along, but out of the corner of his eye he caught a twitch of movement in the compartment behind them, and his chest squeezed.

The man was in his late fifties or early sixties, with heavy jowls, a gleaming bald head, and eyes nested in deep creases. His skin was the colour of walnut. He was not tall, but thickset, dressed in white slacks and a pale blue shirt stretched tight over his large belly. And protruding from his paw-like right hand, Rob saw the forbidding, black steel snout of a pistol.

Dry mouthed, he tightened his grip on the extinguisher and

cleared his throat. "We, uh, we called on the radio, you weren't answering. We saw a small explosion — you were on fire. We came to help you."

The pistol did not waver by an inch. Beside Rob, Sean was like a statue. The man before them was immobile as a block of granite, but he raised a bull-like voice. "Lew! Lew, get in here!"

Rob's palms were sweating on the extinguisher. He tore his eyes off the muzzle of the gun and glanced at Sean's profile. Sean licked his lips, a tiny nervous expression which only Rob would notice.

"We only came to see if you needed help," he said reasonably. The Californian accent that had always fascinated and charmed Rob thickened under stress. "It's none of our business what you do on this boat." He took a half step back, toward the exit. "We'll just get out of your way, so you can go on doing it."

The gun rose a hand's span and Sean froze again. The older man pursed his lips critically. "There's times," he said in harsh, clipped Sydney strine, "when being a good Samaritan can get you into a deep pile of shit, boy. Lew! I said get yourself in here!"

"Hold your horses, Meredith." The voice was deep, with English vowels, smooth as damp velvet against the Australian and American.

Its owner stepped into the room, and Rob was not surprised by what he saw. The man was in his mid-thirties, tall and sparely built, dressed with European flair, as if he had just stepped out of the grandstand at the track in Monaco. He was too blond for the colour to be natural — his brows were shades darker, and arched in surprise as he saw his unexpected, unwelcome guests. His expression swiftly composed itself, and he touched a discreet intercom on the door by the wall.

"Parker, we have a pair of intruders. See to them."

"See to — ?" Sean echoed. He took a rasping breath. "For the love of God, man, we only came aboard because we saw an explosion. We were trying to help!"

"Very kind of you." The peroxide blond head tilted toward Meredith. "How much have they seen?"

"They were in there." Meredith indicated the second compartment with a tiny gesture of the gun. "I reckon they saw the lot."

"We didn't see anything," Rob began quickly. "In fact, I don't even know what you're talking about. If we're trespassing, we're sorry. Why don't you just toss us off the boat, and we'll vanish?"

The Englishman smiled, an infuriatingly seductive expression. "You think I'm a complete fool?"

Sean straightened his shoulders. "I don't think you're any kind of a fool, Mr Lewis, but — "

His use of the name wiped the smile of the Lewis's face. "You know me? Damn it, you know my name?"

In answer, Sean pointed at the silver trophy in the glass case in the corner of the room. "Your name is on it. Geoffrey Lewis. The Admiral's Cup, 1988. I can read."

Lewis relaxed a little. "You're very observant. Which only cautions me not to underestimate you. Ah, Parker. Find somewhere to put these two would-be angels of mercy while we decide what's to be done about them. Make sure they're somewhere where they can't cause trouble... and take that extinguisher from him. They make quite a handy weapon."

As he spoke, a tall, burly man in blue jeans and a scarlet tee-shirt stepped up behind him. Over the tee-shirt was the leather harness of a shoulder holster, but the weapon was already in his hand. An automatic levelled on Rob and Sean, and Rob groaned silently as he set the extinguisher down on the nearest chair.

It was odd, how shock took a few moments to fully impact. His legs did not begin to tremble until he and Sean were being moved deeper into the *Minuette,* but by the time he found himself in the tiny, fire-blackened and still reekingly toxic galley, he was sure he could hear the rhythmic knocking of his knees. Parker was a stone-faced character, all jaw and muscles. He offered no single word as he shoved Sean into the galley after Rob, and slammed the door on them.

It was dim, but there was enough light to see that the fire had stripped the paint off every surface. The source seemed to be the stove in the corner, and a blackened propane tank told the whole story. The air was noxious, the deck was heaving, and abruptly Rob felt queasy. He and Sean stood in a lake of greasy fire retardant, in the middle of the cramped space.

"Well," Sean said quietly as he pulled both hands across his sweat-damp face, "this is another fine mess I have gotten us into."

Two

"LEW, keep your bloody voice down, they can hear every word!" Meredith barked angrily. Geoffrey Lewis was unperturbed. "Since they'll not be leaving this vessel alive, that's hardly of any consequence."

"Sweet Jesus Christ." Meredith was furious. "They'll be reported missing. You want the police turning this whole coast upside down, trying to find them? The tall one's a Yank. You don't just lose an American. When one of them goes missing, there's trouble. Company, consulate, law."

"When the young man was lost in a storm, in an open boat at sea, with the highest tide of the decade on its way, and gale force winds forecast?" Lewis demanded. "A tragic boating accident, Meredith. They happen all the time. The authorities will find that motorboat wrecked, a few miles from here. They won't find the bodies, but these waters are full of sharks at this time. In winter the Gulf is degrees warmer than the open ocean, the sharks always come in."

Their voices carried quite clearly. Sean stood with his ear close to the closed, guarded door of the galley, and his mouth dried as Lewis spoke in that silken smooth English voice.

"Rob?" he murmured urgently.

"I heard." Rob shuffled closer. "Sean, we have to get out of here."

Sean's eyes widened. "You want to tell me how?" Then Lewis was talking again, and he held a finger to Rob's mouth to silence him.

"Have you got through to Chandler yet?" Lewis was asking.

"Not a squawk," Meredith snapped. "He's either not answering the CB, or the lightning's producing too much interference. Knowing Chandler, he's probably just not answering — not even listening. He'll be fucking the legs off something."

"Sad to say," Lewis said acidly, "you're probably right. There are times when I wonder if Chandler is worth the trouble he causes."

"Except he's got the contacts, all the contacts, between here and Thailand," Meredith snorted, "and you just can't get by without him." He paused. "How long are we going to wait for that sod?"

"As long as it takes," Lewis said flatly. "As you said, we can't manage this business without him, bastard though he may be. Damn! He should be in a mental hospital. The man's a snap of your fingers away from totally psychopathic."

"Sociopathic," Meredith corrected musingly. "That's what he told me, anyway. The police had him in custody in Amsterdam a couple or three years ago. He'd been working with a terrorist group, supplying arms and explosives — hand it to the man, he may be a certifiable crazy, but he's good at his trade. You want it, he'll get it. Coke, guns, Semtex, it's all the same to Chandler."

"Sociopath?" Lewis sounded disgusted.

"No conscience, no ability to tell right from wrong," Meredith said indifferently. "He just enjoys the mayhem, the panic and blue lights. You can't do nothing with him, Lew. And if you're asking me to hang about here, waiting for him until the storm hits, or until we get picked up by a bloody police patrol — forget it."

"You may be right." Lewis paused. "Try the shortwave again."

Feet shifted on the deck, and the gale rocked the whole vessel. Rain lashed at the smoke-blackened galley windows, and Sean shifted to keep his balance. He looked sidelong into Rob's face, saw his wide eyes and unaccustomed pallor. Rob was cold, wet and scared — they both were, but Sean felt an absurd surge of protectiveness. The reaction was absurd, because Rob was pretty tough. But he was way out of his depth here, Sean though bleakly. None of this was his own fault, yet every instinct told him it was his responsibility to get them out of this mess.

He pressed Rob against the door and whispered, "Listen!"

"For what?" Rob demanded.

"Listen for them coming in, and warn me." Sean was already moving, opening drawers, searching through the contents. A pair of steak knives would not be much use against the gun in Parker's hand, but they were better than nothing. He passed one to Rob, who slipped it into his pocket, and then Sean lifted his buttocks onto the plastic draining board beside the sink. It bevelled deeply under his weight, he felt it straining to hold him, and ignored it.

The window lock was on the side. He tried it, worked his hands and forearms hard, but it was jammed shut. He twisted around, placed his palms flat on the glass and put his full strength against the panel. It shifted by an inch and a stream of ice-cold air rushed through the crack between glass and windproofing.

"They're using the radio," Rob murmured. "Calling this Chandler... John Chandler. I think he's ashore."

"Drug business," Sean panted. "You heard what the man said. Chandler has all the contacts between here and Thailand. That's Golden Triangle business. Drugs, guns, explosives. This boat's probably loaded with that shit. There's enough to zonk half of this state out of its mind, and start a small war. Ever wondered how it comes ashore?" He braced himself, took a deep breath and shoved on the window. "Oh, Jesus, this won't move. I think it was painted shut. They must've known it's jammed, it's why they shoved us in here."

"Chandler isn't answering," Rob's ear was against the door, he was listening intently. Having something constructive to do was the best, possibly the only way to keep blind fear under control. "I think they're calling a mobile phone now. A car phone, maybe. Meredith said he's 'on the road'."

Sweat prickled Sean's face as he grunted with effort. The window moved a fraction further and at last began to free itself off. "Is he answering?"

"Not yet." Rob chewed his lip. "If he's some kind of maniac, he wouldn't have enough responsibility to listen for the radio. Sociopath, the man said." He looked up, his face a mask of tension. "What the fuck are you doing, Sean?"

"Trying —" Sean panted furiously " — to unjam this window." He gave Rob a glare over one hunched shoulder. "You want to stand around and wait for them to organise an accident for us? You heard them!" As he spoke the window shifted a hand's span more, and it was enough. Wind and rain gusted in.

Broad daylight was now like a thick, steely twilight. Momentarily exhausted, Sean slumped against the glass to rest and nodded at the door. "Anything?"

But Rob made negative gestures. "They're still trying to call their man. It'd be ironic if he was screwing his brains out."

"Giving us the diversion we need?" Sean dragged his palms over his face and held out his hand. "Move it, Rob. We don't have much time."

As Rob's cold hand slid into his, Sean hauled him up onto the sink unit. The plastic cracked under their combined weight, and Sean's heart hammered in his throat as he fed himself out through the window. It was barely wide enough. He compressed his chest, physically shoved himself out of the smoky claustrophobia of the galley into the wild, pitching, rain-filled air.

Outside, there were no hand holds, nothing to grab onto, and an eight-foot drop to the churning water below. But they had two advantages, and Sean placed his faith in both. One, the *Fancy Dancer* was on this side of the *Minuette*. Two, both he and Rob were strong enough swimmers.

"Hurry," he panted as he pushed himself through. "There's no hand holds — just drop down, hit the water and swim for it — it's not far."

Rob was half way out even then, struggling to squeeze through the barely adequate space, and Sean's wet fingers lost their grip on the window. He knew it was only a short fall, but in that moment it seemed he hung suspended in the air for long seconds, before he hit the heaving water and went under.

The sudden cold was stunning, and worse, his clothes were immediately like lead fetters, dragging at his limbs. He kicked out for the surface, threshed his hands and feet to tread water, and blinked his stinging eyes clear. Above him, Rob was still half in, half out of the window, struggling to get his long legs through, and as Sean watched, he froze.

"Rob! Rob!" Sean barked hoarsely, his throat full of salt. "Rob, shift your ass!"

Then Rob was moving, as if fear doubled his strength, and Sean knew why. Voices bellowed in the galley. Parker or Meredith, or both, were in there, and Sean was waiting for the first gunshot. As Rob plunged down toward the water, he kicked out hard, driving himself through the churning waves toward the stern, where the *Fancy Dancer* had tied on, not twenty minutes before. He heard the splash as Rob hit, and at the same instant, noise erupted from the open window.

He hugged the dove-grey side of the hull and threw every fibre of muscle he possessed into the effort as he came up on the *Dancer*'s bright yellow bow. He did not dare waste a moment to look back for Rob. These were the seconds that might be the life or death of them.

Muscles protested unnoticed as he hauled himself into the well of the *Dancer* and clawed the steak knife out of his pocket. It was sharp enough to slice through a beef bone, and it cut the mooring line as if the rope was made of bubblegum.

Shots burst out of the galley, and Sean dropped the knife to his feet. He doubled up, putting the bow and windscreen between himself and that window. As he squirmed into the seat he hit the ignition and held his breath. These outboards had been a pair of bitches for the last week. They started when they chose to — and sometimes they refused.

Perhaps they had simply been damp for days, perhaps the mist of dewatering fluid that Rob had sprayed into the casings only half an hour before was still keeping them dry. Sean let out a breath as the Evinrudes coughed, spluttered and began to growl, and then he looked around for Rob.

Panic was an unfamiliar emotion to Sean, and not one he enjoyed. The light was a poor, twilight grey, the chop was up above three feet and the rain was pelting, stinging cold, half blinding him. It was difficult to recall that at home in California, August was a glorious month, shimmering with heat that lured an entire population onto the beach. Here, it was winter, and though it never actually snowed in this part of the country it sometimes felt cold enough to.

There! A shape broke the surface right beside the boat. Sean thrust down his hand and clawed to get a grip on Rob's wrist. He had gone under and stayed under, out of sight, until his lungs must have been burning, swimming with the desperation of a champion. He wheezed and coughed as Sean dragged him head-first into the well of the boat, dumped him unceremoniously there and lunged back into the driver's seat.

The V8s roared as the *Dancer* spun about in just a little more than her own length, and Sean opened the throttles. Rob was on his knees and the kick of fast acceleration pitched him flat again. He stayed down, shivering in the lake of water in the well, until the boat stabilised, and then hauled himself up into the seat beside Sean.

"We were lucky," he said hoarsely. "I thought I was dead."

"We might have been." Sean's heart had slowed a little as he pushed the throttles out to maximum, but when he twisted to look back the pulse began to beat in his temple again. "Oh shit, those guys are determined."

"What?" Rob turned, and groaned. "I swear, that's the last time I play the good samaritan."

The *Minuette* was under way, inboard diesel engines driving her through the chop as she came about in an enormous arc. The colour of her hull made her difficult to see against the water and sky, and the gale whipped away her engine noise.

"She's not as fast as we are," Sean said grimly as the *Dancer* put a lot of space between them. "They don't have the acceleration, they won't catch us."

"They don't have to," Rob shouted over the wind. "Did you see those weapons? Half of them, I didn't even recognise!" He leaned over, squinted at the fuel gauges and swore bitterly.

"I know, I didn't fill the tanks," Sean said without even bothering to look at the gauges. "We weren't expecting to go far or be out long. There's enough to get us home."

"Home?" Rob wiped the rain out of his eyes and peered aft, at the now distant *Minuette*. "That's not going to do us much good, Sean. Unless we get out of sight of them, we're going to be towing them like a comet tail!"

He was right, but Sean was already several logical leaps ahead of that reasoning. "Try the radio. We need help. Police, navy, a trawler — anything that'll stand by us."

It was a long shot. As Rob picked up the mic the lightning forked like a devil's tongue through the southern sky. Rain sheeted the whole ocean and visibility had closed in until the coastline, only three miles away, was invisible. The *Dancer* butted and bucked over the wave crests, sometimes skipping from one to another, airborne, only to smack down so fiercely that Sean feared for her hull. She was ten years old, patched and repaired, ideal for a quiet fishing trip... not for this kind of service.

As Rob called repeatedly, trying to raise anyone who would answer, Sean peered at the fuel gauges. They would flatten in a few minutes at this gas-guzzling speed, and he transferred his eyes to the west, where he should pick up the coastline any moment.

On a clear day they would be able to see the roof of the shack, but today Sean could only trust to instinct to take him home like a pigeon. He twisted in his seat and saw the *Minuette*, a good distance behind but sticking with them doggedly, and then the gale flung a surge of salt spray into his face and he lost sight of it.

The radio was in good working order, but no one was answering. Thunder pealed like an artillery barrage, and Rob flung down the mic. He shouted over the wind, the outboards and the crash of the surf, his voice almost snatched away,

"It's no good. We're either not getting through, or no one has time to answer." He paused then, and flung out a pointing arm. "There! The rocks, that's our headland!"

Sean put the wheel over a fraction to aim them into the tiny cove. His mind raced, covering every possible route out of here, but every one of them looked blank. To begin with, the phone at the shack was off. It would be insane to attempt to hide in the house. Meredith and Parker were professionals, probably ex-soldiers or professional mercenaries, with enough arms to equip a platoon. What use was a locked door?

To one side of the shack was the boat ramp. Behind and above it, a wooded hillside where an unsurfaced track led up from the rear of the house, winding through the eucalypts and Norfolk Island pines to the road, a good distance above. And that road out was the best escape route they had. The only one they had.

A sidelong glance at Rob's face showed Sean that he had reached the same conclusion. As Sean aimed the boat at the little cove and reluctantly began to cut speed, Rob dug through the pockets of his jeans and withdrew the keys to the Landcruiser. In these conditions, a four-wheel drive gave them back the advantage.

If they could stay out of reach of Lewis's men, Sean thought sourly a moment later, as a shot he had not even heard slammed into the windscreen not a hand's span from his shoulder, leaving a star-shaped scar. He flinched, ducked into the cover of the seat, and Rob squirmed down into the footwell as the *Dancer* cut speed.

She came into the lee of the headland, and the bluestone boulders cut a little of the wind. There was no chance to make a proper landing. The boat would be damaged as he swung her broadside to the bottom of the ramp and let the force of the waves drive her on. They could not even take the time to tie her up, and the tide would steal her away, smash her on the rocks a few hundred yards down the coast.

She hit hard, and Rob yelped as if his own limbs had taken the pounding. Still, he went over the side like a snake, trying to put the pitching, yawing hull between himself and the sea. Letting the outboards stall, Sean was right behind him.

The silver Toyota was parked at the back of the house. A curl of smoke rose from the chimney, reminding them that they had left the stove on, left a casserole in the old brick oven. Inside the house would be warm, welcoming. A death-trap.

The hillside above the shack was so heavily wooded that sliding mud was not much of a problem, but still, it was getting treacherous underfoot. In the morning, they would have to shovel out the yard, as gravel and dirt washed down and piled up around the bins and the boathouse.

Slithering through the mud, Rob dove at the Toyota's righthand driver's door and jabbed the key into the lock. He was inside before Sean had made it to the passenger door. The Landcruiser started as Sean scrambled inside, and Rob nudged the shift into reverse.

The windscreen wipers clawed the cascades of rainwater off the glass, but visibility was bad. The way out was up beside the boathouse, and Sean held his breath as Rob backed up around the corner. They would be clearly visible from the sea until the trees covered them again, hiding them as they headed for the road. They would be visible again when they made it up to the top of the hill, and left the trees behind.

As the tyres filled with dirt and began to slither, Rob switched to four-wheel drive, changed into bottom gear and put his foot gently on the gas. Sean's fists gripped into the dashboard as the Toyota began to make reluctant, grudging headway. He turned and peered back through the curtain of rain, down the slope toward the boathouse. For some time he saw nothing, until lightning sheeted across the sky, illuminating the whole coast, as if with a battery of floodlights.

"Where are they?" Rob did not dare even glance at the rearview mirror. Every erg of his attention was on the trail, which rose away at a steep angle, mounting the hill. The Toyota was slithering like a man trying to run on ice, and she could be off the trail, in the ditch, any moment.

"They just landed, in a dinghy," Sean said tersely. "Just keep this thing on the road, they're not going to catch us."

"And then, what?" Rob licked his lips. He slewed the car around a hairpin bend in the trail and swore as the steering defied him, but as soon as they were around that kink in the treacherous, unsurfaced road, their pursuers would lose visual contact. "The radio's not going to be much use, and the roads around here are practically impassable."

"We'll have to find a phone." Sean settled into his seat and ran up the belt. "There's got to be a working phone somewhere around here. A farm, maybe. Call the police."

"And then sit waiting for them to get here." Rob spared him a sidelong glance. "Those bastards won't let it rest. You can bet your life, they'll be after us."

"Bet my life," Sean whispered. "Now, that's an interesting turn of phrase."

"Figure of speech," Rob said curtly as he fought the slithering, unwilling vehicle. "Shit! I'm going to lose the road if I don't slow down. You're supposed to be the resourceful, brilliant one — what does Aurora Petroleum pay you for? Think of something!"

"I'm trying," Sean breathed as he hung onto the seat belt." God help me, I'm trying."

Three

FOR ALMOST a week the rain had been an intermittent drizzle that had brimmed the creeks and begun the flooding of the lowlands. It took little more to convert the paddocks to lakes, and when the king tide washed inland, only the high ground would be safe.

Farmers were already driving off their stock. Sean saw a 4x4 on the rise, half a mile northward, but the road was empty of city-bred cars. Only rarely had he seen worse conditions, perhaps in the dead of winter on the Gulf of Mexico. Miles from head office in Galveston, Jackson Oil was trying to get a grasp on local politics while Guatemalan troops looked on, much too close at hand for comfort. Rebel activity was low-level, sporadic, but only a fool ignored it. The last time he had struggled through anything like this, Sean had been driving a fifty-year-old bus overloaded with salvaged equipment and bedraggled refugees, while a tropical storm wreaked havoc across the narrowest part of Mexico. That was the hard way to earn a living.

Beside him, Rob was intent on the road and they were making a few miles per hour as they crested the rise above the house. Rob plucked the CB mic from its bracket and clicked the switch to test it. He was about to adjust the tuner and transmit — a mayday, a plea for assistance on Channel 88 — when he heard a voice he knew, and froze.

"Where the Christ are you?" Meredith was bellowing in that strine accent over the almost overwhelming wash of static from the storm. "Chandler!"

The radio crackled and another voice replaced Meredith's. Calm, cheerful, urbane, with an indeterminate accent. His voice was completely international. American, English and Australian vowels combined to confuse the ear. "Hold your horses, Meredith. I'm safe. What's your rush?"

"Oh, you're safe, are you?" Meredith spat. "That takes a weight off my mind. I said, where are you?"

"In a car, five miles out of town. I made contact with the dealer early last night. It was easy." Chandler paused. "Is something wrong?"

Meredith's voice exploded over the air. "Everything's fucked up! We had a little galley fire —"

"Anyone injured?" Chandler interrupted, in a tone which seemed to suggest he would only be amused if there were casualties.

"No," Meredith snarled. "But a couple of tourist boaties got aboard, said they were trying to offer assistance. Chandler, they saw the whole picture."

"I see." The frequency whited out as lightning broke across half the sky. When it cleared again, Chandler was chuckling. "They're fish bait by now?" he asked pleasantly.

"They will be when we can catch them," Meredith breathed. "They got out a window, got ashore, took off in a Toyota 4x4. Now, we can see the car with binoculars, they're on the road above the coast, but they're out of range for a rifle shot at that elevation. It's a silver Landcruiser, headed south. Any chance you can see it?"

A brief pause, and then Chandler demanded, "In this visibility? Use what brains God gave you, Meredith. I'll keep an eye open for your little problem, but don't wait for me. You'd better tell Lewis to up-anchor and go. The roads are all out in front of me."

"Out?" Meredith bawled. "What do you mean, out?"

"I mean, submerged," Chandler told him. "Flooded. And this old bus won't do double-duty as a boat. It's having a hard time even doing duty as a car. Looks like I'll have to make my own way out."

"You should have been back last night," Meredith rasped. "What the hell happened to you?"

A chuckle cut across the channel. "Entertainment," Chandler said roundly. "Quite a ride. Look, pull the yacht out, I'll make contact when I've got myself out of the deluge. Where will you be?"

"East. Lew's got another meeting. Get yourself to the rendezvous place," Meredith told him acidly. "The *Lan Tao* will be picking up a special cargo a few miles down the coast, they can pick you up at the usual place. Winkler and a squad of men will be aboard to take care of it. Just bloody be there. Lewis is going to have your hide."

"Not if I find your runaways," Chandler said cheerfully, "and deliver them to you, trussed like turkeys for Thanksgiving. Description?"

"Two men, about thirty. Both dark, blue eyes, brown eyes,

well built, good looking. And one of them's a Yank. Sounded like one of the Pacific seaboard accents to me, California, probably." He paused. "Be careful, Chandler. They're not fools. They managed to give us the slip."

"Armed?" Chandler asked pleasantly.

"Not that we saw, but they could have a shotgun or a couple of rifles in the car. A lot of Aussies are gun-happy, remember that. And move your bloody arse!" Meredith shouted, before a blast of white noise overrode him, and he shut down.

Very deliberately, Sean hung up the mic and watched Rob's intent profile as he wrestled with the wheel. "If we use the radio they'll hear every word we say, and they'll know just where we are."

Rob took his eyes from the road for a moment and gave Sean a grim look. "Then it'll have to be a phone," he said quietly. "Which way?"

"You're asking me?" Sean's brows rose. "You're the local!"

"I'm a city kid," Rob muttered. "Born and bred on the sun-hot asphalt. This is about a million miles away from my happy hunting ground. This state's about twice the size of Texas, I don't know every square mile of it!" He put the wheel over and let the car drift as it butted into the solid curtain of rain.

It was getting misty, too. Visibility was bad and getting steadily worse as the storm clouds began to settle on the shoulders of the hills. It seemed to Sean that they were headed directly into the overcast, and his breath caught in his throat as a shape loomed out of the dangerous, steel-grey twilight. Rob braked hard, tossing them both in the seatbelts.

A farmer was standing in the middle of the washed-out road, legs braced against the wind as he waved with a powerful flashlight. A second man was shouting and clapping his hands as he drove several cows across and through the gate, into the paddock on the high side. Sean rolled down the window. He heard the crash of the sea, the distant, forlorn voices of cattle, sheep and gulls, as he leaned out and cupped a hand to his mouth to shout at the farmer.

"Hey, buddy, any farms around here?"

The man was a shapeless mass of oilskins and rubber boots. He splashed through the mud, one hand up to protect his face against the onslaught of the rain. He leaned closer to the window and peered in. His accent was so broad, Sean had difficulty making out the words.

"What's that you say? Christ, mate, you shouldn't be out in this! Tourists, are you?"

"No," Sean said curtly. "I said, are there any farms around here? We need to get to a phone."

"There's farms," the man said dubiously, "but the roads are three foot under." He stood back from the car and pointed inland, upward. "You could try that way, keep to the high ground. You might be able to get through to the old Jenkins farm."

"Thanks." Sean began to roll up the window. "How far is that?"

"Four or five mile, I'd reckon." The farmer waved his torch and stood aside to let them pass. "The road goes over the hill to the town," he called after the Toyota, "but don't try to go that way. The other slope's flooded, it's been under since morning."

"Thanks again," Sean called, and closed the window against the pelting, stinging rain.

Rob dropped the Toyota into bottom gear and let the clutch out with exaggerated caution. "Keep to the high ground, the man said," he muttered. "You know, if Lewis's pet maniac is determined to find us, this storm is the best divining rod he's got to do it with."

"You mean, there's only so many places we can run to?" Sean sighed. "High ground." He watched Rob drive for a moment, and then reached over and stroked the long, lean muscle of his lover's thigh. "Hey."

Too intent on the road to look away or take a finger off the wheel, Rob merely grunted. "What?"

"It wasn't supposed to be like this, Robbie," Sean said softly. "It was supposed to me just you and me."

"It was you and me. It is, still," Rob said emphatically. "All we have to do is find a phone, and a nice dry place, and then sit tight. I don't particularly give a shit if the police ever lay hands on this Chandler bastard or not. That's their problem, not ours. All I want..."

"Is?" Sean prompted. "A hot bath, a good meal, stiff drink, warm bed?"

"And you," Rob finished. "Christ, we might as well be saying the moon, the stars, the planet Mars. Look at this!"

The tyres were scrabbling for purchase as the car inched past a sign. Sean peered through the chaos of the windscreen to see its mud-streaked lettering. He had no chance of reading it, but it was bound to say IMPASSABLE WHEN WET. Absurd humour bared his teeth in a grin.

"Hold onto something," Rob said grimly as they crested the rise. "It's going to get a bit hairy here. There's not much of a road left, and it's all water at the bottom."

On either side of the track were ditches, four feet deep, that might have been designed to trap a tank, let alone the average car. The tyres spun and Rob swiftly took his foot off the gas. The trick was to alternate the power, on and off, and maybe he could keep a grip on the road surface. If he didn't, they would end in one of those storm water runoff ditches and it would take a tow truck to pull them out.

"Where the hell does this road go?" Sean peered through the swirling mist of grey cloud.

"Some town. They might even mean Victor Harbour. I don't know, Sean, this is not my natural habitat. I've never even visited here." Rob flicked on the driving lights, but they made visibility even worse and he turned them off again.

The Landcruiser moved down the road like a crab, all four wheels driving hard just to keep it in forward motion. Sean's heart was in his mouth for the fifth time when he saw yellow lights up ahead. Is that another vehicle?

"It might be a house," Rob muttered.

"In which case, it could be the Jenkins place." Sean's teeth worried at his lip. "Can we get that far?"

"I'm trying," Rob breathed. "Some of these wheel ruts are a foot deep." He changed back into bottom gear and cursed as he wrestled the steering wheel.

Down below, the road vanished into a swirling grey lake. Sean could not even guess how deep the water would be. Perhaps the Toyota could make it across. Or perhaps the lake was so deep that the vehicle's buoyancy would literally float it off. As soon as they lost traction they were done for.

To their right, as Rob braked cautiously, was a gateway. Through the cloud mist they glimpsed a house, an isolate bluestone cottage standing well back from the road. Behind it were a cluster of outhouses, a chicken run, a shed, a barn. A small tractor was parked in the lee of the shed, but otherwise the property would have looked just the same in the 1920s. These cottages were built for the 'soldier settlers', servicemen who had returned from the battles of the First World War and were assisted to settle on the land.

The car crabbed through the gates, and as the wheels hit gravel on the driveway the tyres got a better hold. Rob sighed his relief as he regained some genuine control, instead of slithering and sliding like a drunken skater on a rink of half-melted ice.

The rain was pelting as he turned off the motor, but he and Sean were soaked already, and frozen. It was impossible to get any wetter. This kind of rain could fall all day, days on end. Even a steady drizzle would cause torrential flooding as the creeks poured into the river. Sean gave a thought to the evening's high tide, and shivered. The sky was an unbroken pall of battleship grey, and the lightning flickered again, much closer at hand.

The wind cut like a knife. He turned up his collar and slid out of the car's grudging warmth. Rob looked very pale. Sean jogged around the hood to meet him, and they plowed through the loose gravel to the cottage's white painted, wooden front door. Sean rapped his knuckles smartly on it.

Seconds later it swung inward, and the face of an old lady peered out at them. She was a country woman, weatherbeaten, leathery, probably not within a decade of the age she seemed. She was short and rotund as a barrel, her hair a mix of mouse-brown and grey. She wore baggy jeans and a grey jersey, and a colourful shawl around her shoulders

She examined them minutely with hard, shrewd eyes. "You don't look like you're from the police."

Sean and Rob shot a glance at each other. "You called them?" Rob asked. "Could we step inside, ma'am? It's pissing down."

The rain was driving at the cottage from such an angle that the doorway was already flooding. The woman stood aside and they stepped into a room which seemed a cross between parlour and kitchen. She left Sean to latch the door, and as he secured it he heard Rob murmur quietly.

When he turned back, he saw the single-barrelled pump shotgun held loosely in the woman's big, brown hands. A live fire crackled cheerfully in an open hearth, in the chimney corner, a copper kettle had just begun to whistle on the gas. With her free hand the woman lifted it off to silence it. The country welcome Sean might have expected was not forthcoming.

"Are you from the police, or aren't you? I don't recognise you. I know most of the local lads."

"Uh... actually, we're not," Sean confessed. "Look, lady, we're not here to make trouble. We've had some trouble ourselves. All we need is a phone, and then we'll leave."

"A phone?" Her eyes narrowed.

"To call the police." Rob wrapped his arms around himself and hugged as he began to shiver. "What's your trouble? We might be able to help you, since we're here. Would you be Mrs Jenkins? A farmer up on the road told us to look out for your farm."

The barrel of the shotgun lowered a fraction. "I'm Grace Jenkins. And I'm sorry about the artillery, but we've been done once already today, and you can't blame me for being more cautious. After this, I'll trust no one, that I promise it."

Again, Sean and Rob shared a glance, and Sean cleared his throat. He gestured at the hearth. "Do you mind if we get warm? We're half drowned."

"Help yourself." Mrs Jenkins gesture at the kettle. "Could you use a cuppa?"

"Oh, please." Rob knelt close to the antique brass fender and held his hands to the heat. Sean settled beside him, hands outstretched toward the fire. "What did you mean, you've been done?"

"That bloody man!" Clearly deciding to trust them, Mrs Jenkins propped the shotgun beside the door and slammed the kettle back onto the gas. It began to simmer again almost at once, as she produced caddy, mugs and a sugar basin. "He arrived late last night, said he needed shelter, he'd had a crash on the road. I told him he could sleep in the barn, gave him a meal and a couple of rugs. There's no room in the house, you see, what with Susan and me. Susan's my daughter-in-law. And besides, I don't trust strange men." She looked them up and down, and glanced pointedly at the shotgun.

Sean smiled faintly. "You're dead right not to trust strangers, ma'am, of either gender. What did this man do?"

She had filled a brown ceramic teapot, and as the tea brewed she folded her arms over her large bosom. "As I said, I told him he could sleep out there. Susan took a shine to him in five seconds flat — that animal is handsome, if you like the type, and most folks do. Well-built, tanned, looks fit. God knows what possessed Sue to take him out cocoa and crumpets, about midnight, but this morning you can bet she's wishing she hadn't!"

A crawling sensation beset Sean. He rubbed his palms together and looked at Rob as the elderly woman pushed the teapot and sugar basin across the table. "So, Susan took his supper out?" Rob prompted.

A fist gripped Sean's belly. "Is the girl all right, ma'am?"

"No." Mrs Jenkins flushed brightly, as if she could barely contain her anger. "She will be, physically, but it'll take a while. Get this straight: I'd gone off to bed, I was sound asleep when that bloody stupid girl went out to him. This morning she wasn't in her room, and I knew something was wrong. Call it sixth sense. I went out to the barn and found her. He'd trussed her like a chicken, stark naked, spread out like a side of beef, in cold like this! She was purple with hypothermia. I put her in a warm bath and got a pint of warm, sweet tea into her. Prised the story out of her in bits. She blames herself — who else is she going to blame? But that has nothing to do with it. Three times!"

"Three times, what?" Rob shot a puzzled glance at Sean.

"Three times the bastard screwed her," Mrs Jenkins snarled as her fury broke. "She was raped and bloody sodomised. The last time was before dawn, when he stole my car." She paused, fists clenching. "I want that mongrel behind bars so long, he forgets what his dick is for, forgets what it's like to breathe free air. Bring him back here, and if I get my hands on him I'll castrate the bastard with my bare hands!"

She was so furious, in the heat of rage she was capable of doing it. Such rage was awesome. Sean shivered, and a name whispered in his mind's ear. John Chandler. Lewis's pet crazy. A shiver coursed the length of his spine as he got to his feet and helped himself to a mug of tea.

"So you called the police?" he asked as he stirred the strong, paint-like brew.

She gestured at the door. "That's who I thought you were. I didn't know if I'd got through. I tried to call the doctor too, but I don't know if I reached him either. Susan ought to be in hospital. Do you know what it does to a woman, being buggered, and then screwed in the vagina? Jesus Christ." She rubbed her eyes viciously with the back of a gnarled hand. "If you wanted a phone, you're out of luck. Our lines are down. What about your radio? I saw the CB aerial on your car."

"It's... not in working order," Rob said quietly. "Where would be the next place we could find a phone?"

She seemed to force herself to concentrate. "You could try heading northward. There's a few farms that way. The Miller place, and Bradgate, up on Lightning Ridge. Some of them are evacuating, but the phone lines might be up." She stirred, blinking at them as if she was seeing them properly for the first time. "You look half drowned. You had an accident?"

"We had a boating accident," Sean lied smoothly. "Do you mind if we get warm for a few minutes before we go?"

Mrs Jenkins admonished him for even thinking he must ask. "Have you had anything to eat?" Without waiting for an answer, she began to crack eggs into a dish.

In minutes, the delectable smell of ham and onions filled the air, making Sean's empty stomach growl painfully. Mrs Jenkins was shaking a skillet on the gas, making a single enormous omelette. On the table was a platter of hand-sliced bread and local butter.

A little colour had returned to Rob's cheeks, but his eyes were preoccupied. *Wary*, Sean thought. He leaned closer. "You all right, Robbie?"

"I'm fine." Rob dropped his voice. "You know what I'm thinking? The man who stayed here last night and did that to the girl... you heard what Chandler said. Entertainment. He was supposed to be back on the *Minuette*. They were waiting for him to show, and he never did." His brows rose. "The man's a loon, Meredith said."

"A snap of your fingers from totally stone-crazy," Sean added. "You don't expect to find two like that in the same five square miles." He held his hands to the fire. "And he's looking for us. Christ."

They were speaking in undertones and Mrs Jenkins heard nothing as she divided the omelette and slid it out of the skillet. "Get it while it's hot. You there, son," she added with a gesture at Sean. "There's cutlery in the drawer."

Obedient while his mouth watered, Sean rummaged for knives and forks. Rob took a seat at the table and began to butter bread.

Sean sat beside him, and their legs touched under the table. Their thighs pressed warmly. Sean waited for Rob to move out of his reach as he sometimes did when Sean wanted to be intimate in a place which might be called public. Oddly, Rob did not move. He took a piece of bread and ate hungrily, looking into Sean's eyes, and it was Sean who almost fidgeted, as he began to worry that the old woman would notice. What would she would make of them? One could never be certain of the older generation.

"If we find a working phone up the road," he promised, "we'll call the police for you, and a doctor for Susan. Give us the numbers. We're not local."

She smiled for the first time. "I appreciate it." The names and numbers were scrawled quickly on an obsolete sheet torn off the calendar. "You'll not find it easy to get out of this valley. We're on fairly high ground right here. Noah's ark would be afloat before we flooded, but the lower paddocks are already well under. You had a weather bulletin?"

"This morning," Rob said though a mouthful of ham and eggs. "Only rain and gales the whole day, then a king tide tonight to top it off." He paused, mopping his plate. "Mrs Jenkins, when Cha... that is, when the man left here, did you see which way he went?"

"North." She pointed at the cottage's sturdy chimney corner. "Susan saw him turn out of the gate. He took my car, but that won't get him far, not in this."

"What kind of car, ma'am?" Sean wondered.

"Just an old FJ Holden." He mouth compressed. "Getting on for fifty years old, a classic." She shook her head. "He'll wreck it, and that's a damned shame. It's the only car I ever owned."

"Did he steal anything else?" Sean finished his tea and got reluctantly to his feet. They ought to be moving on. This farm was too close for comfort to the very road where Meredith had last seen them, with the aid of binoculars. If Chandler was eager for amusement, and if he could make headway through the storm, he could visit every farm property in the area. Sooner or later dumb luck would bring them face to face.

"He took some money," Mrs Jenkins was saying acidly. "A few hundred dollars, all I had in the house. And about ten cartridges, twelve gauge, and my old rabbit gun." She studied them over the rim of her mug. "You be careful. He's armed, and he's insane. He tied Susan up in the cold, just walked away and left her. When I found her she was nearly done for. I don't think that bastard would think twice about putting a load of rabbit shot in you."

"We'll be careful," Rob promised as he finished his tea and scraped his chair back from the table. "We'd better go. Thanks for the breakfast, we appreciate it. If we find a phone that's still working, we'll make those calls for you."

She went ahead of them to the door, opened it a crack, and Sean eased through into the teeth of the wind and rain. The cold hit him in every bone. Rob went by fast, toward the car. He slapped the keys into Sean's hands and jogged around the hood to the passenger's side. "Your turn to drive."

"Oh, thanks a bunch. Just my idea of fun," Sean muttered as he wrenched open the door and slid in under the wheel.

Four

FOR THE third time in as many minutes thunder rumbled, miles over the sea. It would be rough, and Rob did not envy the crews of ships out there. As Sean wrestled with the car, he described the plunging deck and pitching horizon. He had worked for Jackson Oil for five years, and work had taken him as far afield as Yucatan and Namibia. But oil exploration was a risky, fickle business, and after several gambles went bad even Jackson had begun to downsize its staff. Rob knew how much Sean resented being made redundant by a company in which he had invested so much of his time and energy, but there was no way Rob could regret decisions made by Jackson Oil.

That downsizing manoeuvre had led Sean to Australia, to Adelaide, and a Hindley Street bar. Rob's greatest worry, now, was that after the incredible life Sean had lived he would soon become bored, and leave. Adelaide had little to attract him, other than the offer of the job with Aurora Petroleum.

In the years when Rob was working in a bike shop, taking night classes to finish a previously botched and abandoned education, and trying to figure out some way to get off the treadmill, Sean was in exotic places, doing exotic, often hazardous things. And Sean was footloose. Rob had been seeing the signs of it for months, but until Peter Kramer set flame to fuse he had never known what he could do about it.

A night of confessions, tears and self-reproach was the beginning. Part of the solution was this sabbatical, two weeks away from the city, work and distraction. A winter vacation, where the chill and rain should have guaranteed them the solitude they needed to work things out, once and for all.

Lightning flickered. Sean swore lividly as he spun the wheel over and made a few more feet up the treacherous apology for a road. Rob clung onto his seat straps and held his cold feet to the heater. The first night when they slept together was still as sharp in his memory as if it had been only a week before. He had drunk too much — he always did when he was blue. The pub was crowded, the music was way too loud and one of the kids had spilled a glass of beer right under his feet. The boy who tended the bar was dragging in the grey metal bucket and medusa-head mop when a deep, rich voice Rob had never heard before said over the blasts of Sheena Easton, "Are you waiting for someone special, or can I get you another beer?"

Rob turned slowly toward the voice and found himself looking up into Sean's smooth, tanned, blue-eyed and smiling face. Damn, but the man was a beauty. His hair was very dark and worn short, which suited him. His dress was casual but very expensive. He was at ease, faultlessly elegant in slacks and a sports shirt, a beige jacket, black boots. Not even the anaesthesia of several beers too many could prevent every nerve in Rob's body coming alive.

They had another drink and then got out of the smoke and noise. Minutes later they were in Sean's Celica, heading out toward the parklands. For a moment Rob wondered if they were going to pound that old beat, do it in the bushes, but Sean made a face at the suggestion. He lived three storeys above South Terrace, opposite the park.

Rob remembered pale ivory walls, green plants, polished woodwork and Black Bottle brandy... the rest of the evening was a blur of sensuality. In a bed with chocolate-brown silk sheets and a copper coloured duvet, Sean took him gently to his emotional limits, and way beyond them. Rob had never flown so high or for so long, and when Sean reduced him to an exhausted heap of trembling muscles, he wondered if he should apologise for some fancied ineptitude.

But Sean was enraptured. Captivated. What did he see, Rob wondered, what did he perceive that fascinated him? Rob never knew. But three weeks after they met, Sean gave him a key to the apartment, and two weeks later Rob moved in. For a while, he began to believe paradise existed after all. He was unemployed in those weeks, and the time he had free to devote to the relationship made it blossom like a rose. But work had to intervene, and the moment Rob signed on with his new employer, he knew the job must cause an upheaval in the idyllic lifestyle he and Sean had enjoyed —

"You see that thing?" Sean stamped on the brake and the car bucked to a halt just before it would have put two wheels into a ditch. "You're the Aussie, you tell me what the hell that relic is!"

Rob cuffed the misted windscreen, the better to see, and followed the line of Sean's pointing arm. It took a moment for him to pick out what Sean had seen, and then he swore. "That," he said acidly, "is an FJ Holden."

Ahead of them, abandoned under a tree with its two rear wheels sunk to the axle in the dirt, was a two-tone green four-door family car, many years older than either Rob or Sean. Rob held his hands to the heater and chuckled, a sound devoid of all humour.

"The old lady was right. He didn't get too far."

"About three miles, maybe four." Sean revved the motor to keep it alive. "You reckon he'll be around here?"

"If he is, he'll be on the lookout for us," Rob reminded him quietly. "A silver Toyota Landcruiser — there won't be too many of us around, and God knows, we're pretty visible, sitting on the only patch of high ground left." He paused, watching Sean's finely chiselled profile as he rolled down the driver's window. "Which way could he have gone?"

"He had one choice: uphill." Sean gestured back along the shoulder of the ridge, the way they also had come. "He sounded like a city boy to me, over the radio. He won't like being on foot, and he won't make light work of hiking in this weather. If he was in town doing Lewis's business yesterday, I'll give you short odds, Rob, he's in city clothes and street shoes." He glanced at the rivers of mud, the alpine wheelruts and sodden grass. "It must be five miles back to town from here, even if you walked straight over the hill. Chandler'll be looking for shelter." He lifted an eyebrow at Rob.

The sense of what he had said hit Rob a moment later. "He could go back to the Jenkins farm."

"He could." Sean licked his lips. "If he does, that mean old lady will put several rounds of buckshot up his ass and ask questions later. And good riddance!" He dropped the car into gear and let out the clutch carefully. "You ever meet a sociopath, Robbie?"

"Can't say I ever had the pleasure." Rob ducked involuntarily as thunder rolled overhead like a cannonade.

When he could make himself heard again Sean muttered, "I had the joy of working with one for five sublime months."

"When you were with Jackson Oil?" Rob was surprised.

Sean's teeth bared, not an expression of humour. "Yeah. And the irony is, Dwight Murdoch is still working for them. That maggot got the job that should have been mine when the company lobotomised itself with that paroxysm downsizing." He paused as he took the car carefully through a lake that might have been a foot deep, or a yard. "Chandler sounds the same kind. Can't do without his 'entertainment'."

Against his better judgement, Rob's fascination was piqued. He braced his feet and hung onto the dash as Sean coaxed the car up a slight incline. Something in the way Sean said 'entertainment' made his blood run cold. "What do you mean?"

"Exactly what I said. Murdoch was like that. Under-stimulated. A therapist I knew in the States explained it to me this way. If you lock any ordinary guy in a room by himself he whistles, has fantasies, figures his mortgage. He'll probably beat off if he thinks he has the chance, and you leave him alone long enough. Lock Dwight Murdoch in a room on his own, and... nothing."

"His mind blanks?" Rob frowned. "Is that possible?"

"The shrink explained it to me." Sean released the wheel to let the car right itself, and changed down. "If Chandler's anything like Murdoch, in his sleep the man doesn't even dream. Awake, he needs constant stimulation, work or entertainment. Now, a man like Chandler doesn't work too much. He'll be earning big bucks, peddling crap. So he needs a lot of entertainment, and since he's so warped he'll have to screw his cap on, he'll have a taste for warped amusement." He gave Rob a bleak glance. "Like that girl. That was bad. She could have died."

"He can count on his good looks to snare a victim," Rob mused, "and then he overpowers the prey, feeds off her fear. Or his fear. If it's just a thrill Chandler is looking for, a boy would be just as acceptable. He probably trussed the girl up when he was spent and watched to see how long she lasted. For a while he'd find it interesting, but when she passed out with the hypothermia the show was over."

Sean nodded. "He might even have forgotten he'd trussed her, while he was ransacking the cottage for the lady's gun and car keys. By the time he drove out of there, it might have gone clean out of his mind that he'd left her. Dwight Murdoch was like that. When he was on the town you could hear the screams as the prostitutes yelled rape. One day, he's going to end up strapped to a weird kind of chair, with his head shaved and one trouser leg rolled up."

John Chandler's case was one of the peculiar ones, Rob thought sourly. If the police ever managed to arrest him, a criminal psychologist would examine him and the only possible diagnosis was that he could not be held responsible for his actions. He would probably be classified as ill and institutionalised for care and treatment, or rehabilitation. It might take years, but one day his doctors would decide he had been cured, and he'd be released. Then he would prey on someone else. Chilled, Rob wondered how many other people had suffered like Mrs Jenkins's daughter-in-law.

The motor stalled, and Sean thumped the steering wheel in a fusion of frustration, anger and healthy fear. "Not now, you bastard, not now," he hissed at the car. "Cross your fingers and pray!" He gave the key a vicious twist. The starter motor whirred, the engine coughed and stalled a second time. "Shit!"

"Calm down," Rob muttered as Sean's temper seemed about to explode. Fury would get them nowhere. "Turn the ignition off and pop the bonnet."

"Bonnet?" Sean echoed, eyebrows arching.

"Hood," Rob corrected. "That long shiny thing in front of the windshield. He opened the door and gritted his teeth as the wind caressed him with fingers like icicles.

He peered at his watch in the steel-grey twilight and was shocked to see it was only eleven. They had been out on the water by six-thirty, determined to make the most of an hour's spectacular fishing — testing local lore — before the wind and rain assaulted this part of the coast. It should have been so simple to scoot home, winch the *Fancy Dancer* up into the boathouse, where she would be safe, and then watch the light show in the sky from the warmth and safety of the house.

He could smell the sea. The sharp ozone tang reminded him of summer afternoons, a bike ride down Anzac Highway to the bay. Holdfast Bay, where the jetty thrust out phallically into the blue-green Gulf waters, and Glenelg's gorgeous beaches attracted a scant handful of locals.

Protecting his face with his hand, he looked into the wind and tried to see the sun, but it was no more than a slightly brighter spot in the miles-thick overcast. Conditions like these grounded most helicopters. Only *Rescue One*, the state's Bell BigLifter, would be operating. Its crew must be working at capacity, pulling civilians out of ludicrous situations.

Ludicrous situations? Rob grinned mirthlessly as he hung onto the bonnet — the hood, as Sean would have it. A powerful gust got beneath and almost tore it out of his hands. His fingers clutched the lip of it and he swore. The whole engine was wet and filthy. Dirt had invaded everywhere. The miracle was that it was still working at all.

He jiggled the plugs and leads, tightened the distributor cap, checked the battery leads, and slammed the hood once more, before the rain could do any more damage. That battery was getting old. He had known for weeks, he should get a new one. They had made so many rough starts lately, the chance was, it was simply flattening.

He gave Sean a thumbs-up signal, cupped his hands and bawled over the wind, "Kick it in the guts!"

Sean hit the ignition with his foot halfway to the floor. Rob held his breath, wishing he knew how to pray, or believed in something to pray to. The starter turned over weakly once, twice, and then the engine fired. Rob huffed a sigh of relief as Sean revved it hard.

He clambered back into the car, limbs trembling with cold and encroaching fatigue. "See if you can keep it running. The battery's no good. We might not be able to start it again." Even his voice shook.

"What's the electrical system look like?" Sean asked grimly as he dropped the floor shift into bottom gear.

"Filthy. And I know — I should have got a new battery before we came down here." Rob held his hands to the gusting, roaring heater. "What we need is about two hours in a service garage. And we're not likely to find one here! Do you smell the sea? We must be about five miles from the coast."

"But that gale is covering the distance at the speed of sound," Sean muttered as he eased out the clutch. The wheels spun, lost all traction, and he took his foot off the gas. "Shit, the tread's so full of mud, these tyres are like roller blades!"

"I think," Rob speculated, "Lewis's man will make tracks for the nearest town and look for a nice, dry, warm hotel. I know I would."

"City boy," Sean teased.

"Dead right," Rob agreed emphatically.

The car slithered forward a foot at a time, and Sean puffed out his cheeks. "Here we go again. If I only knew where we were headed, that would help. We're going north. If we can find enough high ground, and if this thing that calls itself a road doesn't turn into a total quagmire, we ought to see Goolwa eventually."

"At the rate we're going," Rob said sourly, "that'll be about seven o'clock tonight."

"You want to drive?" Sean snapped as the car bumped and rocked from one water-filled hole to another.

Rob sighed. "I wasn't criticising." He reached over and laid his hand on Sean's thigh, gripped the big muscle there. "Why the hell would I criticise you? You've always been the best there is, at everything. I never competed with you. How could I? What was I, when you stumbled over me in that pub? Out of work and well on my way to homicidal depression!"

"Homicidal?" Sean quipped, his smile returning like quick-silver. "You sure that's what you mean?"

"No." Rob gave his thigh a companionable squeeze. "I wasn't sure of anything till that night when you found me. Being gay never depressed me, not even as an adolescent. Being lonely did. Always. Even now, I'm only sure of one thing."

"Which is?" Sean braked, slewed the car around a mess of fallen tree debris and accelerated slowly, carefully, toward the crest of the next slope.

"I love you," Rob said simply. "I want you. And I'll do anything I have to do, to keep you."

The smile widened on Sean's beautiful mouth. "Now, that's healthy," he decided. "You hold onto that thought, Robbie, and you won't go far wrong." He changed up into second gear. "Where the fuck am I going? Is that a T-junction I'm seeing at the top of this hill?"

Again, Rob peered through the windscreen. "I think you're right." He scrabbled in the glove compartment for the map, and studied it in the dimness. "Turn right at the top. This road coils around like an old Irish mile, and heads for the sea. There's a farm or something marked right there. It's not a village, but there's nothing else in the area. It's labelled as Bradgate, up on Lightning Ridge."

"Sounds pleasant," Sean muttered as he revved the engine to keep it running. Every forward yard was a battle. "What's the time?"

"Just after eleven. For what it's worth, we've got plenty of daylight. If you call this daylight."

For the first time since morning, Sean chuckled richly. "You know, you're real cute when you grumble." He settled himself more deeply into the seat, and tackled both the Toyota and the road as if they were a physical adversary. "Quit worrying, kiddo. Chandler's probably hoofed it back to Victor Harbour by now. He'll spend Mrs Jenkins's cash on a motel room, seduce somebody and get himself laid. Then he'll head for that rendezvous point Meredith mentioned, and he'll be out of the country. Forget him. What we need is shelter, a fire, and a meal. When this storm's passed by we'll just use the CB and see if we can get a ride out of this mess." He grinned boyishly. "A boat ride, maybe!"

"So, we head for Lightning Ridge." Rob leaned back and braced himself between the seat and the firewall as the Landcruiser bucked and heaved. "Turn right at the top to get there."

"Jesus — if we make it to the top," Scan hissed a moment later as thunder rumbled right overhead, and the Toyota slithered sideways. It missed the ditch at the roadside by a hand's span.

A pulse hammered in Rob's temples. Sean was doing the best anyone could, but a dozen times in every hundred yards his heart was beating at his ribs. If the engine stalled out again it would surely never restart, and it was one hell of a long walk home.

Five

THE HUNDRED yards to the crest of the rise fatigued Sean as much as if he had climbed them up a mountainside. The rain was an unbroken curtain. On the shoulder of the hill he braked gently, brought the Toyota to a halt and peered through the murk, hoping and praying to see the bright blink of orange hazard lights, ambulance spinners, a police accident squad or fire engine. Anything with a powerful shortwave aboard, which would punch through, or over, the storm, well away from the frequencies Chandler and Lewis were using.

He saw only a fog of cloud, rain and more rain. The sky showed no patch of blue, the hills were uniformly sodden, the trees lashing under omnipresent flickers of lightning. The storm seemed to be all around them now. The king tide that was tipped to submerge the low lying paddocks under six feet of ruinous salt water would come up the river in seven or eight hours. The state's emergency services would be working at capacity in their efforts to evacuate people and stock from the outlying farms before lives were lost. Sean did not envy them.

But for the low, dense fog of cloud, they would have seen the ocean, a few miles to the east. When Sean rolled down the window for some fresh air, the ozone smell was strong enough to prickle his nostrils. The harbours would be empty, as cautious skippers hurried their working boats and pleasure craft out of harm's way, beyond the hundred fathom line. Ships at sea must turn their bows to the wind and run their engines at station-keeping. The beast coming in was the breed of Southern Ocean storm that had the power to lift even large vessels, such as the local prawn trawlers and tuna boats, right out of the water and dump them down, wrecked, on the shore.

"Lightning Ridge is that way," Rob prompted as the car stopped.

"I heard you before. Shit, Robbie, I can't see a yard in front of the hood!" Sean's temper was on a short rein, and threatening to get away from him.

"Want me to drive a while?" Rob offered.

"No!" And then Sean heard his own tone of voice, and backed up fast with a deep, calming breath. He was snarling, and he knew without a glance at Rob that he would be wearing that bruised look. The look he had worn when Sean confessed his brief but explosive affair with Peter Kramer.

Sean took a deep breath, and another. There had been days — though not lately, thank God, he thought — when the only times they seemed to communicate were when they were in bed. High on a rush of sexual excitement, action overrode words. The whole reason they were in this place, and in this mess, was the commitment they had made to each other. This vacation was supposed to build a stronger relationship on better, more solid foundations, not tear to shreds what they already had.

"I'm sorry, Robbie," Sean said with enforced calm. "I'm just getting a bit uptight. You know me well enough by now. There's no point you driving, honey. Besides, you look... what's that word you use? Knackered. Done in. You look like you could use a few days in the sun."

"A year or two in the tropics?" Rob produced a faint smile.

"Maybe soon," Sean promised as he shunted the Toyota into gear and took it around the bend in the track. "I might show you Florida. You'd like Florida."

They had climbed up out of the valley now. As he turned right, Rob peered out of the side window and whistled. "My God, it's like a lake! If they didn't get the livestock out, they wouldn't have stood a chance. You'd need a boat to get through now."

"Which means," Sean said quietly, "we're on our own."

Rob looked back at him, over his shoulder, and cuffed the windscreen. It was misting up thickly. Sean had turned off the demisters minutes before. They were straining the ailing battery and could easily flatten it.

"We know one thing, dead certain," Sean mused as he slewed around an uprooted tree. "Chandler had to come by this route, because there is no other way. How would he get back to Victor Harbour from here? He's not a local, he doesn't know the area any better than we do. Probably not as well."

"If you were on foot you could try hiking dead west, and then south again," Rob speculated. "Still, the detours would add miles to the journey. Get off the high ground, and you're going to drown. It'd be a ten mile hike to Victor, and he's not the kind of guy to tackle that. Well, not without a little incentive."

The higher slopes were populated with sheep, cows, a few horses, clustered together in forlorn knots under the trees. They stood with their heads down, as if they knew the worst was yet to come. Animals always knew. The chance was, Sean thought, John Chandler would know, too. The man was a wild animal. And if you trap a wild animal, it turns nasty.

"Look out — shit!" Rob's voice rose sharply as the car slithered sideways, and what had been impending for the last thirty minutes overtook them so quickly, Sean barely had time to register what was happening.

The two left wheels dropped into the roadside ditch, the Toyota skewed, went down onto its left side and almost ended on its roof before it rolled back again. The motor stalled out into silence and Sean grunted painfully as he hung in the straps, suspended like a puppet. His heart was like a mallet against his ribs as an adrenalin overload hit him in every cell.

Survival instinct seized him in a fierce grip. "Robbie! Rob, are you hurt? Robbie!" His voice cut with the razor's edge of fear.

In the darkness, way down in the left side of the car, Rob was stirring, but Sean could barely see him. "I'm okay," he muttered, muffled, as if he was speaking through a wad of cotton waste. "Move it, Sean. Get out!"

"There's no gas spilled, we won't burn," Sean said quickly, panting as his mind began to clear and he felt a dozen strains and pulls in his back, shoulders, hips.

"I know that, but I'm breaking my bloody neck down here, and I can't get out till you do!" Rob's voice became more suffocated with each word.

"Okay, hold on." Sean unbuckled the seat strap and held his weight on the dashboard and steering wheel. He braced himself on his feet and hunted for the door. The lock clicked open and the wind caught the door, lifting it wide. Steel-grey light and rain flooded the car as he pulled himself onto the side, and then reached back for Rob.

Swearing fluently, panting for breath, Rob, clambered clear of the car. Sean supported him as he stood beside it, and Rob cupped both hands at the nape of his neck, for the moment oblivious to the rain. Worried, Sean explored the delicate assembly of bones and muscles where skull joined spine. The human body was so fragile.

"Nothing's broken," he said cautiously, "but I guess everything's strained."

"I just took a knock," Rob puffed. "I'll have a bruise there tomorrow. Stop worrying, Sean, I've had worse than this falling off a bike." He hesitated, working his head around to ease the abused muscles, and gave Sean a rueful smile. "Mind you, I like it when you're concerned about me."

Despite their surroundings and their plight, Sean felt a flutter of pleasure. "You do? Then I'll keep right on worrying about you." He touched Rob's rain-wet face with gentle fingertips. "Right now, in case you haven't noticed, we're in a jam."

"You're the one who's been twice around the world with Jackson Oil," Rob grumbled goodnaturedly. "All that wealth of experience ought to make a cakewalk of this."

Sean gave him a wry look. "Not quite a cakewalk."

"But close to it." Rob tugged his collar up and wrapped his arms around his chest. "Where do we go now? What's the quickest way out of here?"

"What did you do with the map?" Sean leaned over and peered into the car.

"Dropped it," Rob said acidly. "There were several moments when keeping my skull in one piece was more important that holding onto a damned map! And then —" he stopped as Sean kissed his neck. "Sean?" His voice was hushed, breathless.

"I'm sorry, Rob," Sean said, under the wind and the bass rumble of thunder. "I put the car in that ditch, it didn't drive itself in there. And now you're hurt."

"I'm just bruised," Rob insisted. "And the truth is, if I'd been driving we'd have been in a ditch a half hour ago."

"We would?" Sean blinked on the rain.

Ridiculously, Rob smiled. "Bet a month's pay on it."

Sean leaned over and nuzzled Rob's neck deliberately, where the muscles were sore. He took Rob's cold, wet face between his hands, and when Rob's arms snaked around his waist he stepped forward, pressing them together. His mouth covered Rob's, at once hard and gentle, his tongue hunting for Rob's, unsatisfied until it was made welcome in the heat of Rob's willing mouth. Fleeting images of the last time they made love taunted him. The lamplight gilded Rob's skin, they were mellow after a meal and a bottle of wine. He had bought gold satin sheets. Rob put him on his knees, prepared him with a lick of oil and pierced him to the heart, as he knew Sean liked best.

Lightning forked overhead and the thunder pealed almost at

once, wrenching them apart with the sudden shock of noise. Rob licked his crushed lips. "The storm's almost overhead. You see that tree? I guess they don't call this Lightning Ridge for nothing. We ought to get away from the car."

He was pointing at a tree that had been blasted in halves. Twenty yards further along the ridge was the blackened stump of another tree. Rob stuffed his hands into his pockets for warmth. "I don't know if it's just an old wives' tale, but they say you shouldn't stand under trees in a storm. Or beside pieces of metal. They attract the lightning."

"So I've been told." Sean gave the sky a sour look and hoisted himself up onto the side of the car. He dove in, head-first, rummaging for whatever he could find that was salvageable. There was not much. The flashlight, the map, a bag of candy. "Come on, Robbie. There has to be a farm or a cottage, something along this track. You up to walking?"

"I don't have much option." Collar up, hands in pockets, Rob shuffled away into the teeth of the wind. "I'm all right, Sean, just shaken up. My whole life flashed before my eyes, but I'm just bruised. Bradgate, the farm marked on that map, wasn't too far ahead."

Sean caught him up quickly, and set a fast pace down the track, which doubled back and snaked across the high ground toward the sea. One thought nagged at the back of his mind, though he did not voice it.

This was the way John Chandler would have come, because it was the only high ground left.

Street clothes were useless in these conditions. With a sound of disgust, Sean remembered the last time he had made a forced march through such wind and rain, fifty miles south of Acapulco. Then, he had been wearing something similar to army combat fatigues, and oilskins. His pockets had been stuffed with chocolates, and he'd been equipped with a mobile phone, just a Motorola satellite away from Jackson Oil, and help. And inside those oilskins he had sweated profusely in the tropical heat and humidity.

In dense patches of fog, the cloud was sitting right down on the hill. When they had walked no more than two hundred yards he turned back and found he had lost sight of the car, though it was still quite clear up ahead. Rob had gone on, and Sean took the opportunity to hang back, scout the lie of the land.

The wind was so strong, he could lean on it, as if a giant hand physically pushed him backwards at every step. The rain stung any exposed skin like a swarm of wasps. The single consolation was, wherever John Chandler was, he was suffering the same conditions, and he had been out in the chill and storm since before dawn. He would be much colder and tireder than Sean and Rob, and far past the end of a city boy's patience.

Since leaving the car they had trudged up a steady gradient, but as they scrambled to the highest point of the ridge the slope fell away sharply before them, and Rob pulled up.

"We got a problem."

Twenty feet below, the track led directly into a great wind-whipped lake, fifty yards wide and thirty across.

"That could be ten feet deep," Sean said bitterly.

"And it's full of debris." Rob pointed out a bicycle, parts of a wooden packing crate, and the body of a drowned animal, a goat or sheep, Sean could not tell. "I don't know that I'd like to get into that... and I don't see any boat."

"Now, I wonder," Sean speculated, "did Chandler make his way here before the water rose this far?"

"If he did, he's on the other side and halfway home," Rob said caustically. "What worries me is that it could have been like this for hours. In which case —" he hesitated.

"He's on this side, with us," Sean finished. "No easy way forward, no way back, without exploring."

"Jesus." Rob scrubbed his face with both hands. "Sean, I have the traditional bad feeling about this."

So had Sean. He slitted his eyes against the curtain of rain and looked back the way they had come. To either side of the track were bushes, trees, sometimes quite dense. A man could hide anywhere. They could go back and search, but a troupe of police would need a whole day to do the job efficiently, and in these conditions even a Delta Force strike team could miss the man.

"Fuck," Sean growled passionately. "Fuckfuckfuck!" He shoved his hands into his pockets and cast about on all sides for inspiration. He had almost decided that they had no choice, and had better get into the dangerous, debris-strewn water when Rob shouted over the gusting wind, "What d'you make of that?"

"What?" Half blind in the rain, Sean turned toward him and followed the line of his pointing arm.

"Wait a minute, it looks like —" Rob was pointing off to the left. "A signboard. I can't see what it says." He pushed stubbornly into the wind, and beckoned urgently for Sean to follow.

Sean was with him in a dozen strides, and peered at the hand-painted notice. He saw a name and an arrow which pointed to the left, over the lip of the hill, down into the valley. "Bradgate Farm," he read. "Damn, I didn't see it at all. This is the farm marked on the map. The only one in the area, you said."

"Don't let me worry you," Rob muttered, "but it's already flooded down there. The creek in the bottom will have brought down about a million gallons of runoff from the hills, ten miles inland. By six tonight when the storm tide comes in, this whole valley will be like the ocean. The emergency services will have evacuated the people who live here, hours ago."

"But Farmer Brown might have a shortwave, or even a working phone, or a four wheel drive in the garage. An old tractor would do," Sean reasoned.

He was right, as usual. Rob gave him that familiar lopsided smile. He started down the steeply inclined path toward the farmhouse while Sean was still quartering the hillside and the track behind them with wary eyes. Searching for the shape of a man, or some sign that he had passed this way. Chandler.

The name made his skin crawl. His hackles rose each time he thought of Dwight Murdoch's eccentric, cruel antics... and Susan Jenkins. Madness took many forms. The sociopath was among the most dangerous of lunatics, because he was often mistaken for a normal person. By the time his victims realised the truth, it was too late. Sean was certain that Dwight Murdoch was certifiable. It took a lot to faze the hustlers in New Orleans, but somehow Dwight had managed it. One day the law would catch up with him, but not soon enough.

"You there, Sean?" Rob's voice barked. "Sean!"

He had been adrift in time. He snapped back to the present with an uncomfortable start, and kicked himself. Preoccupation could get a man into very deep shit indeed. He picked up his pace, hurried after Rob and found himself on the muddy track that wound at a steep down-angle, around a mass of trees.

Ten yards below the ridge, the road was completely out of sight and Sean would have sworn he was in a wood. Eucalypts — gum trees — seemed to shed both their bark and foliage all year round, and yet never be bare or skeletal, like the deciduous trees he knew best from home. Fallen leaves and twigs were thick underfoot, drifted like snow.

"Where are you, Robbie? Rob!" For a disconcerting moment

as the trees swallowed him, Sean lost his sense of direction.

A moment later he heard the squawks of a flock of chickens as he rounded the trees. He was in the yard behind a small bluestone farm cottage. It had been built on a part of the hill that had been deliberately levelled, but it was doubtful that even this site would be high enough to beat the flood waters. The impending king tide promised disaster, and the family that lived here was probably wise to bug out.

The house was the now-familiar stone construction, with a red galvanised steel roof. To one side stood a shed, also built of the rippled steel sheeting which was so common in Australia. A deeply rutted driveway ran up to the doors, which were heavily padlocked. Rob was peering in through the narrow gap between them, and as Sean joined him he shook his head.

"No joy. We won't get out that way. Whatever was garaged here, they probably left in it." He turned toward the house, then. "I'd settle for a working phone." He hesitated and frowned. "Are we housebreaking?"

"In town they'd say so, but not in the country," Sean speculated. "Country folks have a code of helping their neighbours in an emergency. The next time, it could be yourself in trouble, and you could die if nobody will stand by you."

"You convinced me." Rob peered at his watch. "I make it just before noon. The valley's flooding fast, but we don't have to panic before high tide."

Sean tried the cottage's back door, but as he had expected, it was locked. He tried the windows one by one, and at the kitchen fortune smiled at last. The window there had been left open a tiny crack.

"Just like my mother used to do," Rob commented as Sean slid up the glass. "She always swore you should leave two windows open in a gale, back and front of the house. It equalises the pressure."

"Smart lady." Sean beckoned him closer as the old-fashioned window squealed up in its frame. He parted the pale green cafe curtains and looked in. "Is anyone home? Hello — anyone here?"

He had expected no answer, and when he received none he lifted himself through. He found himself kneeling on a modern chrome sink unit in an attractive country kitchen. He lifted his legs down, gave the green and yellow decoration of the room a single appraising look, and leaned back out to give Rob the all-clear. Rob quickly clambered through.

"Welcome back to civilisation," he panted as his feet hit the quarry-tiled floor. "It's warm! I wonder if they'd mind if we lit the fire and got dry, and made some tea. We could leave some money on the table."

"Go for it," Sean said without hesitation. "Let me check out the phone."

"The eternal bloody optimist," Rob accused as he found a box of matches and knelt at the hearth.

"Optimism is cheap," Sean retorted as he stepped through into the parlour, which overlooked the rapidly flooding valley.

He found the phone in the living room, almost hidden in a corner between the red leather sofa and an antique china cabinet. The cottage was small, with just kitchen, parlour, one bedroom, plus a laundry in back, and a bathroom tacked on as an afterthought. It must have been built in the twenties, and when this generation of houses were new, you bathed in a tub that was stored in the corner of the kitchen.

The gas heater was on in the parlour, and Sean groaned as he felt his extremities begin to thaw. He did not sit on the sofa as he tried the phone — he was soaked, and despite the warmth he was shivering as he held the plastic to his ear and prayed for a dial tone.

Nothing. He had known all along that the lines must be down. He hung up with a resigned sigh and returned to Rob with the news.

Old houses almost always had open hearths. In the kitchen's chimney corner was a box of wood shavings, a pile of cut mallee roots and a carton of fire lighters. Rob had already got a fire alive and was half naked while a kettle simmered on the gas.

He had spread his shirt and jacket to dry in the draft of heat, and peeled off his jeans as Sean watched. Though he was close by the hearth and it was reasonably warm his skin was unnaturally pale and showing a rash of goose bumps. Was he just chilled to the bone, Sean wondered, or was he hurt?

He swallowed as he slapped a hand on Rob's forehead. "You may have hurt yourself more than you realised, when the car rolled."

"Bull," Rob said succinctly. "I'm just frozen. I don't have your body mass to keep me warm. Remember, you've got an easy twenty pounds on me."

"As you frequently remind me," Sean said drily.

Rob's brows rose. "When do I do that?"

"In bed." Sean winked one blue eye at him. "When I'm lying on you, and you tell me I'm squashing you flatter than a flapjack."

"Oh." Rob gave him the impish grin that had always endeared and seduced Sean. "Well, there are times when it's pleasant to be squashed."

"I'll remember that, next time you tell me to climb off you," Sean warned.

Rob was rubbing his arms, still shivering. "I wonder if they'd mind if we borrowed some blankets?" He was already padding away toward the bedroom to search for them.

They would leave twenty dollars, Sean thought, and a polite letter of thanks and apology combined. At that moment his stomach growled with hunger. "Ah, what the hell," he muttered, and began to open cupboard doors.

He had the distinct feeling he was prying, intruding into someone's privacy, but what he had said to Rob about the country code was true enough. A year from now, it could be the people who lived in this house who were in trouble. It would not be Sean's help they needed, but someone's. It was an unwritten law that you always extended hospitality, so that when you needed a favour yourself, one was offered. Like Mrs Jenkins and her daughter-in-law? Sean wondered how Susan was now. She needed a doctor, and she was not likely to get one.

He tried the light switches, but the electricity was off, which was only to be expected. In a cupboard by the cooker he found ham, bread and butter, mustard, pineapple jam, tea and sugar, a jug of milk. He dumped the jars and packets on the table and began to hunt for crockery.

Rob was wrapped in a tartan blanket when he reappeared, and carried another three over his arm. "My God, Sean, are you still in those clothes? They're not going to dry while you've got them on — and even if they do, you know what it does to you, letting ice-cold rags dry on you? What folklore did your dear, sainted old Gran tell you about that?"

"Arthritis gets in, and the rheumatizz, whatever that is," Sean said dutifully, repeating the old lady's home-grown wisdom, right down to that Philly accent of hers. A sudden rush of something like homesickness took him by surprise, but he realised at once it was not a place he longed for, but a time. A time, and people, who were gone. He forced a smile and turned back to Rob. "You can get a 'cold in your kidneys', so she told me." He gave Rob a grin as he began to strip. "Happened to me once, when I was nine. I lived with the old lady for a while, you know? That was after my dad left."

"I know," Rob said quietly. "He leathered the ass off you, beat crap out of your mother, blacked her eyes, took every penny she had, and her car, and vanished."

"I must have told you about it." Sean smiled faintly, mocking himself. "I don't remember telling you. There's not many people who know about that, I'm not proud of it." Old memories reached out and caught him once more, too easily.

"I'm pleased to be one of the people you trust," Rob said gently "I want to know everything about you. Every last thing."

Like a fish hooked on a tight line, Sean jerked back to the present. The past had a way of tugging him back into half-forgotten scenes he wished he did not remember. What he had told Rob was little enough, about a childhood that had been rough.

"What is it?" Rob whispered as Sean's face creased in an introspective frown.

"Nothing, honey." Sean shook himself hard. "Nothing at all." He stripped swiftly, spread his clothes beside Rob's and scrubbed his skin with a corner of one of the blankets. The first tendrils of warmth had begun to lick through his limbs when he turned back to Rob.

Rob's cheeks were a rosy blush as his circulation restarted. His hair was damp, and Sean pushed him closer to the fire. "Get warm."

"I am warm," Rob said in that dark, sultry tone that would have seduced a saint and always made Sean shiver. "I kind of thought I might get a hug." He let the tartan blanket drop. Beneath it, he was naked. Lean and beautiful, his chest almost smooth, his belly concave. His muscles were hard and round with youth, his legs long, coltish.

Yet Rob had no concept of his own devastating charm, and this was the feature that attracted Sean most of all. He opened his arms. "Come here, beautiful."

They embraced tightly, and Sean buried his face in the strong curve of Rob's shoulder. It felt so good to hold him like this. Not in a flashfire of sex, not on heat at midnight after too much to drink, when frustration made them rough and much too quick... but affectionately, in broad daylight, like real human beings.

"God, I'm sorry," Rob said suddenly.

"For what?" Sean nuzzled his ear.

"For getting us into this shit." Rob's grip tightened around Sean's strong torso. "It was my idea to come down here in the middle of winter."

"Far from the madding crowd," Sean added. "It was exactly what we needed. Stop castigating yourself. Okay, it was your dumb idea to see if the fish were biting before the storm came in, but it was my idea to go to the aid of Lewis's boat. If we hadn't done that, we'd be safe right now, with a couple of drinks inside us and a soft mattress under." He drew back to look at Rob, took his lover's face between his hands and brushed Rob's lips with his thumbs. He felt the prickle of midday stubble and smiled. "It just happened. Stop trying to apportion blame."

"You're a persuasive bugger." Rob leaned over and kissed him. "Get some food into you, love. I think we'll be marooned here for a while. Have you taken a look outside?"

The whole sky was almost black as night now. Every minute, the rain seemed to be growing heavier and the thunder broke right overhead. With the electricity dead, they were lucky to have a live fire for light and heat, and the gas supply was still connected. The kettle had started to whistle, and as Sean released Rob, he swiped it off the burner.

Through the veil of steam he gave Rob a rueful grin. "We're warm, we're dry. The only thing we can do now is stay put, wait for the storm to pass. Then maybe we can hike down into Victor Harbour."

"The low paddocks are already under," Rob said doubtfully. "Sticking to the uplands will make it about a twenty-mile route march."

"So we set out first thing in the morning, and take all day," Sean reasoned.

Rob stabbed a finger at the valley below the house. "Always supposing this king tide doesn't rise so high that this building ends up as driftwood by ten tonight!"

"Okay, so we play it by ear," Sean said sharply. "Don't make it worse than it is." He turned his back on Rob, spooned tea and sugar into the cups and brimmed them. And then, not quite unexpectedly, Rob's arms slid around him from behind and soft lips began to nuzzle the nape of Sean's neck. He turned back, caught Rob tightly and held him.

"I'm just trying to be practical," Rob murmured against his neck.

"I know that. And I shouldn't snarl at you. I'm being a... what do you call it?"

"A nong." Rob chuckled.

"Care to offer a literal translation?" Sean challenged as good humour banished his slight annoyance.

"Into English, a wally, a twit or a berk. Into basic modern American — a dummy, I guess."

"Oh, thanks a whole bunch." But Sean also chuckled, and kissed him soundly. "Go on and eat. And then," he added, licking his lips, that salacious expression that always made Rob shiver visibly, "if we're going to be stranded here the whole day, I vote we make the best of it, not the worst."

"You," Rob told him, "have got yourself a deal!"

To be warm, dry and fed felt like unbelievable luxury. Sean relaxed muscle by muscle and watched the rain pelt against the window. With luck the high tide would not endanger the farmhouse and they could wait till morning before they started out on what would be a difficult hike. They could leave a couple of twenties and a letter on the table, load up with all the food they could carry and be in Victor Harbour by sunset, even if they had to make their way across country. Perhaps they would run into a rescue service vehicle, a boat, or be spotted and picked up by a chopper.

The rain lashed around the house, and Sean wriggled down into a nest of cushions and blankets, so close to the fire that his hip was roasted scarlet. In his hands, Rob was pliant and eager, just as he had been on that first night, fourteen months ago. Sean buried his face eagerly in Rob's smooth chest and opened his mouth to the musk-sweet taste of him.

Rob could remember no time when he and Sean had been emotionally closer, and relief rendered his bones to jelly. How many marriages, gay and straight alike, were wrecked when people ceased to communicate? Relationships ended on the junk heap, and more than anything that spectre had frightened him. Sean was all he had ever wanted. He still could not believe his luck in finding him... or being found by him. What incredible fortune had made Jackson Oil downsize its staff, at the very moment when Aurora Petroleum was advertising for engineers, in papers as far afield as London, Paris and Los Angeles? Now that he had Sean, Rob was not about to let him go without a fight.

Sean's mouth was on his neck and chest. Teeth nibbled, and Rob held the dark head against him. Their hair was dry now, their clothes would soon be dry enough to wear, but it was wonderful to lie nude in the nest of blankets and just revel in each other. Sean was sucking firmly on his nipples, and Rob groaned as pleasure and excitement arrowed directly into his groin. He arched his back, thrust the hard, sensitive little nub of flesh into Sean's hungry mouth and murmured in encouragement. Not that Sean needed any. He was always a generous lover. Sean derived almost as much satisfaction from the giving of pleasure as from the taking.

He kissed his way to Rob's other nipple and started over while Rob wriggled and sighed, and his cock came erect. It arched over his flat belly, and Sean knelt astride him. He trapped the rearing shaft between his buttocks and clenched his muscles around it while he lifted his head and laid claim to Rob's open mouth.

"You are all right, aren't you?" he asked. Still trying to convince himself that Rob had not been hurt when the car rolled. Punishing himself, Rob guessed, since he blamed himself for the spill.

"I'm fine," Rob assured him. "I might have a slight case of whiplash tomorrow, but I wasn't lying when I said I've had worse than that, falling off a bike."

"You're so beautiful." Sean sat back to look at him.

Such remarks always made Rob bask, though he could never fully understand what Sean saw in him. Sean's affection and appreciation were the most precious things he owned. He arched his spine and stroked his own belly, slowly and deliberately stimulating himself for Sean's pleasure as well as his own. Sean loved to watch. Rob's own eyes moved down over Sean's tanned, muscular body, and came to rest on his groin.

The pubic thatch was dense and black but his balls were pale, full and smooth, almost hairless, while his cock was heavy and thick. It did not stand right up when he was excited, probably because it was too weighty for its own muscles, but it jutted like a spear. In the natural history museum in Adelaide was a Micronesian statue, often sniggered over by adolescents. The figure was primal, male, aroused. Rob often wondered who had modelled for that statue, which seemed to be a celebration of masculinity. It reminded him in a way of Sean: martial, strong, even daunting. Superb.

In the cold light of day, sometimes Rob wondered how he ever took every inch of that beautiful cock inside him, yet after the first swift pain had eased, the pleasure was intense. He smiled at it, and Sean made a quiet sound of exasperation.

"Now, what are you thinking?"

"Thinking about that." Rob took it between his fingers. It was moist, hot and throbbing. "About having it inside me, and how impossible you'd think it was to jam a thing like that into a man's ass, and how good it feels when it's in there."

"Men have known that for thousands of years," Sean scoffed as he reached over to the table, for the butter. "I have a theory."

"I'm listening." Rob settled back and lifted his legs.

Sean stroked him, tickled his balls, which began to tighten. "In the days before people knew it was sex made women pregnant, there's no logic in assuming male-dominance cultures. They developed when men realised they could make women pregnant, keep them pregnant."

"That makes sense," Rob murmured as Sean stroked him up and down, and his fingers trailed back into the moist crevice.

"So," Sean went on languidly, "they'd figure babies were the gifts of the gods. Women were respected because only they were gifted, but ancient Egyptians believed men could get pregnant. Take a look at their myths! You probably had a whole lot of matriarchal cultures."

Rob groaned and looked dizzily up into Sean's face as Sean buttered his fingers. "Do it. Please, do it to me."

"I will. So, there'd have been no prejudice against male sex." Sean slipped his fingers inside, making Rob cry out sharply and arch his head into the cushions. "You can't say the passive partner would be scorned. Girls are passive, and the gods gift them. The partner in the woman's role would be honoured. True?"

"Yeah." Rob moved luxuriously on Rob's hand. "Men would want to be fucked, maybe it made them closer to heaven. When they learned how it feels, they'd do it for pleasure." The fingers inside him were stealing his mind. "You read that somewhere?"

"Some of it. Some, I thought out." Sean withdrew his fingers very gently and moved in between Rob's legs. "Ready?"

"Eager," Rob corrected, and drew him down, and in.

The big shaft pierced him slowly, deeply. After more than a year together, Rob was too accustomed to Sean to feel more than a brief pang before discomfort turned to fierce pleasure, and they began to move together. Musk prickled the nostrils, excitement curled through every nerve fibre. Rob's legs locked around Sean's muscular torso, his fingers clenched into Sean's shoulders, and as Sean's movements grew more powerful with urgency, he had only to hang on for the ride.

From there, it was the downhill race to pleasure that made Rob forget this predicament, even forget his own name. When Sean was inside him, nothing else existed. Coming was deep, the pleasure was as racking as any pain, and Rob was sure the strength drained out of him along with the last blood-hot drops of his milk. Spent, he could hardly keep his eyes open, and he gave a drowsy chuckle as Sean kissed them shut.

"Go to sleep," Sean whispered. "You need it. You've earned it."

Rob was pleased to comply.

They both slept, while the storm raged like a dragon over Lightning Ridge. Rain spattered down the chimney and hissed in the hearth, but Rob was oblivious. For a blessed hour all he was aware of was being warm, safe and at peace in Sean's embrace.

He did not stir until an icy draft entered the kitchen from somewhere. Sean was still almost asleep, and Rob turned over as the cold air prickled his bare back.

And then he froze as a shape detached itself from the doorway that led through into the living room.

Six

ROB'S HEART squeezed and the blood roared in his ears. His fingers dug like talons into Sean's arm, wrenching him awake, and in that same split second Sean also saw the shape of the man, standing in the doorway behind them.

In his hands was a double-barrelled twelve gauge, levelled on them and rock steady in large brown hands. A hundred thoughts raced through Rob's mind — was this the owner of the farm, had he come back for something forgotten, was it a neighbour, a policeman who had seen smoke from the chimney when this house should have been evacuated? They were intruders, technically trespassers, they were caught in an extremely compromising situation, and straights could be unpredictable, violent.

Before Rob could speak, Sean had gathered his wits and found his voice. "Jesus Christ, where did you come from? You wouldn't be John Chandler, would you?" His voice was like chipped ice.

The man stepped into the kitchen. "Ah, our backyard philosopher. Where do we come from, indeed? Darwin says we share a common ancestor with apes, but he gets an irritating argument from the Creationists."

They had heard the ambiguous, international accent over the open shortwave. Part Australian, part American, part English, the vowels intermingled and deceptive. Rob groaned audibly. Chandler was wearing white slacks, a green and yellow ski jersey and brown leather shoes that looked as if they had been scraped of mud. And he was dry, even his hair, which meant he had been here for some time. Damn the man, he was as handsome as Mrs Jenkins had said. His long, deeply wavy hair was thick and darkly blond, and his features were so classically perfect, he could have modelled for a statue. His skin had a fine marble texture, and his body was long limbed, elegant, graceful. Yet everything about him was dangerous.

And he was certifiable, with a shotgun in both hands, and two captives in the most vulnerable position. Rob's heart was beating a tattoo against his ribs. He swallowed hard to steady his voice.

"Are you Chandler?"

"At your service, sir." Chandler bowed. The American in his voice had been softened by years of living abroad, unlike Sean's accent. He drew out a chair, sat at the table and with a smile balanced the weapon on his knee. "Don't let me stop you. Go right ahead with that you were doing."

"We were sleeping," Sean rasped.

Chandler's smile widened. "You put on a good show, earlier."

Heat and blood suffused Rob's face. "You saw us?"

The blond head nodded at the door. "I've been here for hours. You were a pleasure to behold. All right, I'll have you on your knees, both of you. Hands on your heads, sit right down on your heels, and lean back, way back. There, it's an interesting feeling, isn't it? Do you feel the compression in your ankle joints already? No matter. You will, soon." When they had settled awkwardly, he looked them both over with critical eyes, before frowning at Sean. "What's your name?"

"Sean Brodie," Sean told him quietly.

"Irish-American, are you?" Chandler asked pleasantly. "Half my family's Irish. Black Irish." His eyes covered Rob an inch at a time and came to rest deliberately at his groin. "Now, that's a real beauty of a cock, Sean. Not like yours. Yours is no good. Too big, looks like a cudgel. But his — now, that's pretty. Why don't you give it a little kiss?"

"Go to hell," Rob spat. "You're going to kill us. There's no reason we have to let you humiliate us before you do what you're going to do anyway."

"Rob," Sean said quietly, "don't provoke him. He's a lunatic."

"And we're dead meat, either way," Rob said bitterly. "Don't give him his fun."

"Oh, bravo, boys!" Chandler encouraged. "Dumb courage, amateur heroics, better than a soap opera. This is the best show in town... after the fucking." He smacked his lips. "It's a long time since I've done a boy. I'd forgotten how much I used to enjoy it. How much I enjoy watching." He was devouring Rob alive with dark, smouldering eyes.

Sean's whole spine stiffened and he shifted involuntarily on his knees, unable to stop himself placing his own body between Chandler and Rob. "Don't even think it, you bastard."

"I can think anything I like," Chandler said smoothly. "But I take your meaning. Death before dishonour, or some such sanctimonious bullshit, is it?" He tilted his head at them. "Does the little beauty have a name?"

"I'm Rob Markham," Rob said icily.

"An Aussie lad, are you? Born and bred, by the sound of you." Chandler leaned back in the chair and eased the weight of the shotgun. "Now, what's to become of you, that's my immediate problem. Question is, what are you worth?"

"In ransom?" Sean resettled his buttocks on his heels as his legs began to cramp under his weight. He could already feel his feet growing bloodless and the long thigh muscles were under constant stress as he maintained the backward leaning position. His knees and ankles would begin to lock up soon, and his mouth dried. In ten more minutes his legs would be so stiff, when he got up he would move like a geriatric. Damn Chandler, he knew what he was doing. Had he done this before? "We're not worth a ransom to anyone," he said tersely.

"Not what I meant, old horse." Chandler drew a packet of shortbreads toward him. "You can't imagine the number of markets where people are eager to pay for a healthy young body, and the number of uses they're put to! There's a man I know in Port Moresby who'll have you, though the price won't be terribly high. He needs a constant supply of bodies to test new batches. Drugs, you know. Top quality... pharmaceuticals are always tested on lab rats." He fed a shortbread into his mouth and laughed quietly. "There's another man I know in Burma, and a lady in Thailand, who'll pay much more for white boys. But that's a long way from here, and we're not planning to head that far north."

Sociopath. A shudder inched along Sean's spine. "When did you get here? We didn't see you."

"I've been here quite a while," Chandler said easily. "When you arrived I was asleep, and unfortunately you took me unawares. I'd left the gun propped there, in the corner of the room, and by the time I woke, I couldn't get to it. You'd have heard me in the other room, and reached it first. So I lifted myself up into the loft and just waited until you were... too busy to notice me. All I had to do then was keep quiet and watch the show."

"Ah, fuck," Sean whispered as he shifted his weight a little, trying to ease his knees and ankles, which did not seem to have a drop of blood left in them now. Rob was doing the same thing, little wriggles betraying his discomfort.

"An apt turn of phrase." Chandler helped himself to another shortbread. "Now, if I shoot you — and God knows, I should, I'd like to — I'd have to dispose of your bodies. Under ordinary circumstances I'd just bury you in the woods. This far from civilisation it might be a decade before you were found. However, this rain would wash you out of the ground in a few hours." His brows arched. "How about if I buried you in the shed?"

Rob was shifting painfully on ankles in which a pair of daggers seemed to be buried hilt-deep. "Not unless you've got a jackhammer. It's concreted."

"I see. Pity." Chandler looked into the fire. "Then, I think you'll have to come with me. Lewis may decide to dispose of you at sea. So long as the tide is going out when we throw you over, you're no problem! Or else, you'll fetch a few dollars in that laboratory in Moresby." He cocked his head at Sean. "Where did you leave your car?"

"We rolled it, it's lying on its side in a ditch." Sean's voice was taut. His knees and ankles were like rusted old hinges, and his thigh muscles were aching. "Chandler, can we move?"

"Hm?" Chandler seemed to become aware of their position for the first time since he had ordered them into it. "Oh no, I don't think so. Not yet. You're safest right where you are. Starting to hurt, are you? You stay where you are a while longer. I'll let you know when you can get up."

He knew what he was doing, Sean thought feverishly. If they were kept this way long enough, they would be useless for minutes when they were allowed to move at last. He breathed deeply, concentrating on the sounds of the wind and rain, and on Rob beside him, the rasp of his breathing, the faint, masculine scent of his body.

For twenty minutes Chandler chatted almost pleasantly about 'his work', and questioned Sean and Rob about their own. His mouth never stopped. If a thought crossed his mind it must be vocalised, and he must have input from other people, every moment, until exhaustion made him sleep. If Sean refused to talk, he would turn to Rob.

At last, Rob was too fatigued and cramped to reply. and Chandler regarded him with a frown. "You look unwell, Robbie boy. You're not comfortable?"

Rob moaned softly. Sean had not spoken in minutes. The shotgun never wavered, but at last Chandler got up.

"All right, let's make you two comfortable. You first, Sean. Up you get, quick as you can."

If only Sean could have sprung up. Yards out of their reach, Chandler leaned on the door and watched Sean stand clumsily, painfully. His knees and ankles would not fully unbend, and he remembered that the Vietnamese would treat their captives this way, a unique, effective form of torture that left no permanent injury, spilled no blood, was cheap and could be performed anywhere. Had Chandler read about it, or had he been there? Sean staggered a step and hissed through his teeth at the knifing discomfort.

Chandler tossed his jeans to him. "Put your pants and shoes on. But unloop the belt first, get the belt out of Rob's jeans, throw them both over here."

With thick, clumsy fingers Sean unlooped them and threw them at Chandler. Rob was still on his knees, hands on his head, his face a frozen mask. He wouldn't be feeling his feet any longer, Sean knew. He struggled into his jeans, and was zipping them as he heard Chandler move to the window.

A knife slashed through the curtains' draw-cord, and the next Sean knew, a loop of it was around his wrists. Chandler wrestled his hands behind him, and Sean cursed himself for the painful near-paralysis of his legs as he was tied, tugged backward and pitched onto the floor like a rag doll. Far out of Rob's reach, his ankles were bound, his wrists made fast to them, which bent his back like a bow, and the last length of cord secured him to the table, which was built in, part of the wall.

"Sean, you okay?" Rob's voice whispered under the wind, which howled fiercely under the eaves.

"I will be," Sean panted.

"He's just fine," Chandler admonished. "In fact, he's safest right there. I don't have to worry about him, so I don't have to hurt him. What more could you ask for, Rob? Now, let see about you. I'll fix you up, and then I'll get something to eat and catch a few winks. I had a terrible night last night."

"You raped a woman," Rob grunted as he struggled up, wincing as his knees and ankles unbent.

"I did what?" Chandler actually laughed. He was gathering up the belts Sean had unlooped out of their jeans. "Put your pants on, boy. That little bitch came out to the shed in the middle of the night and took her blouse off, right in front of my face. I accepted what she offered, and you call it rape? That's so much crap, Rob. I just gave the bitch what she wanted."

"You could tell by the screams, could you?" Sean hissed as he watched Rob labour awkwardly into his jeans. "Then you trussed her up."

"Didn't have much choice." Chandler stroked the barrel of the shotgun, as if it reminded him of the act of violence. "She would have rushed inside to mommy and told the old bat I was taking their antique rattle-trap of a car."

"But she almost died in the cold!" Sean snarled.

"Cold?" Chandler echoed vaguely as he watched Rob zip up. "I was warm enough."

"The girl," Rob panted, "was shocked and frozen."

"Really?" Chandler seemed genuinely surprised. "Ah well, if you flash your tits in men's faces, these things happen." He spun Rob around, and before he had his balance, coiled one of the belts tightly around his wrists. The second, he looped around the first, and snarled it around the door knob to hold Rob securely against the house's back door. "There, I think you'll do." Chandler dusted off his hands and turned his attention to the food they had left on the table. "Is there any chance we could get your car back onto its wheels, old son?" he asked of Sean, who was literally under his feet.

Rob almost laughed as he sagged against the cold, painted surface of the door, but it would have been hysterical laughter. The man was insane, but in so subtle a way that if one met him at a cafe on a summer's afternoon, he might be charming. His insanity would not become apparent for some time.

It seemed to Sean that Chandler was simply incapable of connecting his actions with their consequences. Every facet of life was perceived and understood from his own perspective. Like Dwight Murdoch, he had the capacity to be cruel without even realising he was doing it... or to be so deliberately, calculatedly vicious, he was lethal.

"No, there's no chance of fixing the car," Sean said tiredly. He twisted his head, trying to see Rob, but could not. Chandler's legs blocked his view. "Robbie, you okay?"

"Just aching," Rob said honestly. "We heard you on the shortwave, Chandler."

"You did?" Chandler had constructed an enormous sandwich, and his mouth was full. "What did you hear?"

"You told Meredith you'll find your own way out of this mess, and he said you should make your way to the rendezvous point on the coast." He paused. "Is that where the bulk shipments come ashore?"

"Bright lad." Chandler washed down his food with a swig of milk, straight from the jug.

"So, how do you think you're going to get us all the way to the coast — about four miles across country — in these conditions, on your own?" Rob demanded brashly.

He was pushing, shoving, and Sean took breath, wishing Rob would just hold his tongue. Chandler was so unstable, he could turn violent at a snap of the fingers.

But instead, Chandler finished the sandwich, licked his fingers and scooped a handful of raisins out of the jar on the shelf. "How to take you with me," he agreed pleasantly, "is the problem. But I'll think it through, Rob. As Lewis will tell you, I've an excellent mind." He held up one forefinger. "Someone once said, 'To every problem, there is a solution.' But I don't recall who. Or do I mean, whom? Grammar was never my forte."

He pulled open a drawer and rummaged until he had produced the item he wanted. He held the corkscrew up to the meagre daylight. "As to the problem of controlling you... would a little intimidation work?" He rested the point of the corkscrew against Rob's left nipple. "Did you ever want to wear tit rings, Rob? I can pierce both of these for you. And I promise you, Sean, if you give me one second of trouble, I will." He looked down soberly at Sean. "I'll do it, old son. I'll make him yell so loud, they'll hear him in town."

"We'll give you no trouble," Sean whispered bitterly.

For an instant the corkscrew dug smartingly deep, then it was gone. Rob looked down, expecting to see a bright drop of blood, but there was nothing. His eyes were wide as he looked up at Chandler. He almost screamed it — *you're insane!* — but he choked back the words at the last second. If Chandler was enraged, he could do anything. Rob looked down into Sean's drawn face and sealed his lips. He leaned against the door and watched through slitted eyes as Chandler made tea and sat by the fire.

It was surreal. Rob's half closed eyes travelled to Sean, saw the stress in his shoulders. His arms were pulling with all the strength he had. He was testing the cords, the knots. Rob held his breath. A second later, Sean relaxed, looked up and gave Rob a tiny shake of his head. He was not going to get loose that way. His eyes flickered a message at Rob. *Wait.* Rob nodded. Chandler was occupied and saw none of this.

Rob rested against the door. It heaved and moved as the gale sought to blast the house right off the hillside. Thunder growled and the rain lashed more heavily. Chill drafts raced in through the cracks around the door, and Rob soon found his calves and feet freezing. At this rate, the valley below would be filling fast, and he did not like to even think about the evening's tide.

As Chandler propped his feet in the hearth, the clock on the wall showed two-fifteen. Sean could hardly believe it. The morning seemed a year in the past. He looked up worriedly at Rob, seeing his pallor. He was probably hurting, and Sean did not underestimate the subtle injuries he could have sustained when the car rolled. He might not even be aware of them for days.

With a slurping sound, Chandler took the last mouthful from his cup, yawned and stretched to the bottom of his spine. "I'm going to get some sleep." He stooped over Sean to check his bonds, tied up a loose end, and tightened them. "Now, you're going to be good boys, aren't you?" he asked genially as he straightened and turned his attention to the leather binding Rob's wrists. His voice iced over as he unhitched Rob from the doorknob and shoved him onto the linoleum. "Whichever one of you fights me, I promise you, the other one will be wearing those curtain rings in his tits in the next five minutes. You both know me by now. I don't give the proverbial fuck."

"We know you," Sean muttered, trying to ease his spine as he watched Chandler lash Rob's feet together. When he was done, Chandler picked up the bread knife. For a second Sean froze, but the man simply turned the blade, slashed a ribbon from the curtain, and used that to secure Rob's hands to his ankles, so that Rob was as helpless as Sean, though not secured to a leg of the table.

"Uncomfortable?" Chandler tut-tutted. "Well, you'll live. Big, tough boys like you." Satisfied, he stood back, lifted the shotgun from the table and gave them a genial smile. "A small word to the wise. If you even try to get loose, and I find those bonds have been interfered with, I'll be madder than hell. I'll flip a coin. Heads, I'll fuck the daylights out of you, Sean, and tails, I'll do Robbie, as hard as I know how. And believe me, I know how to play rough. So why don't you relax? You've got a long walk ahead of you."

With those words he stepped out of the kitchen, and they heard the telltale rustle of cushions on the sofa in the parlour. The rain drummed steadily on the galvanised roof, and if they kept their voices to a whisper they could talk without fear of being overheard.

Rob had his fear and fury on a rein and his voice was under control.

"I don't believe the man."

"Believe him," Sean said bleakly. "He sounds sane, which makes him so dangerous. If you met him in the street he might charm you."

"He scares holy shit out of me," Rob confessed.

"Out of me, too." Sean fought to lift his head. "You sure you're okay?"

"Like I said, just aching," Rob said honestly, and cleared his throat. "Can you get your hands loose?"

"I'm trying." Sean's voice was taut with strain. "I'm tied so tight, I can't even feel my fingers. And he meant what he said. We either get right out, or we don't even try. Mess with these bonds, bungle it, and..."

"And one of us gets nailed the hard way while the other watches." Rob heaved in a deep breath, tensed and tried his own hands. "I can't budge. Wherever this boy scout learned to tie knots, they knew what they were doing."

"Okay, so we're not going to pull them loose," Sean panted. "Any chance we can get back to back and untie them?"

"Turn over, let me see," Rob grunted.

That was not so easy, and Sean was breathless before he had wriggled over, almost onto his belly, to present his hands to Rob. Rob peered at the ravelled mess of knots and groaned.

"Not a chance," he whispered. "If I had a couple of hours, and my hands in front of me, maybe. But not like this."

"Okay, okay," Sean rasped as he rolled back over. "So we think. Think." He took a breath. "Knife? He cut the curtain with something."

"The bread knife — and he took it with him." Rob licked his lips. "There'll be another one in the drawer. But he's bound to hear, and how can I stand?" He forced himself to relax and use his eyes.

The kitchen looked different, seen from a rat's-eye view. A strong, icy draft blasted under the door, and Rob was getting very chilled. If he stayed put another hour, while Chandler slept beside the gas heater in the parlour, he would be like a block of ice.

And then Sean lifted his head, twisted his heck for a better view. "Just a minute."

"What?" Rob squirmed around to see.

"The farmer's wife sews," Sean whispered. "Other side of the chair, back in the corner — looks like a sewing kit. Needle, thread

... scissors. Can you reach it?"

"I don't know." Rob rolled onto his side, the only position in which he could inch his way across the floor. "Can you see Chandler from there?"

"I can see his feet," Sean said softly. "Go on, try. Anything has to be better than lying here!"

Rob gathered his muscles, bunched them for effort and began to worm away from the table. If he could not reach the box he could always tell Chandler he had been frozen, and just shuffled over to the hearth to get warm. Chandler's peculiar mind would probably accept that.

Moving at all was almost impossible. Rob bruised his shoulder, his elbow and knees, and his back felt wrenched by the time he had reached the chair. The sewing kit was an antique biscuit box, and the lid was off. He wondered at the rush in which the people had left this house — a piece of embroidery work was left on the side of the kit. He saw hanks of coloured silk, several pairs of knitting needles. There had to be a pair of scissors. No sewing kit could be without them.

The box was between a footstool and the chair. Chandler had not even noticed it. Rob manoeuvred himself around, closer, closer, till his hands were in range. This was the point of no return. He looked back at Sean.

"Go," Sean whispered. "He's asleep, hasn't moved. He can't hear over the rain. Move it! It's the best chance we're going to get."

Swallowing his heart, Rob propped himself on the chair and looked into the box. "Scissors," he hissed, "good ones, dressmaker's, they'll be like razors." Then he rolled the other way, got his hands into the box and felt around for the large red handles. Needles pricked him, his fingers delved into the softness of silk, and then he grunted. "Got 'em! Sean?"

"It's okay. He hasn't moved, but be quick," Sean urged.

Rob turned the scissors, worked the handles into his right fingers and quickly, carefully, sawed at the roped up curtain material that fastened his wrists to his ankles. He caught his breath as his body painfully unbent, but the moment he had cut through, he knew the real danger had begun. Now, they either got out of here, or one of them would be punished before the other.

It would be Sean who was hurt, Rob guessed. In an instant, Chandler had zeroed in on him as the senior, the bigger or stronger. Rob was not affronted. Sean was larger, broader, a little older and far more experienced. All that made him Chandler's natural prey, and fear squeezed Rob's heart.

He had no chance of sawing through the leather belts which bound his own wrists and ankles, and he did not even attempt to. Getting back to Sean was easier, since he had much more movement, and in moments he rolled up to his knees at Sean's side. "Turn over!"

Sean rolled, presenting his hands once more. Rob twisted, stabbed with the scissors until he made contact with cord, got a grip and began to cut. Now, his heart beat like a drum. If Chandler found them like this, their lives were worthless.

The same thought punished Sean, and in the instant his hands were loose he shoved Rob down flat and attacked the tangle of leather belts with fingers that had numbed. He was clumsy, and he was desperate. The leather bindings on Rob's hands almost defied him. With a soft curse, he turned his attention to Rob's feet, and sobbed with effort as he tore the leather away.

"You want to try for the shotgun?" Rob hissed urgently. "If we could get it away from him —"

"And if we can't, we're finished. Out!" he panted as Rob's feet came free. "I'll get your clothes — go!"

Their jackets and shirts were still spread out by the fire, dry now, for what that was worth. Ten seconds outside, and they would be sodden again. But outside that door was freedom, and just maybe, the advantage. Sean scooped their clothes up while Rob tried the door.

He opened it a crack. The wind caught it like a sail as soon as the lock released. Rob leaned his weight on it to hold it until Sean was with him. As soon as he opened it wide, the wind and rain would lash inside, and Chandler would be on his feet. Still, he would be woken from sleep on the sofa in another room, which gave them five, even ten seconds in the clear. It would be enough. Sean was at Rob's shoulder now. All Rob had to do was let go the door and move.

The wind exploded in, and they dove through. Instinctively, Rob headed left, down the blind, windowless side of the house, and leaped into the rank undergrowth which flourished behind the shed. Sean was still on his heels as he plunged through into the teeth of the wind. Now, the shed cut off a direct line of sight from the back door, and on the other side of it they were in the woods.

Wet eucalypts smelt like randy tomcats, Sean thought absurdly as he pounded in Rob's wake. The ground was treacherous, sliding away underfoot, and rain sluiced like a cascade down from the higher slopes, into the rising lake. The water was silt-black and could be fifty feet deep in the floor of the valley.

Fear kept their feet on the rocks as they lunged into the trees, and they did not pause for breath until they had put a hundred yards between them and the house. In the lee of a gnarled old gum, Sean caught Rob by the elbow to stop him, and they fought for breath.

"He won't know which way we ran," Sean panted. "We're safe now. Put these on, it's damned cold." He pressed Rob's shirt and jacket into his hands.

The garments would be drenched in moments, but at least they offered a little insulation against the stinging chill. Rob tucked in his tee-shirt and peered at his watch. Daylight was so gloomy, he would have thought it was twilight, but it was still just three.

"We'd better keep moving," Sean insisted, and led the way up-hill, away from Bradgate Farm. At the top, they emerged from the trees into a clear area between two lightning-blasted stumps, casual-ties of storms many decades in the past. When they turned back they saw the farm, a quarter mile away and fifty feet below.

And there was John Chandler.

The shotgun was still in his hands as he paced the yard behind the house, visually searching the hillside, the tree line to left and right, and even the swiftly flooding valley. While Sean and Rob watched, he ran up onto the road, his fury evident in every step. Body language was often more eloquent than speech.

Sean gave a cynical grunt. "He can't search for us. He could run around in circles for hours. Really, he can't not search for us, either. He can't leave us behind. If he does, he'll have to tell Lewis he had us and lost us. We can identify half of Lewis's crew, and the *Minuette*."

"What'll he do?" Rob yelled over the wind. He was not think-ing clearly, and found himself falling back more and more on Sean's ability to reason, literally under the gun. Sean had done it before, he had the experience, almost as if he were ex-army. In his years with Jackson Oil he had seen and done much that Rob could barely im-agine.

For some moments Sean considered the situation, and then gestured over his shoulder, eastward, toward the coast. "Their ren-dezvous — you remember the name of the vessel that's coming in, the *Lan Tao*. If I were Chandler, I'd hike out of here any way I could, and then I'd send back the heavy brigade to cover my tracks. The *Lan Tao*, whatever it is, has Lewis's men aboard, and that probably means mercenaries. You heard Lewis talking about their contacts up north, and Chandler mentioned New Guinea, Burma, Thailand."

"Shit." Rob was shivering, and hugged himself tightly. "Where do we go from here? We have two choices that I can see."

"One," Sean agreed, "get ourselves out, if we can. Find a police station, also if we can. Give them the story and hope to God they can offer us some protection." He wore a doubtful expression.

"Or, two," Rob finished, "we can try to stop this whole ridiculous affair right here, right now. Jesus, there's two of us!"

"You want to surround him?" Sean quipped bitterly. "He's armed, and that puts the aces up both his sleeves. And he's good. Don't be fooled, Rob. He's crazy, but he's good."

"That much, I saw for myself." Rob raked his sodden hair out of his face.

As he spoke, thunder growled once more and the rain began to drive down with double the ferocity. The woods thrashed and bowed under the onslaught of nature. Sean backed up against the trunk of the tree and pulled Rob with him. The rain formed a veil between them and the rest of the world. The other side of the valley was gone, but they glimpsed the black flood waters below.

High water mark was now about thirty feet below the farm house. Sean's teeth worried his lip as he peered at his watch, judged the rate at which the water was coming up, and shook his head. "That house is going to go. This downpour alone would bring the flood right up over the doorstep, and then the high tide comes upriver just after six. By eight, Bradgate Farm will be a pile of driftwood, five miles west of here."

The assault of the rain drove Chandler back inside, and the door closed. Rob pressed tight between the tree and Sean for warmth. "This weather is only an enemy if we make it one," he shouted. "We could recruit it. Chandler's as blind and deaf as we are. We could sneak up on him, he'd never know we were coming."

Sean embraced him, not out of passion but to share body heat. Rob was icy. They could not afford to stand around much longer. Surprisingly quickly, the body began to shed heat, and when a man was lean to begin with, as Rob was, the heat was lost fast. Rob's slim physique was one of the features that had always attracted Sean, but at times it could work against him.

"Okay." Sean tightened his grip as Rob pressed closer. "If we can get that gun away from him, we're half way home."

"We can't get back into the house," Rob mused. "It's too obvious, he's probably expecting us. If he's in a position where he can see the doors and windows, we have no chance — and he's warm, while we're freezing our nuts off. Chris, the wind chill is down to zero."

It was not quite that cold, Sean realised, but when you were wet and tense any wind, let alone a force seven gale, could make it seem you were loitering in a meat locker. In the end it was the same. When the body had lost a critical amount of heat it no longer functioned properly. The shudder reflex must begin, as the muscles tried to warm themselves by spasming, and a man was useless. People were known to die of exposure in Australia's southern states in July and August. Sean did not overlook the danger.

"Then, if we can't go into the house," he said slowly, "we make Chandler come out. A diversion. You make a noise, get him into the yard. I'll get behind him, jump him."

Rob's mouth twisted at the suggestion, but he thought it through and at last nodded. "Okay, I'm buying. What kind of diversion?"

"We don't have a lot to work with. It has to be something that'll carry over the wind. Can't light a fire, and we've no vehicle. How about old-fashioned deception?" Rob was listening intently. "Creep up, hammer on the door." Sean rubbed his lover's hands to chafe warmth into them. "Shout his name. Call him John. This wind will distort your voice enough to make him uncertain. Yell something like, 'Come on, John, we've looked everywhere for you, move your butt!' He might assume it's Meredith or Parker. That self-centred mind of his will jump to fifty loony conclusions. Then, you get out, right back in the trees."

"Two of us could jump him," Rob began.

"I can't watch out for you as well as myself! Trying to look out for you, I'll probably get shot, and so would you, if you try to look out for me. Just give me a chance to get into a place where he can't see me — around the wood pile, beside the door — then shout his name, and get the hell out!"

"I hate this," Rob growled.

"I'm not crazy about it myself," Sean admitted. "You don't have to like it. Just do it."

"I'm starting to shiver like blazes," Rob warned. "I won't be much good in a fight."

Sean managed a wry little chuckle. "Honey," he told Rob with teasing affection, "you never were."

The rain was like a weight on their backs as they made their way along the rise. On their left, above the road, was the old, burned-out ruin of another house. Underbrush had overrun the tumbled stones, only the chimney stack was standing. Sean wondered if lightning had ignited that blaze, as it had struck so many trees. He gave the sky a bleak look as thunder rumbled. This was not the safest place to be, but he was sure those licks of lightning were a few miles further away.

The storm was swirling, its front must cover thirty or fifty miles, and the whole beast would soon have crossed the coast. He peered down into the valley and swore as he saw the water level. It was rising almost visibly. If he marked a point, looked away and then looked back a minute later, he could actually see the difference.

In less than three hours, the tide would peak. They must be out of here, safe on high ground, or they could become statistics. In the chaos, tomorrow, Chandler, Lewis and their men could hunt through these hills without giving a thought to the police. This far from the city, the police were spread thinly at the best of times, and following a storm, they would be at full stretch, trying to salvage lives if not property.

Forlorn, bedraggled chickens had taken shelter under the trees. They flurried away from Sean's feet as he and Rob came to rest not far from the shed.

"Get in there, pound on the door," Sean yelled into the fangs of the wind. "Give me a half minute to get behind the wood pile, make Chandler hear —"

"Then run." Rob zipped his jacket in a vain hope of conserving some body heat, and gave Sean a hard look. "You be bloody careful."

"You got my word on that." Sean swatted Rob's ass to get him moving. "I'll be right behind you. Don't let him see you from the windows."

Together, they clambered through the jungle of weeds at the rear of the shed, and then Rob hung back at the corner to let Sean go ahead.

The wind whipped into his face as he stepped out. He hugged

the coarse surface of the bluestone along the blind side of the house, crouched low and crept into the lee of the pile of axe-chopped mallee roots. They were covered with a flapping tarpaulin, and they were wet. The edges of the tarp fluttered wildly. Sean went down on one knee and gave Rob a cautious thumbs-up sign.

The look on Rob's face betrayed his misgivings as he ducked out from behind the shed. He went by Sean on silent feet, sidled up to the white painted door and bunched his right fist. After a moment's hesitation he hammered a series of heavy blows.

"Hey, you in there, John? We've looked every place else! Do you want a ride out of here, or not? John!"

His fist pounded a second time, he shouted Chandler's first name again to make sure he'd been heard, and then he was off like a jackrabbit. The last Sean saw of him was his backside as he dove into the ravel of geraniums and rhododendrons on the south side of the house. Sean poised on the balls of his feet, ready to spring.

Something rattled inside the house, though the weather blanketed almost all noise. The doorknob turned, the door opened a crack. Sean had not budged a muscle yet.

"Meredith? Is that you, Meredith? Where the fuck are you?" Chandler's voice yelled through the narrowly opened door, before the barrel of the shotgun extruded. He might be insane, but he had the cunning of a lame old wolf. He wasn't putting a foot over the threshold until he saw a face he knew.

Talons of frustration raked Sean. He scooped up a stone and flung it into the yard, where it landed hard. The sound could easily have been a footstep.

On the far side, Rob's face appeared amid the tangle of rhododendrons. He cupped both hands to his mouth. "John, what are you doing, man? Get out here!"

The goad was enough. The door opened and Sean glimpsed the figure in white slacks. Chandler was bare-chested and his slacks were not zipped — he had just put them on. He would have been rain-drenched when he made it back to the house. Not even Chandler was crazy enough to sit in soaked clothes for hours.

The man peered through the curtain of rain. The wind snatched at his voice. "Meredith, where are you?"

His answer was Sean's weight, barrelling solidly into his back. Both of them went down hard, hit the ground with a stunning impact and began to roll. Chandler threshed wildly, and Sean lashed out with his right fist, hunting for his face over and over, while his left hand clenched on the barrel of the shotgun, wrenching it away from himself.

The safeties were off and one barrel detonated with a roar that overrode the noise of the storm. Sean yelled, a sound of shock or reaction, but the buckshot was nowhere near him. Adrenalin surged through him with all the kick of a drug.

He aimed another blow into Chandler's face, but Chandler moved with a speed Sean could scarcely believe. The punch went wide and Sean yelled again, this time in anguish, as his fist drove into the ground with the full force of his arm behind it.

It was luck alone that he did not feel that peculiar, brittle snap of breaking bone. His fingers were whole, but the second's blind dread before he was sure of that was all Chandler needed. The man had the reflexes of a cobra.

In the split second between Sean realising that his punch was going to plow into the gravel, and realising that his hand was not actually broken, Chandler spun the fight around.

Sean was suddenly in a headlock, without knowing how he had got there, and the muzzle of the shotgun was pressed into his neck, below his ear. Chandler backed up on his knees, dragging Sean with him every step, toward the door.

On the threshold he stopped and his grip tightened suffocatingly on Sean's neck. Sean flailed at him with his left hand but the angle was wrong, the blows were useless. His lungs burned as his blood oxygen dwindled, and his senses began to dim. He heard Chandler's voice as if from far away, or at the end of a long tunnel.

"Robbie boy!" Chandler shouted into the swirls of wind and rain. "Rob Markham! I'm going to blow his bloody head off unless you come out here, right now, hands in the air. Don't think I won't do it, Robbie, because you know damned well — I'd enjoy it!"

Seven

IT WAS over in seconds, but Rob knew that to Sean it would have seemed an eternity. A fist gripped his insides as he saw Chandler seize Sean. Chandler was not as tall as Sean, but he was heavier, perhaps stronger — certainly warmer, and more agile because of it. With the shotgun stabbing into Sean's neck and a wild, murderous expression on Chandler's face, Rob was abruptly out of options.

"All right! For Christ's sake, all right!" Hands high over his head, he stepped out of the shrubbery.

Not for a second did Chandler relax. Rob walked toward him as he dragged Sean over the threshold. The door slammed against the lashing wind and Chandler snarled at them, a violent tirade. The wind screamed against the door, blowing it half open, and Chandler paused at last.

"Shut that, and lock it!"

As Rob turned to obey he heard a dull, solid smack of bone on bone. He spun back, wondering if Sean had got in a lucky punch, but Chandler was sucking carnivorously on the split, smarting knuckles of his left hand. Sean was out cold, and one side of his jaw was already growing puffy.

"That was pretty good, Robbie boy, almost clever enough," Chandler said grudgingly as his fury abated. "I wouldn't have thought you could get loose. I'll have to take more care in future. I found the scissors on the floor. I'll bet you play a wicked game of chess, too."

Rob swallowed repeatedly to steady his voice. "We're expected at a friend's place for dinner tonight. If we don't show, they'll come looking for us. In this storm, they'd fear the worst and turn the dogs out."

The handsome face smiled frostily. "Or, I wonder if poker is your game? You bluff with a straight face... the only part of your body that is straight, eh?" He looked Rob up and down. "Nice. I could fancy you, Robbie. A nice gay boy. Good looking, clean and healthy."

The blood chilled in Rob's veins. "I'm not bluffing, Chandler. If we don't show up by seven — "

"I've played a lot of poker in my time," Chandler snapped. "You're good, but I can spot a bluff a mile away. And even if I'm wrong, and your friends assume you're victims of the flood, it'd take a helicopter ten hours to find you in these conditions in the dark. They wouldn't even start searching till morning." He frowned deeply at Rob. "I'm puzzled. Why did you come back? You could have kept running."

Furious and frightened at once, Rob jammed his hands into his pockets and fought down his shivering. "If you want the truth, we're not local to this area, you probably know this part of the country better than we do. We wouldn't know where to run to, and the valleys are all under. If you'd made it to the rendezvous place, and turned Lewis's troops loose, we wouldn't have much chance of survival. We figured the best option we had was to jump you." He gestured at the house with a nod. "Shelter, at least till high tide tonight. Then, food, maybe some oilskins in a cupboard somewhere." Rob shook his head slowly. "You were just lucky, Chandler. That was a hundred to one shot. Sean nearly took you down."

"So he did. And that's logical reasoning," Chandler allowed. "Still, I am lucky. I always am. The sun shines on the righteous." Deliberately, he placed his foot on Sean's throat. Sean was too deeply unconscious to know what was happening. Chandler's eyes became predatory. "Now, will I get nasty with you, or will you cooperate?"

"What do you mean?" Rob's heart was like a trip hammer. The barrel of the shotgun never wavered by an inch.

"I can kill him, just by stamping down," Chandler said thoughtfully, as if Sean's death might be entertaining. "Now, I don't want to kill him or you, because I can't hide the bodies, and I have no desire to leave you behind me, dead or alive, like a pair of signposts pointing after me. The police are not complete fools."

"And Geoffrey Lewis would draw and quarter you," Rob guessed sourly.

"He would." Chandler pursed his lips. "Also, you're worth money, a straight sale, fresh meat for the laboratory. Lastly, you're under my skin like glass powder, boy. I want to know you're in that lab, shot up nine ways from Tuesday, batch-testing the product that's making me so rich, you can't even imagine what it's like." He gave Rob a fat smile. "Knowing where you are will give me a lot of satisfaction."

The smile, the note in his voice, chilled Rob more than the wind and rain. Now was not the time to push, or try reason. Chandler was mad, and the only thing to do with a madman was humour him. "I'll cooperate," he said quietly. "What do you want me to do?"

"Thank heaven for small mercies." Chandler sighed as if it was a genuine relief. "Pull down your pants, turn around and clasp your hands, back of your head."

"What?" Rob's mouth was dry.

"You heard every word." Chandler's tone hardened and his foot shifted on Sean's throat. "Move. You'll find this interesting, if nothing else. A little treasure I picked up on my travels. You ought to travel, Rob. You learn the most amazing things."

Rob unzipped his jeans, pushed them down around his thighs, turned around and clasped his hands at the back of his neck as he had been instructed. From the corner of his eye he saw Chandler snatch up one of the lengths of cord that had secured them before.

"Come here. I've no intention of taking my foot of your friend's throat until you're secure." He spoke genially now. "That's a beautiful little ass. Does Sean worship it? He should. He made a lovely job of fucking it. I love watching men fuck — in the flesh, that is. Videos just aren't the same."

The constant chatter had become like a series of physical blows, which Rob endured with gritted teeth. The cord looped tight about his wrists, at his nape, and then Chandler shoved him forward and down, until his face was between his knees, pressed into the folds of his jeans. The loose end of the cord hung down his back, and Rob was not even breathing as Chandler used it to bind his genitals. He pulled Rob up straight, and shortened the length of the cord with a knot in the middle. It tightened, and Rob choked off a yell. Before he had his balance, Chandler roped his ankles with a foot of slack between, so that he could manage a shuffling walk.

"Get the idea?" Chandler stood back and set the shotgun on the table. "You can't kick me, you can't take a full step. If you try to take your hands up over your head, it feels as if someone's pulling your nuts off, doesn't it — and you've no one to blame for the pulling but yourself." He waved Rob away. "Stand by the fire, if you like. I'll attend to Sean now, before we leave. You see, I can only manage one of you at a time, and it's a two or three mile hike."

Even thinking was difficult. Rob blinked his eyes clear and focused on Sean's face. A blue bruise had begun to show on the side of his jaw, but he was still out. Rob almost envied him. He thought back to dawn that morning when they had made love, dressed warmly and taken the boat out for the cheap thrill of a couple of hours' fishing in the sharp, exhilarating pre-storm gusts. He wondered how they had blundered into this nightmare, and how they were going to blunder out of it. For the moment, Sean had it easy. He was dead to the world, but that beat just plain dead.

Rob shuffled closer to the hearth and tried the cord binding his wrists. He pulled, felt his skin abrade, but he would never force it. He tried ducking to see if he could get his hands over the top of his head, and in moments decided not to try that again. Chandler was right. His balls might have been in a vice.

"I have something a little more special for Sean," Chandler mused. He had fetched his jacket, a large, quilted green anorak with deep pockets. "Have you ever hated a man you've only known for an hour or two, Robbie?"

"Before today? No," Rob said bleakly.

"I like a guy who speaks his mind." Chandler's smile was stunning. From one pocket he had taken an antique Chinese enamelled case, and this he opened to display a set of seven glass ampoules, a syringe and a set of needles, still in cellophane. "Now, this," Chandler said thoughtfully as he primed the hypodermic, "is the best stuff money can buy. Not mine, Rob. I don't use it. This is a birthday gift — for a lady, if you must know." He snorted with laughter. "Better than a dozen red roses."

The pulse in Rob's temple hurt. "For godsake, Chandler."

"For God's sake, what?" Chandler gave him a curious look. "This is the best merchandise on the market, a lady's birthday gift, worth a fortune, and I'm going to give it to Sean. Be reasonable, Robert. What do you want me to do, hit him again?"

"You could tie him," Rob said, rasped and stammering as he focused on the tip of the needle.

"Like you?" Chandler looked him up and down. "I could. But I don't like Sean. And I'd love to see what effect this little narcotic concoction has on him. Do you know much about drugs? You ever use them?"

"Not recently," Rob whispered. "Ten years ago, I experimented. What is that stuff?"

"This is what we call a speedball." His eyes restlessly skimmed

Rob's body salaciously, and his grasshopper mind moved on. "Interesting way of being tied, isn't it? You know where I learned that?"

"I..." Rob licked his lips as Chandler checked the needle. "I wouldn't know."

"Morocco," Chandler confided. "That's the way the rebels tie their prisoners, till they get out of them what they want to know. You see, you can't take a pee or a crap, you can't sit properly, or walk or lie down, and in two hours' time your arms are going to feel like they're falling out of their sockets, but if you relax them you'll give your balls such a yank, you'll wish you hadn't. They're not dumb in Morocco. Now, let's see to Sean."

As he spoke, he had opened Sean's shirt wide. The dose seemed to have been pre-measured in the ampoules, and Rob's only prayer was that it had been carefully done by an experienced user. The tip of the needle pricked Sean's left nipple, and a drop was injected. Then the right nipple was attended to, and Chandler unzipped Sean's jeans, tugged them down. The drug was skin-popped in a dozen places down the length of Sean's cock and into his scrotum, before Chandler sat back on his heels and put the equipment away.

"You ever see a user shoot up that way, Rob?"

"At a party, just once," Rob admitted hoarsely. Sean had not even twitched, and when the first rush of the drug hit him, he would be even further from consciousness. At least he would not feel cold, or fear, or hurt. Rob struggled to hold onto his rationale. "There's some kind of druggie lore, something about shooting up that way producing a sexual high, isn't there?"

"You've been around a bit," Chandler observed as he came to the fire and warmed his hands. "Then again, who hasn't these days?"

All at once, the pleasant small talk was like bamboo under Rob's fingernails, and the shout was torn out of him, as involuntary as breathing. "Stop it! Just shut up, shut up!"

Chandler arched a brow at him. "My, you do have a temper. There, do you feel better now?"

Useless, absurd tears blurred Rob's eyes. He shifted his arms and winced as his balls pulled, as if he was carrying a weight on his testicles. "What have you planned for me?"

"I told you." Chandler held his hands to the fire. "You're coming with me. There's a quick way over the hills, to the coast. We can stick to the uplands, we'll make it. We've been using this route into and out of the state for the last year. The police are such rural dickheads, they don't even know we've been here! I know the area reasonably well, I just can't handle the both of you at one time, which is why Sean received Geraldine's birthday present. I hope you realise, that little lady is going to be furious! Sean'll be out about ninety minutes. And by that time, to quote Arnold — I'll be back." He chuckled at his own wit.

"And where will I be?" Rob fidgeted miserably.

"Waiting for the *Lan Tao*." Chandler reached for his shirt and jersey, shrugged into both and pulled on the anorak. "Sean'll keep, right where he is." He smiled that stunning, male model smile. "Hey, don't you trust me? You should. Your lives are in my hands."

The discomfort of Rob's bonds was growing by the minute, but Chandler did not even seem to notice. This was not an exercise in sadism. Chandler's mind was so object-specific, as soon as he was concentrating on something else, in this case the route of their hike, he did not even notice Sean or Rob. Rob gritted his teeth and growled,

"How do you expect me to walk, trussed up like this?"

"Hm?" Chandler turned toward him. "I'll show you. It's time we left anyway. Did you hear on the radio, there's a storm tide coming up the river."

"I heard." Rob was intent on Sean as Chandler untied his ankles. He could have kicked now, but his arms were so stiff, his balls so sore, Chandler would make mincemeat of him. He would have better chances. For the moment, his best option was to wait. The cord that had restrained his ankles was tied to the one which hugged his spine. It looped over his throat like a noose and tied again, tight. Chandler plucked it like a bass string.

"You felt both ends of that, didn't you? So I don't have to warn you to be careful," Chandler warned as he untied Rob's hands.

After so long forcibly doubled, pain burned through his shoulders and elbows. Rob would have hunched if he had been able. Blood rushed back into his muscles and joints and his eyes watered as Chandler caught his hands and wrenched them down. They were tied again, this time before him, and Chandler stood back.

"You'll do, Rob. You can pull your pants back up and zip them. I'm going to walk behind you, just like this, and I'm sure you're going to be completely cooperative."

He had the shotgun in his right hand as he stepped behind Rob, and Rob struggled his jeans up. Chandler's fist caught the cord against his spine and tugged, which had the double effect of choking him and giving his genitals a painful wrench. His shoulders and elbows were still useless, and as the barrel prodded into his back he blinked down at Sean.

"Is he all right? He much did you give him? He hasn't moved."

"Sean's a big boy," Chandler said dismissively. "He must weigh around one-seventy. Now, Geraldine weighs about half that, so I gave your friend a measure less than double her dose. That sounds about right to me." He jabbed forward with the gun. "Let's get moving. We don't have a lot of time before that high tide starts to come upriver."

And if Sean was still out when it rose, he could slither down into the stormwater lake when the foundations of this house washed out. Rob blinked down at him, in that moment fighting impotent tears. Somewhere along the way, he would get his chance to jump Chandler, and when the opportunity arose it would be Rob's delight to reduce the man's handsome face to pulp. Then he would get back here, the fastest way he could.

The dose Sean had received was large, but if a scrawny little woman who weighed less than a hundred pounds could take half that much, he should be able to handle it. Sean had never done drugs, and he was fit, strong. *Keep telling yourself that*, Rob thought as he stumbled out into the wind and rain.

The chill was shocking. His bare torso stung with the needle-sharp, heavy raindrops. Chandler tugged the cord to stop him and Rob yelped breathlessly. Much of this, and he would be badly bruised. *Be careful. The man's insane, don't provoke him, take your time till you get the chance, and then —*

Thunder rolled down Lightning Ridge like the brass section in an army band. Rob was steered up the path, through the trees, by the farm's half-hidden signpost and onto the unsurfaced road. Then up the opposite bank and through a gap in the broken fence, into the paddock beyond.

"On a clear day you can see the ocean from the top," Chandler remarked. "It's not as far as it looks. And I can just about pick out my landmark."

"Your what?" Rob panted. He glanced back, wondering if this was his chance, but the jab in his kidneys told him otherwise. He glanced down and saw the truth. The safety was off the shotgun. He forced himself to relax and plodded stubbornly onward.

"My landmark," Chandler repeated. "Keep your eye open for a white roof. It's a shed, clearly visible from the sea. That's our usual rendezvous point. I got a phone call through from the Jenkins farm, did you know? Geoff Lewis's crew will be there, aboard the *Lan*

Tao, on the high tide, and our next stop is Port Moresby." He gave Rob a push. "I've had enough of Australia. It seemed like a good idea, to do business here for a while, but this is a terrible country, and the market is too small to make it really worthwhile. I'll be glad to leave. There's richer pickings elsewhere."

Rob listened sourly, catching one word in three as he plowed through the mud and ducked his head into the icy wall of rain. Chandler kept a good grip on the cord, tight enough to let him know he was a prisoner. In the first half mile, Rob knew he was in trouble. He looked up, trying to see Chandler's white-roofed shed, but as yet saw nothing.

Was Chandler in a world of his own, fantasising the power he commanded? But that was not the manner of Chandler's insanity. Rob shook his head hard, to clear his thoughts. He must keep his mind alert, watch out for a shed, a ship... and never forget that the highest tide of the decade was on its way in.

With the effort of putting one foot in front of another, he lost track of time. Every quarter mile, he was less capable of turning around and jumping Chandler even if a priceless opportunity presented itself. His shoes were thick with mud, it was difficult to keep his balance, but if he fell Chandler would not let go of the cord, and the results would be dire. Rob stayed determinedly on his feet.

The rain continued without a break as they slithered off Lightning Ridge onto a hiker's trail that would be a pleasant scenic walk in good weather. Today, it was a nightmare. The sky was black, the distance lost in mist. Rob could not see the sea, though he could smell it. He put his head down and butted into the wind while the thunder rumbled.

Maybe a farmer or a police rescue squad would be out this way, looking for stray lambs. One man half naked and obviously tied, the other behind him with a gun — they made such an odd couple, even a blind man must notice them.

But they saw no one. Rob listened for an engine, rotors, voices over a loudhailer, anything that promised relief. All he heard was wind, rain and thunder, and Chandler's incessant prattling, mercifully whipped away by the gale.

Was Sean all right? He could be overdosing. Yet even if Rob was with him, he could do nothing for him. What chance was there of getting an ambulance, getting him to hospital? Sean would live or die on his own strength and tenacity. Rob's last shred of hope was that the dose had been well judged, the drug well made, the needle

86

new, clean, and properly prepared. Making mistakes with a hypo could cause embolism. Chandler's hands had looked expert as they opened the cellophane, primed the hypo, slipped it into the tips of Seàn's nipples. Rob shuddered, remembering all too clearly the scene at that party, where a five-year veteran addict had performed that shoot-up like a cabaret act, for a wide-eyed audience.

For some reason Chandler had neglected to take Rob's wrist watch. Perhaps he had not even noticed it, or considered it unimportant. It was twenty minutes before five. They were running out of time, and Rob lifted his head to peer through the curtain of rain.

He swore hoarsely as he saw the shed Chandler had described, no more than a hundred yards away now. Chandler was still talking, but Rob had closed his ears. He was prattling about a threesome he had done not long before, with a blond Swedish track star and a black Nigerian stud.

The cord tightened suddenly, making Rob come to a halt with a wince. "Stop here for a jiff," Chandler said. "I'll have a look around. Can't march you down to the shed if there's people there! It'll be good to get out of this rain. It looks like it's never going to stop. D'you know, Rob, there's crank religious cults out there, building arks? True!"

Rob blinked his eyes clear and looked about for some sign of life. He saw only a stony beach, the outlet of a creek, and on the near bank a shed made of galvanised sheets, from which the white paint was slowly being stripped by the sea wind. Forlorn seagulls nestled in the dunes, but there was no trace of people.

"All clear," Chandler bawled after a full minute's observation. "Hurry now. I've got a long way to go! By my reckoning, that boyfriend of yours should be coming around by the time I make it back to Bradgate Farm."

"You —" Rob's voice was rasping, alien in his own years. "You sure about the dose you gave him?"

"Oh, ye of little faith!" Chandler laughed. "Good Lord, you think I want to have to carry him all this way here? And I can't leave him. The pigs get obsessive, every time they find a dead body. This whole area — our route in and out — would come under police scrutiny. Geoff Lewis would paralyse me! Walk on." He gave Rob a push. "How long have you two been lovers?"

"Fourteen months." Rob struggled to keep his footing. His genitals were aching and felt bruised.

"Are you happy with Sean?" Chandler sounded genuinely interested.

"I was." Tears stung Rob's eyes, invisible in the rain. "I expect you'll change all that."

"I expect so. You see, old horse, killing is a matter of survival. The law of the jungle. Tell the truth: if you had the chance, you'd kill me right now. Wouldn't you?"

Panting, Rob slithered to a halt in the wet grass and weeds beside the shed. "I might not be responsible for what I did," he said sourly, and shocked himself with the admission. With the hate that rushed through him.

The shed's door was padlocked, but from the pocket of his anorak Chandler produced a keyring, and sorted through the assortment of keys to produce a set of six fine picklocks.

"You any good at picking locks, Robbie? It's an art. Here, watch this."

If ever there had been a time for him to jump Chandler, this was it, but Rob was so cold, so tired and sore, he was literally unable. Chandler shoved him down full length into the mud, and he cried out sharply as he rolled over to take the tension off the cord. By the time he could see clearly again, the door was open and the muzzle of the shotgun was in his face.

"It just takes a couple of minutes. Nothing to it," Chandler said cheerfully as he pushed the door wide, braced it against the wind, and waited for him. "Christ, you're a mess. Still, it won't be much longer. All you have to do now is wait for the launch."

Rob stumbled into the shed. The sudden dimness blinded him and he peered helplessly about. "What launch?"

"You haven't been listening to a word I said!" Chandler sounded annoyed. "I've told you twice at least. You trying to make me angry?"

"Why should I do that?" Rob stood swaying in the middle of the shed as his eyesight gradually adjusted. Overhead were long, open steel rafters holding a set of commercial-length ladders. Scattered underfoot were card boxes and wooden crates, a mountain of paint cans, a litter of general hardware.

"Well, I imagine you're not listening too well," Chandler allowed. "I should think your balls are pretty blue. There's a ship coming. The *Lan Tao* is a freighter belonging to Geoff Lewis. She'll be along here at about six or seven o'clock, give or take the storm, the tide and her rattle-trap engines. She'll put a launch over the side, take us aboard. This is our regular rendezvous point... and today's delivery day! Planning, Rob, is how you stay six easy jumps ahead of shit-head police. The further out of town you get, the easier it becomes."

"Brilliant," Rob agreed hoarsely as he watched Chandler ambling about the shed. He was clearly looking for something, perhaps for inspiration, and it took only moments for him to hit on an idea.

A tea chest was dragged into the middle of the shed, right below the rafters. A coil of what looked like tow rope was untangled, and one end thrown over the steel beams overhead. Once again Rob found himself on the ground.

"You stay down," Chandler warned. "I don't want to put a bullet in you. You know where I want you."

"Batch-testing the same crap you shot into Sean," Rob said bitterly as he looked into the muzzle of the shotgun and thought, for the hundredth time that day, how much he hated guns. He always had hated guns, as if he'd instinctively known the day would come when he would be looking into the wrong end of one. The public use of firearms, even hand guns, was very common in the States, Sean said. But not here. Not yet.

A moment later Chandler set the gun on top of the stacked paint cans and applied his hands to the rope he had found. Rob saw in the first few seconds what he was doing. He was tying a hangman's noose, and Rob's bruised throat clenched. He cast about for any option, any avenue of escape, but Chandler was too quick.

"That should do it," he decided. "Come on, up you get, Robbie. I want you standing on the tea chest. Move it! You know the ropes — pun intended!" He chuckled at his own joke.

Heart pounding, racing, Rob struggled up. He was determined to bolt through the door, when Chandler caught his shoulders and dropped the noose neatly around his neck. It pulled tight and fear froze Rob like a statue. Chandler's weight on the other end of the line stretched it tight over his head, and he was physically tugged to the chest. There, Chandler pulled again, and if he did not step up, he would choke at once.

He clambered up, and before he had even found his balance the long end of the line was tied off to one of the main posts which supported the roof. Instinctively he clawed at the rope, but Chandler's hands closed about his wrists and pulled them way down. They were not untied, but a spare length of rope looped around his bonds, and simply knotted about his ankle, effectively preventing him from raising his arms.

"Now, just be a good boy," Chandler said reasonably. "If you try to get down, you'll stretch your neck. Do yourself a favour and stay put. I'll be back in an hour or so, with Sean. It'll all be over soon. You ever been to Moresby? You'll like it there. For one thing — it's warm!"

Rob did not even attempt to answer. The chest shifted under his feet and he held his breath until it stabilised. It was sound enough to hold his weight, but the wood was rotten, cracking. God knew how old it was. The rope above him was so taut, he could have plucked it like a mandolin string. If he even ducked his head, he was in trouble.

At the door, Chandler pulled up his collar. "Damn, it's cold out there," he said conversationally, looking through the gap as he inched the door open. "And it looks like this rain's going to get worse before it gets better. There's nothing I hate more than hiking in the rain." He looked back at Rob and nodded. "I can't stand around here, there's not much time. Ciao, Rob."

With that, he was gone. The door slammed, and Rob listened as the padlock snapped back into place and locked. He heard the steady squelch of footsteps, padding away... then nothing but the gale, the drum of rain on the steel roof, the crash of the surf and the rumble of miles-distant thunder.

It was dark, and now that he was standing absolutely still the cold began to strike with a vengeance. Rob was shivering badly, which meant that hypothermia was imminent. Part of his trembling was due to stress, anxiety, as Sean haunted his thoughts. But the greater part of it was genuine cold. And Rob was tired. Not drowsy yet, but weary, aching, and sore. Several of the more tender parts of his anatomy felt friction-burned.

How in hell was he going to get out of this? He looked up, his eyes followed the rope which looped over the rafter and ran down to the post where it was tied off. It was far out of his reach. He could not lift his hands to climb. If he could have got a hold on the rafters he could have got the noose off his neck, but to do that he had to get his hands loose.

He pulled with every ounce of strength he had, hoping he could dislodge the cord. If his skin scuffed through, a little blood would lubricate the rope — the idea was right out of classic fiction. The trouble was that the characters in those books had not been bound by a professional. Chandler was too good, and Rob bit back a sob of frustration as he realised it was futile. There was no way down off this chest, no way out of this shed.

The wind moaned around the roof, lifting the corrugated sheets. Now and then he saw a bright swatch of sky where one moved, buckled. The whole shed heaved as it took the broadside of the wind and he sucked in a breath. It was not impossible that the structure could be blown down in the gale, and he would be in the middle of the wreckage.

He closed his eyes, already shuddering as his muscles tried to generate heat. By the time Chandler made it back to Lightning Ridge, the water would be almost up to the house. Sean should be coming to, if the bastard had judged the drug correctly. But he would be too groggy to give Chandler a hard time.

They had one option left, and Rob seized on it. When they were picked up by Lewis's crew they would make a break for it either on the beach or on the ship. Sean would be hung over, but Rob placed his faith in Sean's strength, the fitness in which he prided himself. Sean was physically stronger than any other man Rob had ever known, not merely in the muscular sense. He had a will spun from strands of iron. And Sean had the best reason in the world to fight his way out of this nightmare.

Revenge.

Eight

HIS DREAMS had been wild beyond all imagination. A kaleidoscope whirled in Sean's head as he hovered near the brink of consciousness, never quite reaching the surface of the dark waters that had swirled over him and sucked him down.

Faces and voices he had not seen and heard in years grinned at him like death's heads from his memory ... Rob's face peered at him out of the mist of the present, lined with distress, fatigue and worry. Then Rob was gone, replaced by Dwight Murdoch, who needled him, prodding and mocking.

"Hey, Brodie, do you wanna take the jet over to Haiti for the weekend? Fag heaven." He smacked his lips. "I won't rat on you. Go on, take the jet. You can be up to your balls in black ass in a coupla hours. I might even come along. There's nothing I like better than a slice of sweet, black ass."

Sean locked his jaws to shut in the protests. The price for misusing the jet, which was Jackson Oil's company property, was his job. He would be fired automatically, and Dwight knew that. He loved to torment. Once, just once, Sean had made the mistake of letting Dwight take him to bed, too late realising his error. Dwight was not gay, nor even genuinely bi. He was a predator, who loved to seduce a gay guy, get the poor bastard on his knees, get that WASP, middle-American horse cock down a protesting young throat, and then laugh fit to break a rib.

Fingers tickled the back of Sean's neck as he leaned over the computer terminal. It was humid and oppressively hot. The air conditioning amounted to a fan in the ceiling that worked intermittently at best, and an open window which Sean had closed an hour before, when dusk began to lure out the mosquitoes. Mexico was almost the last place on earth he would have chosen to be, even if it were the only location where he could have avoided Dwight.

He ducked to evade the tickling fingers and gave Dwight a solid shove in the chest. "Why don't you just get on with your job, leave me to do mine?"

Dwight pulled monkey faces, which he thought was hilarious. "Touchy, aren't we, darling?"

With a supreme effort of will, Sean backed up the file he had been working on, took his disk out of the machine and with sharp, jerky movements packed his briefcase. His shirt and slacks adhered uncomfortably to his skin. He wanted a shower, a meal, a beer and some sleep, in that order.

Two large, deliberate hands groped his backside, and as he jumped out of Dwight's way he swung a powerful roundhouse slap at the man's head. Not a closed-fisted blow that would put him on the ground, perhaps break teeth and leave a bruise which would be visible to the company officials. Jackson Oil did not take kindly to brawling among its employees. The boys who worked out on the rig, the exploration platform in the bay, would be fired off the staff at once for fighting. The engineering crew — among whom it was not quite Sean's delight to work — would be severely reprimanded, perhaps fined.

The blow landed hard and slammed Dwight into the filing cabinet. A wilted pot plant teetered, and Sean's hand shot out to catch it before it could fall and smash. Dwight cupped a hand over his cheek and mouth, where a fleck of blood showed redly.

"Get out of my way, and stay out, Dwight," Sean said quietly, in a voice like ice crystals. "You had me where you wanted me once, and you made a king-sized fool of me."

"Queen-sized," Dwight snorted.

"Have it your way. You got what you wanted, you had your laugh, so now you leave me alone."

"You wanna play rough?" Dwight mocked as he clambered back to his feet. He was a big man, but graceless, like an ox. "I like it rough."

"I don't want to play at all." Sean stepped around him to get to the door. Through the long plate-glass windows, the Gulf of California was twilight mauve. Palm trees waved in the early evening breeze and the beach was deserted, save for the poverty stricken local kids who would beg or steal or hustle, if they got the chance. Sean wanted to swim... he wanted to get away far from here, maybe even right out of the country. His feet were itching, telling him plainly that the time had come to go.

The door slammed behind him. Five minutes later he was in a dingy hotel room, a large double Jack Daniel's in one hand, a cigarette in the other. He should give up both. They were the rot that would prematurely age a man, cost him his looks, and when he hailed from a community that prized youth and beauty above almost every other quality, a guy had to be careful.

Still, Sean swallowed a second whisky too fast, dragged deeply on the cigarette and then stubbed it out. He dropped his sweat-damp clothes with an expression of distaste and sprawled across the bed, face down. Just ten minutes rest, he promised himself, to take the ache out of his spine, the throb of tension out of his head. Then he would hit the shower, go out and find some congenial company.

He was drowsing when the door cracked open. He turned his head on the pillow, ready to curse Dwight with the full volume of his lungs. But Rob's face smiled at him... swimming a little, blurry, out of focus.

"Robbie? What you doing here?" Sean rolled over and opened his arms. The relief he felt at seeing Rob was physically weakening. "Come here, honey. God, I've been missing you so much."

Rob's shape drifted toward him, hands outstretched as he leaned down to kiss. Their fingers almost meshed, lips almost touched, and the welcome apparition was gone.

It warped into Dwight, and Dwight embraced him. That thick-lipped, slobbering mouth suffocated him with its prehensile tongue. Sean lashed out, but his fist seemed to bury itself in cotton waste, before the apparition of Dwight was gone too.

The room was empty and stifling, with just the buzz of a dying insect and the constant phwap-phwap sound of the ceiling fan for company. Sean groaned, flopped back onto the bed and punched the pillow. He gripped his aching skull between his hands.

"What's the matter with me? I've got to get out of here! I'm starting to lose my fucking mind!"

A travel brochure was tucked under the pillow. He teased it out, flipped it open and scanned the well-known, well-worn pages. Australia was a land of opportunity, from the sun-drenched shores of the Great Barrier Reef to the Red Centre, where the sacred site of Uluru reared over the Martian-red deserts in the north of South Australia. It was the only state that had been populated and developed by free men, colonists, rather than convict slaves. Sean liked the sound of that. The mile-square of the city of Adelaide, which had become the central business district, had been planned by a British Army officer, Colonel Light. His statue stood over the north of the city, pointing away toward the horizon. Victorian antique iron lace still decorated buildings that were filled with old world charm, yet modern skyscrapers reared over the city's skyline. Eucalypt woods and white beaches called to Sean. Barossa vineyards and Coober Pedy opal mines, beckoned from the pages of the brochure.

In the back was a litho photo of Rob, sitting astride the big Honda that was his pride and joy. The 1100RC was a race bike, with the streamlined, red-white-and-blue fairing that made it look like it was racing while it was standing still. Rob was bare-chested and brown, dressed in the familiar, too-tight, ass-moulding blue jeans he liked best. His hair was mussed up by a warm summer wind, and he was so beautiful, Sean felt a tug of helpless longing. He was a dream, Sean's dream, come to life.

A sheet of paper was slipped into the back of the brochure, and he frowned as he discovered it. It was a letter, addressed to him, but he had never seen it before. As he unfolded the single page he saw the blue and silver Jackson Oil logo and the company's pale grey watermark. Beneath the bold header were four words in heavy red type.

Brodie, you are fired.

The signature underneath was barely legible, but he could recognise the initials. 'D.M.' Anger seethed in Sean's belly, but he was too tired to hold onto it. He slumped down, let the mattress swallow him and closed his eyes. So he was fired. His hands closed on the travel brochure as if it were a lifeline. Sudden unemployment suited him just fine. He knew where he was heading, he would be on a plane... as soon as he had slept a little. An hour or two would do. Just an hour or two...

The dead sleep shattered and his eyes opened with a start.

Slate-grey quarry tiles under his cheek. A fireplace with the embers burned out, almost black. A window framing a square of sky that was twilight-dark, ripped curtains.

Bradgate Farm, on Lightning Ridge. Sean rolled over onto his back with a deep groan. His jeans were pulled down, his shirt was open and he felt like a chunk of ice. He had been lying here, God knew how long, in the draft that streamed under the door. His head felt like a bag of cotton candy, his throat was raw with thirst, and his tongue tasted like... like acid. His cock and nipples were inexplicable sore, while every erogenous zone in his body felt swollen.

He peered at his chest, touched himself there and found a little crusting of blood on the tip of each nipple, the residue of a tiny puncture. He peered at his genitals and saw multiple tiny bruises. Shot bruises. So. Little wonder his senses were so dislocated, he felt as if his brain had been disconnected from his eyes and ears.

"Oh, Christ," he groaned. The last thing he remembered was the fight. Chandler had him in a firm grip, they rolled and pitched through the mud ... his hand slammed into the ground and the pain rocketed through his arm. He peered at his knuckles in the poor light, and swore.

They were bare to the bone. Pieces of gravel had embedded in the ragged wound and the entire hand was a single enormous bruise. He had not broken the fingers, and he knew he was lucky. He remembered Chandler getting him into a headlock in the split second when he was paralysed with dread that his hand was broken. Then the muzzle of the shotgun jammed into his neck, and Chandler began to bawl Rob's name into the wind.

Rob must have surrendered himself, or Sean would not have had a head left on his shoulders. He had been half conscious, half suffocated as he was dragged back over the threshold. He felt just a single blow, and then blessed darkness.

With careful fingertips he explored the side of his jaw and, sure enough, it was swollen, not quite like a pudding, but tender and puffy. But one punch was not enough to keep him out for long, and he groggily touched the dozens of tiny punctures. The dense fog in his head, the fever-dreams, the partial numbness in his extremities — all this made sense, if he had been drugged.

"Rob?" He called, and listened intently to the house, but heard only the wind and rain, the sporadic rumble of thunder, retreating into the distance as the storm passed. It sounded like artillery, a long way off. "Rob!" Louder. He hauled himself to his knees, tugged his clothes about him and hoisted himself to his feet.

Dizziness made him clutch the edge of the table until the moment of white-hot nausea settled, and then he lunged through into the living room. His body was some peculiar mix of soreness and numbness. His heartbeat was too heavy and too slow.

And he was alone. The parlour was empty, but the gas heater was still on, and he warmed his hands until his raging thirst demanded to be assuaged. Propped at the sink, he drank a glass of water. His belly churned but he kept the drink down, bathed his face and washed his eyes with the stream.

He had no idea what the drug could have been. Drugs were not Sean's speciality. He had always given them a respectable distance, but he knew Chandler had shot him with a lot. That crap had mingled the past and present in his mind, producing an unholy confusion of images that fascinated him even while he wished he could forget them. They could drive a man insane.

That word led him back to Chandler, and he rubbed his face hard with both hands. Chandler must have taken Rob, but where? The man was capable of anything, and a pulse beat hard in Sean's throat. He peered at his watch and saw that it was ten minutes after six. The short winter daylight was waning fast, the storm tide would be approaching its highest point.

He stumbled back into the living room, pried the curtains apart and peered down into the valley where Bradgate's livestock paddocks should have been. The cattle or sheep were gone, and in their place was a wind-tossed, steel-grey lake that broke about two feet below the foundations of the house.

"Oh, my God," Sean whispered.

After five minutes he looked back at the water level, and could see at once it was still rising. The king tide, highest of the month — some locals said, the highest of the decade — was peaking. High tide was somewhere around six, but this valley was upriver. The water level could keep rising through another half hour.

He could not know how sound the foundations beneath him were. This house could break away, slide down the hill. If he was going to find Rob, or even live to tell the tale of this, he had to get out.

His jacket was still sodden, but he zipped it on and made for the back door. The moment he opened it, the strength of the wind tore it out of his hands, slammed it back on its hinges. Rain lashed in, turning the whole floor of the kitchen into a lake, but none of that mattered. In ten more minutes, this house would be under, perhaps ever gone in a vast mud slide. Sean did not even bother to shut the door behind him, but stepped into the yard as sheet lightning exploded across the sky.

He was blind for a second, and still blinking when a voice which froze his bone marrow said clearly, "Well, well. I timed the shot pretty nicely. You're a big boy, Sean — I told Rob not to worry. You had a nice trip?" He chuckled and sang, "*Come fly with me...* Now, move your pretty ass, Sean. We don't have a lot of time. Unless you fancy drowning!"

John Chandler's cheerful prattle tore into Sean like broken glass. He blinked his eyes clear of rain and the lightning after-images, and looked into the man's face, which smiled over the double barrel of the shotgun.

Rob's worst enemy was fatigue. Standing still as a statue, balanced on a chest, four inches away from oblivion while his body temperature gradually bottomed out, would have been called torture in most First World countries. His wrists were bloody and impotent tears scalded his eyes. It was insane — there was always a way out! Always.

Yet, not this time. He could only wait. He held his arms and legs tight together to conserve what body heat he could, and watched the time. The storm beat mercilessly at the shed. The whole structure was moving, but it seemed to be solid. Thunder growled like a trapped animal and the wind had a voice of its own. It whispered to him.

Never get out alive, Robbie, this is the last time around, you know you've been pushing your luck, you've been pushing it for years. Bikes and boats and risky one-night stands... you've been on borrowed time, and this is the payoff.

All of it was true. He had run stupid risks and he had been lucky, perhaps for too long. He closed his eyes, and his thoughts began to drift. He and Sean could have had a wonderful life together. Rob had never had the opportunity to travel, and Sean promised to show him places he had never even heard of. Perhaps they could have a house, a few acres, horses, and —

"Jesus!" Rob wrenched awake in the last second before he began to drowse. He was going to kill himself if he was not more careful. If he was to get out of this — and fuck the voice in his mind's ear that told him there was no way! — he must stay awake, stay on his feet. When the launch came, he and Sean would get their chance to run.

"Stay awake," he told himself. "Stay awake! Okay, you son of a bitch. Breathe." He forced a breath to the bottom of his chest, and then another, until he began to dizzy with the flood of oxygen. "Now, you talk, you concentrate," he snarled. But his mind was as numb as his body and no words would come. All right, he would sing.

He shook his head the little he was able and coughed. His throat was dry, croaking, as he began. Anything that kept his mind and body harnessed together. His voice was a little more than a rasp as he began, "My wild Irish rose, sweetest flower that grows, I've searched everywhere, but none can compare ..."

His mother had sung it to him when he was very young, he

knew it by heart, could have sung it in his sleep. It reminded him of days long gone by. The house in Glenelg, the red brick primary school where his emotions had come awake, and where he endured his first schoolboy crush, on another boy. The Esplanade in summer, where the cruising was pretty good... the jetty, after dark on warm nights, when the tide was out, and boys could meet. Those were happy days, long before the word Aids had been coined, before it was necessary to sift the sand regularly for the discarded syringes on which pensioners could tread next morning, and the condoms that were swallowed by, and choked, the seagulls, who thought they were edible. Happy days, fifteen or twenty years in the past. Rob wished he could go back, so long as Sean was with him.

"My wild Irish rose," he sang again, as if he were singing it to Sean now. Sean was third generation Irish-American. That name, those looks, the complexion and eyes. His family were from Sligo. "Sweetest flower that grows. I've searched everywhere, but none can —"

"Oi, you in there!"

What? Rob gasped. A voice, outside?

"Hey, Elvis bloody Presley in there!" the voice yelled once more, and a fist hammered on the door. "We can hear you! Open up, will you?"

"I... I can't!" Rob yelled desperately, his voice cracking on the words. "Help me, please. I'm locked in here. Smash the lock, break the chain. Help me!" He heard scuffling sounds, and two men arguing against the wind, which whipped away every other word while his heart began to race. "Please!" he shouted, "just break the lock!"

"Calm down, mate," the voice bawled through. "We'll have to get something to break the chain. There's a crowbar on the boat. We took her out of harbour before this mother of a storm could make shrapnel of her, but it's too dangerous out here. You could get drowned, trying to save a bloody dinghy. We just wondered if you had a shortwave in there."

Rob could not have cared less why the men were out here. "Just break the lock, get in here," he begged. "Hurry."

"Hey, are you hurt?" The voice was concerned now.

"Yes," Rob panted. "Please don't be long."

"Sit tight, mate. Couple of minutes."

And how long did they have before Chandler arrived? he could already be on the slope leading down to the shed, watching. He could whisk Sean away. Rob recognised the onset of hysteria, even delirium, and clamped down on it fast. He would have time for hysterics later, but not now.

Footsteps squelched through the mud with a disgusting slurping noise, and the voice he knew by now said, "That'll do the trick. You want to do it, Bernie? This bloke sounds a bit rough. He could have been shut in there for a week. Christ, how did he get himself locked in?"

"By accident," Bernie shouted. "It's easy. When I was six, my parents took me on a trip. Got myself locked in the gents' lav when the place closed. Okay, gimme some room, stand back."

An iron bar rattled, scrabbled, and Rob heard sounds of pulling and cursing. It took the weight of both men to snap the thick chain, but at last it broke and the door swung open with the force of the wind. His saviours stepped inside, and Rob blinked his vision clear.

They looked like weekend fishermen, dressed in oilskins and rubber boots. Both were forty or forty-five, clean shaven, pale with the cold, and shocked as they saw him.

"Christ almighty," Bernie swore. "Jimbo, get in here!" He hurried forward, swiftly searching his pockets.

Rob caught a glimpse of a thin blade before the rope over his head tumbled down. His knees buckled and if Bernie had not caught him he would have fallen. The knife was against his throat then, sawing at the cord, and all at once the pressure on his gullet and genitals eased. As his hands were cut loose he sagged to his knees, barely hearing what the men were saying.

"He's like ice." Bernie was shocked and angry. "Somebody's tried to kill the poor sod. Another hour or two, and they'd have done it. Get a move on, Jim, he's half dead."

"I'm going," Jim promised as he hurried away.

With an effort, Rob lifted his head and looked up at the fisherman. "I owe you." He held out his hand. "Let me have your knife. Just for a minute."

It was given to him, and Rob unzipped his jeans. Bernie swore again as he watched. Rob's hands were shaking dangerously as he sliced away the cord, and when the pressure was gone his startled veins protested. He braced himself, pressed a hand to his groin until the pain dwindled to a level he could disregard.

"Holy shit," Bernie whispered. "Who did this?"

"Later," Rob panted. "You don't have a radio?"

"It's busted," Bernie explained, "which is why we knocked on your door. We thought you might have a CB. You sounded... well, to tell you the truth, we thought you were drunk. Singing. We figured you'd probably got in here for shelter, opened a bottle to keep out the cold, had a few too many. You know."

"I know." Rob zipped up and chafed his bare arms and chest. "How far is it to the nearest town or village, somewhere with a rescue station or a phone?"

"A couple of miles, this side of Victor." Bernie jerked a thumb over his shoulder, down the coast. "There's a property development, a new housing estate. Mind you, the phones won't be on. There isn't a working phone for miles, it's all been evacuated. High tide broke about a mile inland, all their fancy houses were three foot under. You'd never believe it, but this shed is supposed to be up a hill, above the beach."

Rob forced himself to his feet, determined to get his legs moving and keep them moving. "Can you get to Victor Harbour? Find the police, give them a message."

"We'll try," Bernie said doubtfully. "You ought to see a doctor."

He was probably right, but Rob put the thought to the back of his mind. "Have you got a pen? Take down a message."

From a voluminous pocket, Bernie produced a tattered notebook and ballpoint. "Go on."

"Find the police or emergency services. Tell them..." his mind seemed to jam a gear and he struggled for the capacity to think. "There's a lunatic out here. His name is John Chandler, he works for an English guy called Lewis. The police might know them. They bring drugs in, here on this coast. Chandler's got my friend. There's a ship called the *Lan Tao* coming, it'll be here soon."

The fisherman gaped at him. "Drugs?"

"We saw a whole lot we weren't supposed to." Rob hugged himself, and nodded at the rope that had noosed his neck and was now tangled at his feet. "That's what all this is about."

He was chafing his arms as Jim hurried back into the shed. In his arms was a bundle, wrapped in a piece of tarpaulin, and as he opened it Rob saw a bottle of Frigate rum, two heavy grey wool jerseys and an anorak, not waterproof but quilted. Rob pounced on the bottle and took one large swig. Two might make him dizzy, but one hit the spot. Warmth spread outward from the pit of his belly while Bernie gave Jim the gist of the story he had been told.

"I owe you — again," Rob panted as he struggled into both the jerseys and the jacket, and gave the men a look of gratitude. "Tell me where I can reach you. I'll pay you back."

"Hey, forget it," Bernie scoffed. He shoved his hands into his pockets for warmth. "Look, why don't you get in our boat? It's only a dinghy, and the motor's on the fritz, but we might be able to get you to Victor."

The temptation to agree was fierce, but Rob shook his head. "I have to find my friend, while I've got a chance. In fact, you two had better get out of here, fast. Chandler strung me up there, and you don't want to be here when he gets back." He heard the panicky note in his own voice, and neither Bernie nor Jim needed to be told a second time.

While Rob chanced a second swig of the dark brown Queensland rum, stashed the bottle and took a grip on the crowbar, the two men hustled back through the stony twilight, toward the twelve-foot 'tinny', a steel-hulled runabout that lay beached on the pebbles.

Lightning still flickered, as it had since morning, and the thunder drummed out at sea. Rob was jumpy, and the noise quickened his pulse. He was at the door, peering out at the tide which lapped only eight or ten yards from him, when he heard a sound that congealed his marrow.

The roar of the shotgun seemed to cut through Rob's own body. One single terror consumed him: where was Sean? He held his breath as he took a half step out of the shed, and the rain sluiced into his face. Bernie was already on his face in the mud. Jim was doubled over, trying to drag him along, or pick him up. It was impossible, and Rob heard his own voice yelling at the man to drop him, get out. Jim never got the chance.

He had just turned to run when a second shot pierced the whirling air, and Jim was tossed down. The shot was not clean, and he rolled, whimpering, in the mud, just short of the dinghy. Rob's mind was a white-hot, half-formed swirl.

Two barrels, two shots. Chandler had to reload, and that took time. Rob bunched his thigh muscles, metabolising the adrenalin of fear, and launched himself out from the shed.

Through the twilight he saw the shape of Chandler, watched him lock the barrel of the old-fashioned weapon back into place, saw him bring it up into his shoulder like an experienced skeet shooter. Of Sean, there was no sign, and with a cry of frustration and dread Rob dove back into the shed.

A third shot exploded, much closer at hand, and Jim's whimpers were silent. How long had Chandler been out there? He might have been there the whole time, just waiting for the intruders into his private scene to leave. Rob's clenched fists battered the iron wall of the shed. Where was the justice, where was the sense? Those two men had probably saved his life, and in return for their kindness they lost their own.

"Rob! Robbie, boy!" Chandler shouted, so near to the door that Rob gasped. "Come on out, now. I saw you! Don't make me put a round in Sean. He's safe and sound. You don't want him hurt, do you?"

"No. Wait, for godsake." Some instinct made Rob kick the crowbar out of sight before he stepped outside.

The whole world was a deep, steely blue. Daylight was almost spent, the sun was half an hour down. And there was Sean.

He was on his feet, but not standing up straight. He was stooped, muddy from head to foot after numerous falls, and he was still so groggy, he was weaving as if he had drunk too much. Rob's heart sank. Even if the opportunity to run came, Sean would never make it. Chandler was still smiling, and an animal nerve in Rob wanted to batter that cheerful grin off his face, and keep on battering until his face was gone too.

Shrugging the jacket up about his neck, he stepped toward them. "How are you, Sean?" He voice was a hoarse croak.

Doped blue eyes peered at him. "I've been better," Sean admitted. His voice barely carried over the wind. "You look rough."

"Makes two of us." Rob grabbed him, propped him up and held him tight.

"Get him into the shed," Chandler said briskly. "There's not a whole lot you can get up to in there, and our ride out of this bloody awful country will be along soon."

Rob almost carried Sean inside, and sat him down on the tea chest that had almost become an executioner's block. While Sean caught his breath, Chandler collected the lengths of rope. Rob poised to pounce on him, but he was never close enough, and the shotgun never wavered. Memories of Jim, whimpering in the mud, froze Rob's legs into place.

"I'll have to rope the door shut, since your friends have contrived to pulverise the lock," Chandler said ruefully. He saw the crowbar too, and shoved it outside with the toe of one foot. "You're an enterprising young bastard, Rob, I have to hand it to you. And you've got luck. You've given me more trouble than I bargained for!" His eyes sparkled, as if the challenge had been just what he wanted. "You know, I expected to find you'd hung yourself by the time we arrived."

He backed through the door then, slammed it, and Rob heard a faint scrabbling sound as the rope ran quickly through the bracket handles. For some moments his mind was blank, until Sean made some quiet sound of distress and Rob turned back.

He knelt beside Sean, and as his arms circled the bigger, broader body he discovered Sean's trembling. "Christ, where are you hurt?" He peered into Sean's eyes in the near darkness. The pupils were vast, dark, dilated. "Sean!"

"I'm okay," Sean mumbled.

"That's a lie." Rob's grip tightened on him.

"I woke before he arrived back." Sean scrubbed his face and blinked owlishly. A little light made it into the shed through gaps between walls and roof, just enough to see by. "I got a breath of air on the walk over here, Rob. My head's starting to come clear."

That was probably the truth. "You're frozen," Rob fretted.

"I'm soaked, and there's a gale blowing," Sean slurred. "I'm still pretty numb, Rob, with the shit he gave me."

"I know what you're describing," Rob said awkwardly. "I wish I didn't, but I was a fool once or twice, a few years ago." He gripped Sean by the upper arms. "You'll have to move around. If you sit still, you'll be an ice block in ten more minutes."

"Right." Sean hauled himself up and plodded in circles in the gloom. Rob shadowed him, afraid he would fall, but Sean's mind was slowly beginning to work again and he gave Rob a anxious look. "You okay?"

"Bruised," Rob confessed. "He had a handful of me where it hurts most, but I'll live."

"I'll kill him," Sean whispered.

The barely audible words frightened Rob almost as much as Chandler frightened him. As Sean came to rest, Rob caught his lover's stubbled face between his palms and hunted for his mouth in the darkness. Sean's tongue was acid, and Rob was sure he could taste the drug, but the trembling had begun to abate. Blind, Rob's hands covered him, searching for injury, and when they came to Sean's own right hand, they stopped.

"It's bare to the bone," Sean said bitterly. "I'll need some stitches, when we get out of here."

When. Not if. Rob peered at Sean's hand, assessing the damage. It was bad enough to demand prompt medical attention, and he doubted that Lewis's crew would see to it. Sean let him fret for a time, then slid an arm about him and hugged.

"Honey, have you looked around?"

"What for?" Rob asked dully.

"Tools." Sean gestured at the shed. "Anything we could use as a weapon. I'd be surprised if we can't find something. This place ought to be a goldmine."

"I haven't had a chance to look."

"You kidding? You were locked in here for an hour!" Then Sean saw Rob's averted face, and he choked back his anger.

"You were tied."

"Like a Christmas turkey, and I'm bruised," Rob said sourly. "Feels like I've had a kick in the balls. If those fishermen hadn't found me —" He shook his head savagely.

Sean caught him in the crook of his left arm. "We're getting out of here. The only question is, how." He kissed Rob's ear and fended him off. "We haven't time for this. Save it, Robbie. You have to help me."

Rob shook himself hard and dragged both hands through the tangle of his hair. "Okay, let's see what we can find."

The shed was cluttered with junk. Ladders and paint, mineral turpentine, several pairs of stained old coveralls. A wrecked model airplane; a box of crashed kites. Years' worth of ancient newspapers, camping gear. The place seemed to be used by someone who operated a house painting business, and kept the overflow junk of his own home here.

Almost blind, rummaging by touch, Sean grunted as he produced a screwdriver, and Rob watched him use it to lever the tops off several cans of plastic paint. Rob peered over his shoulder into a box.

"You found something?"

"Paint," Sean said grimly. "Lots of it. Highly flammable, burns like blazes. If we had some way to ignite it we'd have a great diversion. Shock tactics. You don't have a cigarette lighter, do you?"

"In my jacket, back at Bradgate Farm." Rob searched the pockets of the anorak, hoping for a box of matches, but he knew he would find nothing. The jacket had none of that clinging odour of stale cigarettes that always betrayed a smoker. "No joy," he reported at last.

"Okay." Sean continued to rummage. "Keep looking. Dry rags, dry wood, newspapers. Pile them up."

"How about oily, painty coveralls?" Rob plucked them out of a box. "These'll burn."

"Great." Sean stooped woozily and cleared a space in which to work. He held his watch to the tiny glimmer of twilight. "We don't have much time. Chandler was chattering about the ship, a freighter belonging to Lewis. It can't be far away."

Rob arranged the filthy coveralls and searched with growing urgency for some means to set them alight. "Tools," he grunted as he dug through into the back of the shed. "Christ! It's so dark, I can't see shit." The rain drummed on the roof with renewed vigour, almost drowning out his voice. And then, for the first time that day, luck smiled. "Sean," he called as he kicked aside a stack of card boxes. "Sean, there's a grindstone back here, the kind they use for sharpening knives."

"We'll start a small fire, keep it alight," Sean said breathlessly as he spun the grindstone over. The rusted old machine squealed and rumbled, but the grinding surface was good enough. He held the screwdriver against the spinning wheel and a shower of magnesium-bright sparks cascaded from the steel. "Perfect," he muttered. "Now, what will we light a fire in?"

This time, Rob was there before him. "This." He lifted the remains of a concrete birdbath out of a rusted wheelbarrow, and trundled the contraption over to the grindstone. He left Sean propping himself up beside the machine, and fetched the coveralls and an armful of newspapers. These filled the barrow, and he pecked Sean's cheek. "For luck."

Sean actually chuckled, but the sound was shaky. "You spin the grindstone, I'll hold the screwdriver... spinning it makes me dizzy. I feel hungover."

So Rob spun it over and Sean pressed the tool against the wheel, producing a cascade of brilliant sparks which spilled into the old oil and dry fabric. It was only a matter of time before they caught — this was the way domestic accidents happened, and home handy-men burned down the house.

First the fabric smouldered, and Rob knelt beside the barrow, blowing on the tiny orange glow. It caught, he saw a lick of flame, then a tiny fire, and he grunted in victory as he held his hands to the sudden heat.

"Rags and newspapers." Sean gestured at the boxes.

"Turps," Rob added as the light enabled him to properly see what was around them. "There's half a bottle of turpentine here. I won't let it go out." In the scant illumination he peered into Sean's drawn, smudged face. "You look like hell."

"Thanks." Sean pulled his back straight and worked his neck to and fro. "Open some of these cans. We need a lake of paint just inside the door. Plenty of it. Move, Rob, we don't have time to waste."

"You're a logical son of a bitch," Rob observed as he did as he was told.

"Leave us space to get out," Sean called after him. "Remember, burning paint gives off toxic fumes. We can't hold our breath for long. As soon as it's alight, we have to get out. All this is, is a diversion."

"And we need a weapon," Rob added. "Keep looking."

The paint spilled to the right of the door. Rob went on opening cans and pouring till the lake was three feet wide and four long, cream and green, like swirls of candy as it ran together. The stink soon filled the shed, and he felt his head begin to buzz.

When he returned to Sean, he saw that Sean's clumsy fingers were messing with the remains of the kites and model airplane. Rob watched for a time, and began to see what he was doing. Sean produced a grim, humourless smile in the flickering firelight.

"Clever enough?"

"It'll do," Rob agreed shakily. "Move over, let me help you. We must be out of time." His voice trembled more with fear than with cold.

Sean's good arm circled his waist. "Are you sure you're all right, Robbie?"

"Scared," Rob said hoarsely. "My father used to get furious with me when I was scared. He'd go red in the face and yell at me, 'Be a man! Be a man, or you'll be nothing.'"

"That was cruel," Sean said, under the drum of the rain on the roof. "You hated him, didn't you?"

"About as much as you despised your old man, who beat up you and your mother, robbed her blind, and left you both." Rob rested his head on Sean's for a moment. "And still you survived, and made good. I love you."

"You think I don't know that?" Sean's breath was warm against his ear. "Help me, Robbie. This hand's giving me some trouble. I can't move it much. Bring the barrow closer so I can see better. My eyes are still blurry."

Card, newspaper and paint rags kept the fire burning. The light was adequate, but it allowed Rob to see how badly damaged Sean's right hand really was. The bones were whole, but the flesh was torn, black and blue. Even if it was treated here and now, he was going to carry a scar.

Still, Sean forced his fingers to work. He was snapping off the string tails of several kites, and Rob helped him strip away the bits of rag which had flighted them. To the thick, coiled jute strings, he was tying pieces of the model plane, the radio control gear and the motor. The result was two crude versions of the simple Argentinian weapon, the bolo — basically just a couple of weights on the ends of a couple of lines. Whirled around and released, they would bring a man down, if not actually injure him. A now razor-sharpened screwdriver substituted well for a knife.

They were done, with the two 'throw weapons', a makeshift knife, a lake of paint and a fire burning fiercely in the rusted wheelbarrow. The absurd spectacle aroused Rob's humour as he lowered his buttocks onto the crate beside Sean.

"This is just ludicrous enough to work."

"It had better." Sean flexed his back and shoulders continually. "There's not much more we can do." He paused, peering into the shadows above them. "Help me get those ladders down."

The task was easier said than done, but hard work got the blood moving, which kept them warmer and would also help to dissipate the drug in Sean's bloodstream. Sean yelped and swore as he tried to use the injured hand, and Rob took the weight of the ladders as they tumbled out of the rafters. He propped them on the blind side of the door and at Sean's quiet suggestion, tied a length of rope to them. The same rope that would have strangled him if he had fallen. Now, they could stand back, beyond the burning lake, and a single tug on that rope would bring the ladders down on whoever came through the door first.

"Not bad," Sean decided as Rob trundled the barrow closer. "Now, we wait, and we listen." He held out his good arm, inviting Rob to hold him, and they hugged tight. "You're going to be okay. Trust me."

"I always trusted you," Rob said tiredly.

"Then, tell me the truth," Sean prompted.

Rob blinked at him in the firelight. "About what?"

"When Chandler had you alone here, did he touch you?" Sean

108

licked his lips. "Back at the farm, he said he could fancy you. If he put one finger on you —"

The suggestion made Rob wince. "There wasn't time for him to even think about that."

"Truth, Rob?" Sean's brows rose.

"You want the truth? He tied one end of a rope around my gullet and the other end around my genitals, pulled it tight and jerked me around by it. Let me tell you, I did as I was told. That was all — it was enough!" Rob took a deep, calming breath.

For some moments Sean was silent, looking into the fire, and Rob studied his profile. His jaw was stubbled and the bruise was spreading. To Rob, he was beautiful, and he might have said so, but before he could speak Sean's dark head rose.

"Listen."

A nerve in Rob's gut coiled up like a watch spring. He took a step closer to the door and waited intently, trying to hear the sound Sean had already picked out of the wind. Then, there it was, a steady grumble under the background noise of the weather: the engine of a boat. And it was coming closer.

Nine

THE ENGINE was old, Sean thought, a rattle-trap V8. The launch probably belonged to a ship that should have been scrapped years before. Many shipping companies made a fortune, keeping worn-out ships on the water, registered in unscrupulous Third World countries when no legitimate government would touch them. They were a scourge, and there was no way of getting rid of them. Was Geoffrey Lewis playing with fire, underwriting his own hulls? It was a recipe for disaster, but once in a while a man grew very, very rich out of blind luck.

The launch was coming in on the tide, which was turning now. It butted across the current and the engine worked hard to drive it up onto the stony slope below the shed. Sean half-heard the rasp of keel on pebbles before the engine cut out.

Thunder was grumbling again and flickers of lightning glared through the gaps between the east-facing wall and the roofing iron, but the storm was no longer overhead. Sean came to his feet as he heard voices. Chandler was shouting excitedly against the wind.

"Winkler! You took your sweet time getting here!"

"We were lucky to get here at all in this storm." The voice was deep, the accent unmistakably South African. "The sea is rougher than I've seen it in years, and that garbage-barge is not exactly seaworthy. I've told Lewis a hundred times, if he doesn't sell it for salvage, it'll be on the bottom — and it'll take us with it. What the fuck are you doing, John? Get in the boat, let's move — the skipper's having kittens!"

"I've got us a bonus," Chandler said smugly. "Fresh meat for the lab."

"Prisoners?" Winkler sounded sceptical.

"The men Meredith managed to misplace this morning." Chandler's voice was right outside the door now. "You heard about the intruders aboard the *Minuette*?"

"I heard," Winkler said dubiously. "You ran them down?"

"I just bumped into them. They were going my way, trying to keep to the high ground, so I thought I'd bring them along for the walk."

"Nice and neat," Winkler allowed. "No bodies to leave behind, a financial reward in Port Moresby, and no live witnesses to Lewis's business." He paused. "Hodges, Prescott, move your asses! Two prisoners in the shed — get them out, get them in the boat."

Footsteps slurped through the mud toward the door, and Sean licked his lips as he tried to derive a mental picture from the sounds outside. He was sure it was four pairs of feet, which accounted for Chandler and the South African, and the men who had crewed the launch.

He moved back from the door and stooped to gather up the first of the crude throw weapons. He would be useless in a fight, but he could whirl and throw the weight, and tumble the ladders down on whoever stepped inside.

He was untangling the coarse jute strings while Rob lit a rolled newspaper from the barrow. Their eyes met in the flickering red light, and Sean nodded. He trusted Rob more than Rob trusted himself. Rob was strong. One day he would discover the strength in himself that Sean had always been aware of.

The door's bracket handles rattled as the rope was cut. Sean took several breaths to clear his head, and held the last one in his lungs as Rob prepared to throw the burning paper into the lake of paint. When that paint began to blaze they would not dare take another breath. The smoking fumes would be poisonous. They must disable the intruders and get out, or they would go down too, victims of their own makeshift weapons.

The shed's doors opened outward and the wind seemed to glue them shut. Rob waited until they were swinging before he tossed the paper into the middle of the green and white chemical pond, then jumped swiftly out of the way. It was a scant second before the paint became an inferno, almost exploding into a wall of flames. They leapt up fiercely, and through them Sean glimpsed John Chandler.

Shocked by the sudden glare and heat, he had thrown his left hand up to cover his face, and in the right was the shotgun. All four men were stunned as they opened the door to a sea of flames, but the element of surprise would not last long. Sean lashed the rough bolo around his head in a wide arc to generate some power, and released it when his intuition told him to.

Each weight spun on four twisted strings which had the strength of a light rope. Like a coiling snake, the unlikely weapon tangled around Chandler's legs and he fell, perilously close to the fire. Rob was moving at once. He had snatched up the other weapon the moment he lit the paint, and was beginning to swing it as Sean threw the first. Rob's was aimed at a tall, white-blond man who stood directly behind Chandler. It could only be Winkler. Behind them were two characters who seemed to boast a close kinship with the great apes.

The absurd weapon rushed out of Rob's hand. The weights were only about three pounds apiece, but it was enough. A mess of twisted strings wrapped around Winkler's torso, and as Sean watched, one of the pieces of model airplane junk struck his temple hard. He went down as if he had been punched.

With self-preservation foremost in mind, Hodges and Prescott were on their way to the ground in a headlong dive, and Sean did not hesitate. "Go!" he yelled, and shoved Rob out through the fringe of the heat and flames, into the cold, turbulent night air.

Grogginess, dizziness, filled Sean's head, but his eyes were on the shotgun which had threatened and humiliated them both. He pounced on it while Chandler was still trying to untangle himself, on the edge of the fire, and snatched it up in his left hand. His right was so useless now, it might have been made of wood.

Sean was not as ambidextrous as he liked to pretend, and using a shotgun one-handed was almost impossible at the best of times. With a supreme effort, he levelled it and turned back toward Winkler's men just as Hodges and Prescott began to regain their wits.

They were armed. Sean would have been astonished if they had not been. Hand guns were cheap and commonplace, not so customary on Australian streets as they were at home, but still far from unknown. He caught a glimpse of two automatic pistols being clawed from a holster here, a belt there, and with a single, instinctive spasm, his finger tightened.

The recoil of the shotgun almost knocked it out of Sean's grasp, and wrenched his wrist painfully. As they went down in the mud, Prescott and Hodges had rolled close together, well within the spread of the buckshot. Pellets peppered them both in the chest and belly, enough to wring a scream from one and a winded curse from the other. The kick of the shotgun had been like a body blow, and Sean's vision blurred. His right hand and arm seemed crushed in a vice.

The whole action was squeezed into seconds. "Rob! Rob, grab the guns — for godsake, what are you waiting for!" Sean bellowed as the dimness spun around him. He fought his groggy senses and felt numbly for the shotgun with a hand that could barely feel at all.

But Rob was already moving. He snatched up both the pistols before Hodges and Prescott were lucid once more, and as Chandler began to struggle toward his feet, the butt of one of them hammered into the back of his head. Chandler plunged down again, not quite unconscious, but sufficiently incapacitated for Rob to ignore him.

"And them, too," Sean shouted, with a gesture at Hodges and Prescott. "Rob!"

"Them?" Rob blinked at him in the weird light from the fire.

"Hit them, for Christ's sake!" Sean bellowed. "Put them out — you want to fight? Buckshot's not going to slow them down for long!"

Realisation widened Rob's eyes, and he spun back toward the two men. They were still down, clutching a dozen wounds between them, but none of the injuries was enough to stop them. The pellets were lodged in muscle and fat, each one worth a scalpel-probe and a stitch, exquisitely painful but hardly lethal. Rob seemed to realise this all at once, and fear galvanised his whole body.

Sean had never seen him fight. A brief flirtation with karate as a young teenager was Rob's only contact with mock-violence, but he swung the butt-end of the pistol like a pro, before Winkler's men even knew he was coming. Sean heard the dull thuds as it impacted firmly with bone, and then their moaning and cursing was silent.

Lightning flickered, a long way out at sea, and the rain eased a little. Sean took a breath of the salt wind and looked out at the ship. The *Lan Tao* lay about a quarter mile offshore. It was a 1950s vintage break-bulk freighter, the design of cargo carrier which plied the oceans before the advent of the roll-on, roll-off container ship. With every flicker of lightning, he could pick out the enormous derricks and the immense forecastle amidships. A torch flashed out from the side, blinking a coded message.

"They're watching us," Sean said grimly as Rob came toward him, handling the two pistols as if they were venomous insects.

"It's almost dark," Rob protested.

"Remember the arsenal we saw on the *Minuette*? Several of those weapons were night 'scoped. Vision intensification gear. Oh, they can see us, Rob. Bet on it." He paused, and a moment later his heart began to race. "Can you see that? They're putting another boat over the side. If we don't get out of here, as soon as they get in range they'll shoot first."

"Holy bloody shit," Rob whispered, half heard under the wind.

"Their launch," Sean rasped with a gesture at the beached runabout that had brought Winkler's party ashore. "It's either that or make a run for it, and I'm too dizzy to run far enough or fast enough."

He tucked the shotgun under his arm, plucked one of the pistols out of Rob's hands and pushed it into his left jacket pocket. Way out across the water, another engine started. They were out of time. The launch was a battered geriatric motorboat — not a powerboat, but a ten foot dinghy with a steel hull and a single Johnson outboard on the stern. It had run itself aground against the tide with its own power. Without Sean's urging, Rob put his shoulder against the bow and began to shove. Deliberately, Sean threw the shotgun he had come to hate into the water, and turned his left side to the boat to help.

The keel rasped back over the pebbles and into the water. The outrunning tide unstuck the boat for them, which was sheer luck. An hour earlier, it might have stuck like glue. Icewater surf broke about Sean's knees, stealing the breath out of his lungs, but all at once the boat floated off. Rob hauled himself aboard and reached back for Sean.

Feeling heavy, clumsy, useless, Sean let Rob hoist him bodily over the side. He fell into the well and rolled against the stern, under the tiller. Rob zipped the Johnson twice, three times before it gargled into life. Sean pulled himself up at the side and gazed at the boat which had been put over the side of the *Lan Tao*. It was making headway, and he thought he counted four murky figures aboard.

The Johnson barked, roared, and Rob grabbed the tiller in both hands. Sean was about to ask which way they should go, but Rob had already decided. The nose came about, battering into every wave as it headed south, parallel to the coast. They were headed toward the town, but it seemed a long way off indeed. In the general power blackouts, no light showed anywhere as far as Rob could see.

Not fifty yards away from the shed, they passed another grounded dinghy. It could only be the craft belonging to the fishermen who had found Rob. Sean gave the men a moment's thought, and then banished them from his mind. He would grieve later, but first he and Rob must survive.

The wind was blowing from one direction while the current ran in the other, and the chop was a bad dream come true. The Johnson sounded sick, and Rob was cursing as he coaxed power out of it. To Sean it seemed they were making decent speed, until he fixed his eyes on a stationery point, a signpost on the shore, and saw the truth. Running into this current, driven by one ailing outboard, they were hardly making headway at all.

The rain dribbled away almost to a stop as he crawled up against Rob in the stern. "Can you get any more out of it?"

"The throttle's already wide open," Rob shouted over the din. He twisted to look back at the other boat. "Conditions are the same for them. We've got about a quarter mile on them, but we're not going to outrun them. Not in this bucket."

'Bucket' was the right word. The dinghy was thickly rusted, and Sean was uncomfortably aware of water lapping around his legs. He cradled his right hand against his chest and looked back at the shore.

"Ah, fuck! Look at that — we're making about two miles an hour. We're going nowhere."

"Neither are they." Rob jerked a thumb over his shoulder. "One of the fishermen said there's a new housing estate up ahead. We'll see it long before we see the town. At this speed, it's going to take half an hour to get there!" He gave Sean an anxious look. "We won't make it to the town before they overtake us."

Sean had taken a breath to shout over the engine noise when it seemed an insect buzzed past his head. More by intuition than experience, he realised what it was, and he caught a fistful of Rob's collar to pull him down into the well of the boat. Rob grunted, trying to keep a grip on the tiller.

"What the hell are you doing, Sean?"

"They're shooting at us! You can't hear the shots over this racket!" Sean bawled.

Rob's picturesque language was smothered by a rumble of thunder. His grasp on the tiller did not budge, but he moved against Sean, and Sean felt his shaking. Rob had never been in any situation even remotely like this. He could scarcely imagine some of the scenes Sean had seen. Working for Jackson Oil might have been hard, tedious, sometimes dangerous, but it had provided a wealth of experience which Sean had never properly appreciated before.

Think! he demanded of his fuddled mind. *You can think your way out of this!* He hugged Rob tight with his left arm and lifted his voice over the noise. "Head inshore."

"You sure?" Rob looked anxiously at him.

"Positive," Sean insisted. He bobbed up for a moment, and his eyes raked the dark coastline. "I can see rooftops, right there. Rooftops mean cover, some place to get lost in. If they can't see us, we're in with a chance. Come on, Robbie, land this thing while we've got a few minutes' head start."

"But they're shooting!" Rob yelled into the wind.

Sean clawed the rain out of his eyes. "Sitting on a heaving deck, getting tossed around by the sea, shooting into a gale, in the dark — I wouldn't give a nickel for their chances of hitting the side of a barn!" He sounded a good deal more confident than he felt, but the last thing Rob needed now was for Sean to falter.

The argument was basically sound, and Rob bought it. He put the tiller over and sent the boat angling sharply toward the shoreline. The tide was running out fast now, and the old Johnson fought the millrace of the water. The surf was rising, too. In fifteen more minutes it would be six or eight feet, high enough to capsize a dinghy. Even these breakers gave them a furious pounding before the keel rasped up onto a rocky slope.

The engine stalled out, and Rob hopped over the side at once. A wave crashed over him, almost dumping him back into the boat, and he fought to keep his footing as he gave Sean both his hands to help him out. The water sucked and tugged at Sean's legs, like a creature intent on dragging him back into the sea and down.

They had landed at a cleft in the hills that would normally be a half mile inland of the tidal zone. Through the cleft, they glimpsed the new housing project. The storm and the freak tide had completely changed the face of the coast. The houses were all brand new, modern designs with one or two storeys, tiled roofing, stylish fencing. All had one factor in common. They were ruined.

As Sean forced his legs onward, pounding in Rob's wake into the gloom, he saw that the creek had burst its banks. The houses were flooded out and several roofs had been ripped away. Windows were smashed, trees uprooted. Before their eyes was five million dollars' damage in a half square mile. He peered in the dimness, looking for people, but nothing was moving. Not even a dog barked.

"Bernie and Jim told me it was evacuated," Rob panted as he slithered along on the hill slope, just above the waterline. He pulled Sean down into the scanty cover of a stand of trees. "That boat's going to be with us in about another minute. We'll have to get into the water, if we're going to make it to the houses. Can you do that?"

"I'll have to." Sean was kneeling, hugging his hand against his chest. In the cold, every extremity was numb. He could scarcely feel the injury. When it began to warm, it would hurt like the devil.

"Sean?" As he failed to move, Rob caught his collar and gave him a vigorous shake. "Sean!"

"I'm okay." Sean pushed up to his feet and knuckled his eyes. He dragged in several breaths and willed the fog in his head to clear. Lightning sheeted out in the east, but overhead the sky was steel blue and for the first time in ten hours the rain stopped. He peered at his watch and saw ten minutes after seven.

Offshore, the lights of the freighter cast yellow beams through the gloom. She would be on station-keeping, her old but powerful diesel engines running, her bow turned into the wind. With an effort of will, Sean mobilised his legs and took a handful of Ron's sleeve.

"Hurry. Let's see if we can get among the houses before they make it ashore."

"Find someplace to hide?" Rob panted.

"You got a better idea?" Sean slid precariously down the slope, and into the flood water. It lapped to his knees for a few strides, then to mid-thigh, and he gritted his teeth as it swirled up around his groin. "You want to sit there and wait for them to come get us?" He nodded ahead, at the inundated houses. "In this case, you can hide, but you can't run!" His teeth bared with effort as he forced his way through the water. "We got one chance left, Robbie."

"Ambush?" Rob guessed breathlessly.

In his pocket, Sean's left hand closed about the pistol Rob had taken from Winkler's man. It was a long time since Sean had used a hand gun, but they swore it was like riding a bike. Rob had never used one at all, but there was not much to learn, and necessity made an excellent teacher.

A pace ahead of him, Rob almost stumbled and caught himself before he could go under. Sean's hand shot out to catch him, but Rob fended him off. "Blind leading the blind," he panted. "How's your balance?"

"Getting better," Sean told him. "Quit worrying about the drug — I've just about worked it out of me." He lifted his right hand. "If you want to worry about anything, fret about this."

In this gloom he could not see it, but he knew it was bleeding.

Even trying to use it had opened the lacerations. The flesh over his knuckles was in black and blue tatters, and Sean knew full well it was the sort of wound that could turn nasty if it went untreated. The kind of 'nasty' that cost a man some fingers. The cold and the salt water would control the injury a little, but Sean punished himself mercilessly.

Of all the stupid things he had ever done in his life — aiming a punch at Chandler, letting the man roll out of the way and then slamming his hand into the ground. He deserved to have a fistful of broken bones.

Save that he had not *let* Chandler do that. Chandler was good. He was a professional. Sean gave the man his grudging respect as he struggled after Rob through the black, swirling water.

Ahead of them was a house. This morning it would have been a home, someone's two storey, red brick pride and joy. Now it was a wreck. The roof was torn away and a tree had plunged through the front windows. But it would provide them with protection, get them out of direct sight of the shoreline. Then, Winkler's men must actually hunt for them, and they would have minutes or an hour in which to plan.

Dogged, determined, Sean plowed through the water after Rob. As he shoved his way through the wind he felt like a pit bull up against a bear.

A pace ahead of him, Rob grasped a wrought-iron gatepost and pulled himself through toward the house. At every step since they had left the boat, he had expected to hear the crack of a rifle, but Sean must be right — he usually was. The conditions were so bad, Winkler's men were not about to simply waste their ammunition.

He dragged Sean after him into the lee of a brick garage, and paused to scout the lie of the land. They must get in, get out of sight. The only course Winkler's men had left was a pattern-search, and that would take time. Rob prayed they would quit, pull out and go. Sense told him they would not. Much more was at stake than an hour's frustrated inconvenience.

They needed to find a house with an intact roof. The ground floors were all flooded, three feet under, and Rob would sure the water level was still rising. It was probably still raining over the hills, and the runoff was sluicing down that creek. By midnight, the water might be six feet deep, and it was good sense to get the people out of here.

How far was it to the town? It could be another mile, it could be five. Darkness, storm and a degree of panic had cost Rob his orientation, and he kicked himself for the lapse. Sean needed a partner, not a parasite.

As he caught his breath, he tried to bring to mind the navigation charts of these waters. Where was the nearest lighthouse? It was sure to have a shortwave. Sean's hand on his arm dragged him back to the present.

"That one!" he was shouting. "Third on the left, with the bushes at the side!"

The house had somehow kept its roof. A well-grown tree had come down against the side wall, but by some good fortune it had missed the windows. The weight of the water had sprung the lock, the front door was half open, so breaking and entering was not a concern.

They could hope for no better, and Rob pushed away from the garage, with Sean clinging stubbornly to his heels. "Will they search for us?" he called over his shoulder.

"You know they will," Sean panted. "But that's going to take time."

Time, Rob told himself, *for me to have a look at that hand of yours.* It was typical of Sean to keep silent about how bad the injury was. The cold and the drug had helped to keep it numb, but he could hardly be unaware of it.

The swirling water concealed debris, objects that loomed like pitfalls before them. A cry from behind him spun Rob around, and he caught Sean the instant after he stumbled. Deep under the water, Rob's foot made out the shape of a child's tricycle, abandoned like a landmine at the gates. That child would be homeless if this water got much deeper. Rob wondered fleetingly if the insurance company would pay out in a situation like this, or if the whole calamity would be deemed an 'act of God'. Most victims finished out the disaster with nothing.

They stumbled up the garden pathway, and Rob dove in through the half-open front door. A step inside, they found themselves in a hallway with cream-painted walls, bedraggled plants, and the half-seen, menacing shapes of furniture. To the right was the living room. Sean forced his way through and peered through the grimy window glass.

There, he braced himself against the wall to rest, and for five endless minutes kept watch. Nothing moved in the lake which would have been a front street that morning, and as Rob tried to make out shapes closer to the shore, rain began to pelt against the glass.

At last, Sean was satisfied and turned his back on the window. "I think we're safe. Let's get upstairs, out of this water."

From the hips down, it was icy enough to make Rob's balls ache, and he was grateful to clamber up the stairs. Sodden jeans and shoes felt disgusting, and as he climbed out he became aware of a myriad of minor hurts, bruises and scratches.

The house was almost completely dark, and he felt his way into the bedrooms. The electricity would have been turned off hours before, when the estate was evacuated — and even if the power had been connected, switching on a light would have signalled their presence like a beacon.

The master bedroom faced west, away from the sea, and there, Rob looped back the curtains to let in what light was available. "Sit tight," he told Sean hoarsely. "Let me see if I can find some candles. You know what this state's like. You could set your watch by the power cuts, so everyone keeps candles around. Open some of these closets, see if you can find some dry clothes." He touched Sean's face, though his features were invisible in the darkness. "You okay?"

"No, I'm not okay!" Sean said stridently.

"You sound more like your old self," Rob observed. "That shit must be wearing off. Just wait there."

He felt his way back down the stairs, slid into the water with a curse, and pushed through into the back of the house. Hunting for candles, he had two choices: the cheap household variety which everyone kept for use in the frequent blackouts, or ornamental candles, intended for the dining table.

By touch, Rob investigated the cooker, and grunted as he discovered it was gas. Now, did the lady of the house use matches, or a gas gun? He felt along the back of the cooker, and felt something move against his hand. Jackpot.

The box was almost full. He struck a match, held it up and peered about until he had located the cupboards. From here, he was down to luck. The cupboards under the sink were out, since they were submerged, but he inspected the wall cupboards, and stumbled over a stack of expensive china, Waterford crystal... four silver candlesticks, eight coloured candles and several boxes of matches.

"Eureka," he muttered to himself as he scooped up four of the candles and two candlesticks, stuffed them into his pockets and hurried back to the stairs.

He set up the candlesticks on the dressing table in the master bedroom. As Sean drew the curtains over, Rob coaxed two candles to light. Sean was still working through the closets, and throwing out odds and ends.

The people who lived here would have packed in haste, taken their best and left anything that was not essential. Old clothes had been abandoned. Shirts and jerseys, several sizes too large for either Rob or Sean, lay on the wide double bed, along with a jacket, a man's cardigan. It was not worth changing their trousers. As soon as they left this second storey they would be hip-deep in the water again.

"Come here," Rob called quietly as he cupped his cold palms around the candle flame, hoping for a little warmth. "I want to take a look at your hand."

"It's pretty bad," Sean warned. "There's nothing you can do for it."

"You let me be the judge of that!" Rob was waiting, and Sean stepped reluctantly into the light. His face was smudged, his features drawn, but Rob was intent on the hand. He had never been particularly squeamish, but he shivered as he saw the wound. "Christ, Sean, you call this pretty bad?" He looked up into Sean's eyes in the fluttering light. "If this turns septic, you could lose your fucking fingers!" He straightened and rubbed his face hard. "Let me see what I can find."

This bedroom boasted a stylish en suite. Rob took a candle and cupped his hand about it to keep it burning as he stepped into the alcove which housed a shower stall, basin, toilet, and a small cabinet on the wall.

The door was mirrored, and he spared his face a single glance. He was filthy, and he was showing the mileage of stress and fear. Shadows played wickedly about his features. "Bloody gargoyle," he accused himself as he slid the door across and peered into the cupboard.

Inside were a bottle of Detol, a tube of Savlon antiseptic creme, manicure scissors, tweezers, a plastic packet of fresh washcloths, and a man's shaving mug shaped like an antique Toby jug. Rob took the bottle and tube, and filled the mug with tap water.

That water would have stood in the pipes for hours, and would be clean. As soon as the pipes were empty, no one could guarantee the integrity of the water. He gathered up all the clean towels which were piled on top of the cabinet, and stepped out of the tiny en suite to find Sean stripped to the waist.

Rob scrubbed him with a towel to dry him, and got both of the well-worn jerseys onto him. His natural body heat would begin to warm him a little, although from the hips down he was still wet. Then Rob clenched his teeth and turned his attention to the injured hand.

"I think there's some gravel and wood splinters in it," Sean said quietly.

"I can see them." Rob looked up at him. "They'll have to come out."

"Do it." Sean looked away. "I know how bad it is."

Rob wondered if he did. He laved his own hands with the Detol, washed the wound with water and splashed it with the antiseptic liquid, which made Sean hiss in pain. He worked with the tiny scissors until he had cut away the tattered, dead skin. When the injury was tidy, he felt very gently, very carefully with his fingertips. Finding the sharpness of a piece of stone or stick, he plucked it out with the tweezers. Sean was silent, unmoving, until Rob let go his hand.

"All out," Rob whispered as he dashed it with more Detol and thickened it with Savlon creme. He scissored the washcloths into strips, and with these bound the whole hand as tightly as he could. "That's the best I can do, Sean."

Wheezing with reaction, Sean held the hand against his chest. "That's a decent imitation of a field dressing. It'll hold me, till we get out of here."

"Maybe," Rob said doubtfully. "By morning, that's going to be a mess. Infected." He screwed the cap onto the Detol bottle and handed it to Sean. "Soak the bandage, as often as you can stand to, and..."

"And I'll save my fingers," Sean finished. He set the plastic bottle aside and cupped his good hand around Rob's nape. "I've seen wounds you can't even imagine."

"On the oil rigs," Rob said hoarsely. "Engineering sites, where a good loud shout brings a squad of paramedics, at a flat gallop."

"Yeah." Sean leaned over and pressed his lips against Rob's forehead. "Get yourself dry. I'd dry you myself, but you'll have to forgive me if I just sit and watch. Then I'll return the favour, and check you over."

"I told you, I was only tied up," Rob protested, much too quickly.

"And you told me how," Sean added. "Drop your pants."

Rob groaned. "Sean, it's all right."

"So let me see, and then we'll both be sure." Sean's good hand clenched into Rob's shoulder muscles. "Right now, you're cold and numb, but I'll give you odds that rope scuffed right through your skin in places. You've been slithering around in mud and immersed in flood water. These houses are almost certainly plumbed into septic tanks, and those tanks will have overflowed. The water out there could be toxic. Stop being a prima donna and drop your damned pants!"

None of that had even crossed Rob's mind. He felt his cheeks flush as he unzipped the wet, clinging jeans and turned toward the candles. "I'm bruised," he saw awkwardly.

"You're black and blue." Sean knelt before him, the better to see. He hesitated. "How the hell did he tie you?"

"With a rope," Rob said ruefully. "Is the skin broken?"

"Abraded a little. You were lucky," Sean observed. He palmed Rob's balls in his good hand, explored him with careful fingers. "You're a bit swollen."

"I'd expect to be." Rob worked his neck to and fro to ease its tense muscles. "So's your jaw. That was a pretty good wallop he laid on you. And I'll bet your nipples are sore."

Sean looked up sharply at him. "You watched the bastard shoot me up?

"Of course I did. He skin-popped most of it into your cock and scrotum. You're too cold to feel it, be grateful for that. There was nothing I could do to stop him." He tried to move away, out of Sean's hands. "I'll be fine."

"Let's be sure." With a determined effort, Sean twisted the cap off the plastic bottle and groped Rob's genitals with a stinging palmful. "There, you'll do. Now, get dry! Like I said, I'd do it for you, but —" He lifted the bandaged hand.

"You always did like to watch me." Rob stepped away from him, stripped to the waist and began to scrub his skin with a towel, short, vicious strokes that brought up swathes of scarlet. "You watch me in bed, that is." He looked levelly at Sean in the light of the candles, and Sean gave him a faint, curious smile. "What? What are you thinking?" Rob's heart squeezed.

"I love you," Sean told him simply. "I just want to say it."

"Because it's occurring to you that we might not get out of this?" Rob guessed. Tears blurred his eyes and he blinked them away.

"I don't believe that," Sean said stubbornly. "I just want to say it, because I'm damned proud of you."

"Proud?" Rob's brows rose in surprise.

"Of your strength." Sean gestured vaguely at the house, and by extension the stormy night, their predicament. "You've never had the training to cope with any of this. Home, school and a few Hindley Street binges while you kangaroo-hopped from one job selling motorbikes to another — none of it prepared you for this." He reached over and placed his left hand flat on Rob's chest, where he could feel his heart. "You're doing good, Rob. If we were warm and dry, and if we had a safe half hour... but we haven't, so words will have to suffice. I love you."

Emotions which Rob could not even identify seethed through him, scalding him. "Jesus, you're saying goodbye to me."

"Bullshit," Sean scoffed. "I'm just grabbing the chance to tell you, before we get down to brass tacks."

"Brass tacks?" Rob's mind spun. Sean caught his shoulder, pulled him closer, and he surrendered to a brief but thorough ravishing of his mouth. "Sean?" Muffled against Sean's face.

"Brass," Sean repeated, "tacks." He let go Rob's head and looked into his eyes. "Have you ever handled a pistol?"

The question was so unexpected, Rob just shook his head dumbly.

"Then it's time to learn. Where did you put it? Come on, Rob! You took two from those bodyguards, gave me one and kept the other for yourself!"

It was in the pocket of the anorak Bernie and Jim had given him. Rob pulled it out and handled it awkwardly. On television, the damned things always looked so small and easy to use. The reality was a solid weight of machined steel which did not fit his hand particularly well. Sean seemed to know what he was doing, and Rob forced his mind to concentrate.

"These," Sean told him quickly, "are just a couple of old Smith & Wesson automatics, early or mid-1970s. There's nothing magical about them. You release the magazine here, see? It drops out, goes in again like this. Got it? Cock it like so... and it's ready to shoot. You can get the rounds off as fast as you can pull the trigger. That's the safety. When it's on, obviously the gun doesn't shoot. Now, drop the magazine out of that and see how many rounds you've got."

Annoyed by his own clumsiness, Rob slid out the magazine and held it to the candles. Incongruously, it seemed to be newly manufactured, while the gun was old. Through a narrow slit in the side he could count the rounds. "There's eight rounds in it," he told Sean as he checked the other weapon.

"And seven in this." He sat on the end of the bed and looked up at Rob, wide-eyed in the dimness. "We're not going to hold them off forever with fifteen rounds between us."

"Where did you learn all this?" Rob gestured with the gun.

Sean produced a wry little smile. "Don't laugh. My mother had three pretty good guns. After Dad left we moved around a lot, must have covered half the states, looking for someplace where she could find decent, regular work. We never knew where we'd be next. She was a good looking woman, twenty years ago. Men noticed her. She took to keeping one of these in her purse, and another at home, and one for spare. I spent a lot of time home alone as a kid, and I was a pretty little boy, so..." he shrugged eloquently. "She taught me how to use a gun. Took some of the anxiety out of her mind. Mine too, come to that."

"She's dead now, isn't she?" Rob turned the gun over and over in his hands, and wished he had a few dozen rounds spare, and several hours to practise on a shooting range, with proper tuition, before he had to use this thing in earnest.

"Yes." Sean held out his good hand, and Rob took it. Their fingers meshed. "I was doing an engineering course at college, she was working nights. We just drifted apart. I left home and a few months later I figured it was high time I came out. My circle of friends changed, some of the old family didn't want to know me anymore. Mom and I lost touch. She died four years ago. I didn't even know she'd been sick, but my uncle told me it was cancer. We'd been drifting so long, she wasn't even sure where to write me."

"Drifting," Rob echoed as he studied the mesh of his fingers and Sean's. "That's not going to happen to us. Not again."

"You got that right," Sean said softly. "You want to know something dumb?"

"Try me." Rob sat beside him, leaning warmly against him.

"I've been thinking about a home," Sean confessed. "Not an apartment, a house, out of town. I mean, you may laugh, but I'd like to have a dog. I never had a dog."

"I'm not laughing." Rob's eyes stung and he blinked the tears away as he turned toward Sean and embraced him with both arms. "I had a little blue heeler when I was a kid."

Sean kissed around his mouth. "What's a blue heeler?"

"Australian cattle dog." Rob's tongue flicked Sean's lips. "A horse property, maybe? It'd cost a packet."

"Not these days, when farmers in this country and the States are walking off the land, broke," Sean scoffed. "You can pick up an old farm for a song, so long as you don't mind fixing it up. We could get a couple of horses too."

"Ambitious," Rob warned.

"Give me one good reason why not?" Sean hugged him.

The wind lashed against the window glass, and Rob clearly heard the sound of water lapping against the walls outside. Chandler's men were out there somewhere, and by now it was imperative that they find the fugitives. They could not afford to leave Sean and Rob alive and loose. Geoffrey Lewis would never dare return to Australian territorial waters, and for the loss of this easy route in and out of his marketplace he would probably skin Chandler alive.

Weariness tugged at Rob's body as well as his mind. He held Sean, breathed the earthy scents of his damp body, felt the rasp of his evening stubble. They had been running the entire day, and they were both hurt. *Let it end soon,* Rob thought tiredly, though if it was a prayer, and to whom or what he prayed, he had no idea. God or gods — was anyone listening at all? But with or without divine interest, it must end soon. They were almost out of rope.

For long, silent minutes they clung together, resting and listening, and at last it was Sean's sharp ears that picked up the sounds of intrusion. He tensed, and Rob lifted his head as his tired body jerked awake.

"What is it?" He blinked at Sean as the candles flickered.

"Someone outside." Sean leaned over and quickly snuffed out the candles. In the sudden darkness, he grasped Rob's arm. "You'll be fine, Robbie. Got the gun? You don't have to hit anything. They can only come up those stairs, and it's a narrow staircase, like a bottleneck. It's a cop's worst nightmare. The noise of gunshots alone ought to send them running like a bunch of jackrabbits."

"You sound sure," Rob said quietly as a pulse began to hammer in his temples and throat.

"I am sure," Sean said firmly.

He moved to the bedroom door, which was right at the top of the stairs and cracked it open. He pressed against the wall, just out of sight of the stairway, and in the dense darkness, Rob heard the gun cock.

Ten

IT WAS a long time since Sean had felt the weight of a pistol. He shifted the old Smith & Wesson into his right hand and winced quietly. The fingers were like sausages, and if he tried to use it the recoil would pluck the weapon out of his grasp. He would never hold it on target. He shifted the gun into his left, and muttered the kind of language for which his father had leathered him when he was a child.

He could control the gun with his left hand, but his aim would be a matter of sheer luck. He looked over his shoulder and saw Rob as a half-shadow in the corner of the room. A wisp of light fell through the window, just enough to make him out. A thousand things flittered through his mind, words he should have said to Rob. Things they should have done.

And then, at the bottom of the stairs the door creaked inward, water slopped and lapped, and Rob was suddenly right beside him.

"They're here," Sean murmured. "They only had to check a dozen houses to find us." He pressed Rob against the wall, beside the closet they had ransacked. From there, he had a view down the stairs and could see the shapes silhouetted dimly against the open door.

Two men were in the hallway, and they performed the search strictly by the book. They would search the ground floor first, the living room and kitchen, the back of the house, the exit into the yard. Sean listened as they investigated the door there, but it was still locked from the inside.

Satisfied, the two men returned to the stairs. A third form lumbered through the front door, hunched and holding his chest. Sean grunted. It could only be either Prescott or Hodges, back on his feet, tenacious as a bulldog. Buckshot had its limitations.

The flood water swirled darkly. The men moving down below created ripples, like a tidal pattern, which caught a glimmer of light from outside. Perhaps the clouds had cleared as the storm passed on, and the moon was up. A stair creaked as the intruders began to climb, and Sean held his breath.

One of the two able-bodied men was on his way up. The strength of this ambush, as Sean had told Rob, was in the darkness, the narrowness of the stair well and the element of surprise. Even a novice could hardly miss. The only question was, when to fire for best effect.

He held the gun in his left hand, supported by the heel of his right palm, laid flat against the wall, unmoving. He waited until the man was two-thirds of the way up, out of the water, then he peeled himself off the wall, leaned out through the door and squeezed the trigger twice.

His reward was a hoarse scream, the thuds of a large body tumbling back and down, and a resounding splash as a weight hit the water at the bottom of the stairs. A moment later voices began to yell. Now, the need for stealth had gone.

A voice bawled in what could have been Afrikaans — Winkler? Another voice was so thick with Aussie 'strine' that it might have been any language but English. Sean did not get a word of what was said.

He slammed the bedroom door, and he and Rob seemed to be thinking with one mind. They dragged the dressing table across to block it, hold the door shut. But now they had locked themselves in, and Rob paced like a trapped animal.

Sean's first thought was to open the window and look for a way up or down. The glass slid sideways, and he wrenched out the screen of insect netting. It fell into the murk below and he leaned out, but saw no drainpipe within reach, no handy shed roof. The eaves were too far overhead and the brickwork was wet and greasy. Wind and drizzling rain spun about the house, and Sean closed the window again.

"We're not going to get out that way," he said bleakly.

"We could jump," Rob said doubtfully.

"It's a long drop," Sean argued, "and you don't know what's right beneath the surface. You could break a leg."

"I know." Rob hugged himself. "Oh, Christ, Sean."

"Hey." Sean's left arm snaked about his waist. "We've got plenty of ammunition. They're still going to have to come up those stairs and through that door. The deck's stacked in our favour. Come daylight, people are going to start showing up here, to see what's become of their houses."

"Daylight?" Rob looked at his watch. The face illuminated for a moment in the darkness. "Sean, it won't get light for ten, maybe eleven hours. Dawn will be late and dim, in this weather. We can't hold them off till then."

"Then think of something," Sean hissed. "Come on, Rob, where's that sharp mind of yours, that loves to do crosswords and guesses the end to every mystery by the time the movie's half over?"

"Okay — calm down. Think." Rob began to pace again, between the window and the bed. "They have to come up those stairs, but now they know we have at least one gun, so they'll be cautious. We can hurt them, we just proved it. We just can't get out of here." He paused and turned back to Sean. "Why the fuck would we want to get out? We're tired, it's dry here, and we have a place to defend. High ground. They're hip-deep in water, freezing their balls off, it's raining, and they're looking at a narrow flight of stairs with one gun, maybe two, at the top. Would you take that on?"

"No way, it's a death trap," Sean agreed. "They're in a mess, and they know it. So they'll call Lewis, on the *Minuette*. He had a meeting, so they said on the radio, eastwards of here. He might have snuck out, of course, and be about a hundred miles away by now. International waters."

"Maybe, but don't count on it. The success or failure of a million dollar business is riding on this — on us." Rob sat on the end of the bed and hugged himself. "Any way you look at it, it'll take Chandler's merry men some time to work out their next move."

Sean sat beside him and slung his left arm around Rob. "You reckon that water is still rising?"

"Must be. The creeks carry runoff from the hills. The water'll rise until it stops raining twenty miles inland." He rested his head against Sean's. "How's your hand?"

"Throbbing. Not too bad," Sean lied. He flexed it, and gave thanks for the darkness. Rob did not see him wince. "How are your balls?" he asked to cover the moment's discomfort.

"Throbbing," Rob said drily, "not too bad. What about climbing out of that window? There's enough sheets stored in the closet to twist together into a rope."

"I don't think I can make it, one-handed," Sean whispered.

"No," Rob agreed, "but I could. I'd climb down, go around the blind side of the house and give them one hell of a surprise. There's only one able-bodied man down there —"

"That we know of!"

"Right. But it'd still give them the very devil of a shock," Rob said stubbornly."

"You going to shoot 'em?" Sean demanded, both impressed and appalled by Rob's audacity, the courage — or was it desperation? — it took to make the suggestion.

"There's such a thing as beginner's luck," Rob said tartly. "I've got seven shots, and I've got the element of surprise. I couldn't miss with every one of them. I'm guessing there's two moving targets out there, and one of my them is lumbering around, already wounded." He paused. "You tell me what other choice we've got!"

Sean hated every syllable of it. He hated anything that sent Rob into danger, and yet he knew Rob was right. "You sure you're up to it?"

"Physically," Rob said bitterly. "Mentally, I'm tired, I'm stressed out, and I'm desperate. Look, Sean, I'm not going to kill anybody, if that's what's worrying you." He gestured with the gun. "I've never used a hand gun in my life. I'll be satisfied if I manage to even scratch the mongrels, hurt them enough to stop them running after us!" Deliberately, carefully, he put on the safety and slid the weapon into his pocket. "In my history classes, they used to call these siege tactics. You keep people cooped up long enough, and in the end they go cuckoo and defeat themselves."

He was right. Sean knew he was right, and still he hated it. "Okay. But you be careful. Stay out of sight. Don't even try a shot till you can see both your targets. Give me your magazine, I'll fill it up out of mine. When you can see both of them, you'll have the advantage for a whole second, maybe two. Like you said, they'll be pretty shocked. Aim for the broadest part of the body, give yourself a chance of connecting. Take the able-bodied man first — it's probably the South African — because he's the one who can move fastest. The other one'll be slow. Pull the trigger gently and steadily, understand? Three rounds a second, gentle pressure. As you fire, keep correcting your aim till you hit something. You hear a yell, then you go on to the other one at once and do the same again, don't hesitate. Got it?"

As he spoke, he had filled the magazine and returned it to Rob's weapon. Rob took it from him and slid it to his pocket. "I think so." He made some unidentifiable sound. "Thank Christ one of us knows what he's doing."

"You scared?" Sean took him by the shoulders.

"Terrified," Rob affirmed, but he lifted his chin. "And I'm going to do it anyway."

He struck three matches and lit the candles, which generated just enough light to work by. The tiny, curved-bladed scissors were frustrating, but it was easy to rip the fabric of sheets length-ways, as soon as a seam gave. The strips were six inches wide for adequate strength, and when three were twisted together the rope they made was good enough.

It took a quarter hour to get sufficient length for Rob to tie onto the leg of the heavy divan bed and have enough left to come within a few feet of the ground, so that he did not have far to fall.

"Remember," Sean warned, "the water's got to be four feet deep by now. You won't move fast through it."

"And they'll be just as slow," Rob added as he peered at his watch. "I make it half past ten. Jesus, time flies when you're having fun."

They had been here amply long enough for Winkler to get a message through to his bosses. The margin for error they were working with was by now perilously slender. Sean caught Rob's cold face between his hands and kissed him.

"What, for luck?" Rob murmured.

"You watch yourself," Sean said thickly, hardly trusting his voice.

"Count on it." Rob touched the side of Sean's jaw, which was bruised and tender. "You think we've come this far only to lose the lot? Providence doesn't work that way, old son."

Sean wished he believed that sentiment. He opened the window and looked out. "There's no one around. Give me the rope."

The bulky length of rags and scraps filled Rob's arms as he brought it to the window, but it snaked smoothly down toward the water, so far below. Sean frowned at it, and did not envy Rob the climb.

For the moment the rain had stopped. The clouds were racing and a half moon showed for a second, ringed around by a chestnut coloured halo, before it was gone again. Rob lifted himself onto the window sill, bent his knees into his chest to feed his legs out, and grasped the rope tightly. He looked up into Sean's face as he swung out and began to lower himself.

"Give me three minutes, then make some noise. Shove that dressing table around, shout. Just don't let them start taking potshots at you!"

"I won't. Three minutes." Sean steadied the rope as Rob climbed down. His figure became dim as he approached the water. He clawed the gun out of his pocket, held it up to keep it dry, and Sean heard his quiet gasp as he deliberately immersed himself in the cold. Then Rob plunged determinedly through the waist-deep water, toward the corner of the house.

Three minutes, he had said. Sean marked the time, and mentally formulated an image of where Rob must be. Christ, he thought, this was courage. Rob was not a soldier, he had received no formal training from the police or rescue services, he had no experience with firearms. But he was out there, in pitch blackness and four feet of icy water, with a gun in his hand, though he had no real idea of how to use it.

Dread squeezed Sean's insides and he pressed against the wall by the door. Strange, how time dragged like a bad movie. Down below the stairs, he heard two voices. One was groaning in pain, the other rasped in undertone conversation. The men were in poor shape. Maybe Rob was right, and this was not as hazardous as it looked.

One minute.

And then a new sound entered Sean's audio picture of the world, and his skin crawled. It was an approaching engine, and could only be a boat. Sean hurried to the window, leaned out and called Rob's name, but Rob was gone, out of earshot.

Surely he must be able to hear that sound. He might even be able to see the boat. Sean's teeth worried painfully at his lip and he held his bandaged hand against his chest.

Still, the rain did not begin again, and the wind had begun to die down for the first time in twelve hours. Sean listened intently at the door.

"John! Here, John!" It was Winkler's voice, with those clipped South African vowels, there was no mistaking it.

Another voice answered, almost certainly Chandler's, but the words were muffled by distance and engine noise. So Chandler was back on his feet, probably nursing a king-sized headache. He would be nursing a fine fury, too, since he had been dragged out through a night like this, to do a lousy joy, when he could be on the ship, warm and dry.

But what could Chandler do, here? There was no way up those stairs until Sean was out of ammunition. His skin prickled with foreboding and he returned to the window. He called Rob's name, louder now, and still there was no sign of him. He must be at the front of the house, out of sight. And the equation had changed. Chandler's arrival altered everything.

Was he alone in that boat, or did he have help? Almost as the thought rushed through Sean's mind he heard another voice, male and strong, and he groaned. These men were determined, and every instant lengthened the odds on the fugitives making it away.

Get out, Robbie, get out and run! Sean thought feverishly. *Just vanish, keep going, don't stop till you're five miles from here!* At least one of them would make it. In that moment, all Sean cared about was Rob's life and safety, which seemed so much more precious than his own.

When he saw no sign of Rob, he pulled the rope back up and closed the window. That would prevent Rob from conceiving any foolish notions of returning to captivity. For the moment he was free, and out there he had a chance. In here? Sean looked bitterly at the room, which had assumed the characteristics of a trap. What chance, indeed!

At the bottom of the stairs, the deep, angry voice snapped an order and the wounded man groaned. Sean guessed that he was being moved, probably lifted, carried to the boat. Standing beside the cracked-open door, he took a grip on the pistol. He had left himself three rounds. Every one of them would have to count.

Very carefully, he heaved until the dressing table slid away from the door, which afforded him a clear shot. Memories crowded his mind: a summer's evening in upstate Michigan, in a back yard, where his mother taught him how to handle a gun... a crisp winter's afternoon in New Jersey, when he was so sure he would have to use it that his palms were sweating inside his thick woollen gloves...

A shape moved, shadow-like, below him. Steel-blue light silhouetted it from behind. Sean took aim, squeezed the trigger, but his reward was cursing, not screams. In the background Chandler barked urgently, water splashed as men scrambled this way and that. Sean forced a breath to the bottom of his lungs.

Two shots remained in the magazine. Another shadow taunted him but this time he dared not waste a round. He must wait until he saw a figure on the stairs above the water level, too close for him to miss. But the shadow came no closer, and instead Sean heard a sound that at first he could not place, though it was peculiarly familiar.

Something metallic hit the wall, bounced to the floor, rolled like —

A grenade? Sean had only ever heard that odd metallic sound

on the soundtrack of films, but animal instinct sent him diving away across the bedroom. He flung himself down behind the bed, and with his good hand dragged the mattress off it, on top of himself.

Seconds slithered by like snakes, and the only sound in his ears was the thunder of his own heart. Sean had just begun to chide himself for the total, paranoid stupidity that had left that door undefended, when every sense he owned overloaded.

The intolerable noise and stunning shock wave knocked the breath out of him, and consciousness dimmed. Colours swirled, sounds echoed, as if he could half-hear someone singing, close by. He floated in the dazed stupor, trying to pick out the tune and wondering where he was. He knew something was wrong, but could not remember what — he knew only that it was urgent. He had no time to lie here and rest. He must get up and do something vital. He wondered if he was in bed, waiting for the alarm.

He shifted uncomfortably and gave a start as he discovered that his legs were wet. If he was in bed, he had a problem, and he jerked awake. It was dark, but no, that was the floor under him — and reality punched into him like a blow.

His skull throbbed. The tune in his head resolved into the off-key warbling of aching, abused ears. He remembered the grenade then, diving and pulling the mattress onto himself. He sucked in a breath and at once coughed on the plaster dust that filled the air. The weight on top of him was suffocating, as if a wall had toppled and buried him alive.

Footsteps crunched toward him and voices called out. Sean tried to move and found himself trapped more securely than if he had been manacled. He could do nothing but wait. With his fingertips, the only extremities he could move, he felt around for the gun, but it was gone. He had dropped it when he grabbed for the mattress, and it could have fallen anywhere.

But Rob's out and gone, he thought feverishly. His heart beat harder and his tongue flicked dust-dry lips. Rob could be two hundred yards away by now, lost in the darkness and still running. Safe.

Unless the little fool was still watching this house. Sean groaned.

Rubble tumbled away and the weight pinning him down steadily diminished. All at once the mattress was lifted up and off, and a brilliant flashlight beam shone full in his face. His irises shrivelled, he could see nothing beyond the light, but he knew Winkler's voice at once...

"Ah, you're alive. You're the American. Brodie, is it?"

"Yeah." Sean coughed. His throat and lungs seemed full of powdered cement.

The light angled this way and that, into the corners of the room. "Where is your friend?" Winkler asked sharply.

Sean sealed his lips.

The light probed into his face once more. "I said, where is he?" Winkler repeated, raising his voice.

"Fuck yourself," Sean told him succinctly.

"Ah." Winkler stepped back, and a moment later saw the makeshift rope, which Sean had dropped by the window. "So your friend climbed out. You did not go with him?"

Sean displayed his bandaged hand, which was answer enough.

"You were unable to climb." Winkler's blond head nodded. "All right. John! Tony!" He stepped over the mound of rubble as two half-seen shapes moved into the room. The light fell back into Sean's face. "They're going to take you down. If you give them a fight, they will kill you."

The warning was elementary, a bald, matter-of-fact statement. It pierced Sean to the bone. He struggled to sit up, and while Chandler stood back, observing with a face like thunder, Sean allowed the man called Tony to hoist him to his feet.

He felt out his muscles as he stood, and was relieved to discover himself more or less intact. He was not badly bruised, but he was dizzy again. He had taken no harm in the fall, but the shock wave from the explosion was like having his ears boxed. His brains were rattled, and he could not expect to regain his full coordination for an hour or two.

Worse than the physical aches and transitory mental confusion was the deep, grinding sense of dread. Sean had never felt anything like it before, but he recognised what it was. It was dawning hopelessness.

As he picked himself up and let the half-seen man called Tony handle him like a rag doll, he felt the first tendrils of pessimism weaving through his mind and body. A voice whispered to him that there was no way out of this nightmare, he was dead, or bound for a laboratory so far away from any legitimate authority that no one would ever know what had become of him. How many 'missing persons' took this route to oblivion?

The cold was startling as he was propelled down the stairs and into the flood. The shock jerked him back to a disoriented, premature awareness, and Sean was breathless as the chill hit his groin.

More shocking was to return to his senses and remember the defeatist thoughts he had been entertaining just moments before. He could not afford pessimism. Time for that when he felt the wall against his back, and he really was out of options.

As he waded down into the water he thought of his mother. She had fought to survive every day of her life. Should have kept in touch with her. Should have stayed closer, been family. Sean shook himself hard, trying to keep a grasp on the present as the icewater made him pant. He glimpsed his father's face through the gloom of memory, and for the thousandth time wondered what had gone wrong. Frank Brodie had been a good guy in the early days. It was not until Sean was eight or ten years old that he began to smell whisky on his father's breath, and the leatherings began. The black eyes that marred his mother's pretty face. One night leaped out of Sean's memory, his parents' last fight, before Frank took every penny in the house, and the keys to the pickup, and walked out. They never saw him again, never knew what became of him.

"Stand up!" Chandler bellowed directly into Sean's ear, so close that Sean could feel the warmth of his breath.

He gasped, horrified to discover that his mind was slipping again, and he had begun to slither down into the water. Concussion? He pulled himself up, stood between Chandler and the thickset young man called Tony and forced himself to alertness.

The waters were waist high, and the current was strong, plucking at his legs. Chandler, Winkler and the others were braced against the swirl, and Sean discovered three guns aimed on him. An outboard runabout, what Rob called a 'tinny' because the whole hull was metal, aluminium, bobbed three or four yards away, where it was tied up to what must be a gatepost.

Two men lay in it, groaning and cursing. One was the survivor of the brief struggle on the slope below the shed; the other was the man who had tried to make it up the stairs. Sean could not tell which was which.

At last, the wind had begun to die down and the clouds overhead parted. Squinting upward, he saw a few stars and the white half-disk face of the moon. Thunder still grumbled, as it had since soon after dawn, but it was a long way off now. The storm would be venting its fury over the Coorong, and by the time it reached Melbourne it would be spent.

The flashlight probed into the murk around the house. Chandler was hunting for any sign of Rob. Sean clenched his teeth and prayed that Rob was at least a mile away by now, and still moving. Chandler saw nothing, and turned angrily toward Winkler. His face was a taut, bleak mask.

"That little asshole could be halfway to town."

"Or not," Winkler mused. "You said we've caught ourselves a couple of gay boys?"

"I saw them fucking." Chandler angled the light into Sean's face. "This one was on top."

"Then, there is such a thing," Winkler said slowly, "as loyalty between lovers. That little bastard might be somewhere very close. You know we only picked up one gun in the room. That leaves one Smith & Wesson automatic missing, and at least a dozen rounds. Now, what's that sound like to you?"

For several seconds Chandler considered this, and then without warning he took Sean by the collar, kicked one of his feet out from under him and shoved him under.

Sean barely had time to drag in a breath, and he struggled fiercely. Other hands joined Chandler's, and held him under until his lungs began to spasm. He had lost track of time when they released him. He came up wheezing.

Air was his first priority, but Chandler was already shouting, and Sean forced open his eyes, willed himself to listen. An automatic rifle, a Kalashnikov, was still aimed on him.

"Robbie boy, are you watching this?" Chandler bawled into the night. "I think you are. He's half drowned. Next time, who can tell?" He paused and panned the flashlight this way and that. "I swear, I'll drown him unless I see you in the next twenty seconds, Rob. Let me see you, hold that gun up over your head, or he's dead. You hear me?" For a count of five he waited, and then gave a nod to Winkler and Tony, who held Sean between them.

This time Sean was forewarned, and took a deep breath. He was completely passive as he went under. He had two choices: struggle, or not. If he struggled, he would exhaust his oxygen and his strength, but if he hung limply in their grasp he would buy himself time, and the men holding him would never be sure if he was conscious or not.

Totally still, he let the water close over his head, shut his eyes, listened to his heart and waited. Rob was a mile away at least, he told himself. Halfway to town, where he would find a police officer, give him the whole story, and then maybe the coast guard would stop the *Lan Tao* —

Dizziness swamped him, his chest was burning, and when they let him up the world spun around him. He wheezed for breath, but he could still make out Chandler's voice, and forced himself to make sense of the words.

"Smart boy, Robbie," Chandler was saying. "Give the gun to me and put your hands on your head. Now, get in that boat. Tony, put the American in the boat, and don't take your eyes off them. These two are more trouble than they're worth."

"You should have killed them," Winkler said acidly.

"Maybe I should have," Chandler agreed. "And maybe I will."

"You play too many games," Winkler added accusingly. "You do this too often, John. One day, one day soon, Lewis is going to feed you balls-first to a pack of hungry fish."

When Sean's vision had returned to normal he blinked at the bobbing, pitching boat. Iron hands lifted him into it, and as he began to see properly he focused on Rob's face. His belly felt as if it contained a great weight of bricks, and he shook his head over Rob as Tony and Winkler climbed into the small craft beside them. Two guns remained levelled.

"You idiot," he whispered to Rob as they were shoved together in the middle of the boat, in the puddle of salt water.

Rob did not answer, but turned his head away as the outboard was zipped and began to snarl. Chandler untied the tiny craft, hoisted himself over the side, and Winkler leaned on the tiller. The boat turned about in its own length and Chandler headed it for the creek which emptied into the sea not a hundred yards away.

The tide was running out fast now. The surf was high and the way back to the sea was a nauseating ride, like being mounted on a wild horse determined to break every vertebra in Sean's spine. He was jostled against Rob, and Rob took a grip on him, bracing him until they were out across the tidal waters.

The boat steadied, and Sean looked out to sea. At once he saw the yellow lights of the freighter. The skipper had brought her about, perhaps to make it easier to handle her in changing wind and tidal conditions. The ship was much closer inshore than it had been, and he could hear the deep, rhythmic thud-thud of her old diesel engines.

The runabout was making good speed, with the current. It was only minutes before they were alongside, and Sean could pick out the name on the bow. The *Lan Tao* was probably registered in Cambodia or Laos, and more than likely laden with the kind of cargo which would make a customs officer's nostrils flare, like a hound scenting the fox.

Shapes moved up on the deck as the runabout came in at the waterline. The *Lan Tao* was very old. The break-bulk cargo hauler was a pup by comparison to modern freighters. She would have been launched years before Sean was born, and was showing her mileage. Where the sea had stripped her paint, cascades of rust ran down her sides.

A cable snaked down, swiftly followed by another, and Sean watched as their guards scrabbled to hook on. A derrick had swung out, high overhead. A winch began to growl and squeal, and of a sudden the sea fell away beneath them. The feeling of weightlessness was nauseating, and the roll of the ship made the boat swing like a pendulum. Sean swallowed hard, clenched his teeth and looked up, not down.

The crane swung them in and slammed the boat down into its cradle. As it was secured, the muzzle of a gun protruded into Sean's face. On trembling legs, he clambered out just as a light patter of rain began to fall. His eyes were on Rob, who looked as skittish as an unbroken thoroughbred colt. Sean pulled his shoulders back and turned toward Winkler as the man began to speak.

"Move it!" he was shouting, not at the regular merchant navy crewmen who stood well back, reluctant spectators, but at a squad of Lewis's people. The crew were in denim, wool, oil skins and rubber boots. Lewis's people wore designer clothes, trendy city garb, and most were armed. "Have you got Lewis by radio?" Chandler shouted at one older man. "Where the hell is he?"

The man leaned out of an open doorway in the forecastle which towered, a mountain of rusted steel, thirty or forty feet above Sean's head. White light spilled out of the doorway around the big, burly man; he held a Colt assault rifle easily between his hands.

"Lew headed east, he had a meeting. The *Minuette* will rendezvous with us in the morning to take you and your shipment off. Your merchandise is safe, stop worrying. We stacked it in the chart room, told the regular crew to keep their noses out or get bloody. They're mostly a bunch of kids, running scared. What about your prisoners?"

"What indeed?" Chandler agreed. "Where's this bucket headed, Duggan?"

"Christchurch, Auckland and New Caledonia, then on to Port Moresby, no stops."

"Drugs for New Zealand, and guns for a couple of rebel factions," Sean whispered, for Rob's ears.

Chandler studied them with a deep frown. "Get these bastards inside. Stash them somewhere safe — and I mean safe. Don't underestimate them. They're trouble. Hold them while I talk to Lewis. If he wants them drowned, I'd be delighted to oblige, right now. The tide's running out, there'll be no better time than this." He waved for a couple of crewmen to assist. "Somebody get me some dry clothes, and a drink."

Roughly hustled along, Sean and Rob moved in through the open door, and stumbled up the ringing steel stepway which climbed to the bridge, high above the deck. Sean listened to the thud of his heart as he forced his legs on, in Rob's wake, until the hands which still grasped his upper arms from behind brought him to a halt.

He stood swaying in the sudden light. Up ahead of them, through a wide open door, was the chart room, and just forward of that space, the bridge itself. He saw the steering, navigation and radar gear, chart table, ship's log, and several young men wearing pale, shocked faces. Aft was another stepway, leading on and down into the body of the ship.

To Rob it was an alien environment, but to Sean it was so familiar he could have groaned. Jackson Oil ran a number of older freighters as tenders for the big exploration vessels. They were cheap, in the mid and late 1980s they were readily available, and when they got into trouble it was no tragedy to just cut them loose and let the weather have them.

This ship was a classic 1950s hull, almost identical to the *Rosie Malone*, which had worked the Gulf of California 'grocery run', servicing the *Jackson Pioneer*, for ten out of the twelve months that Sean had worked in that part of the world. This rust bucket should have been cut up for scrap years ago. No sane underwriter would touch it.

Two robust young men held him and Rob by the shoulders, and as Sean's head began to clear, his ears pricked up. The bridge and chart room had been customised and refitted, not once but several times, that Sean could see. The radio station was in back of the bridge, fitted into the port side lookout wing. Through the open door Sean could hear Chandler using the shortwave.

"*Lan Tao* to *Minuette*, come in."

A burst of static answered, and then a voice Sean knew all too well. So cultured, so British Public School: "*Minuette*. Is that you,

John? You're bloody late! Over."

"I've got a good enough reason," Chandler snapped. "You wanted two prodigals returned to the fold? You got 'em. Only question is, what do you want done with 'em."

A long pause delayed Geoffrey Lewis's response, and then he said clearly, "They're in working order?"

"Alive and kicking," Chandler reported. "Couple of good looking gay boys, worth an attractive fee to that dope lab. Moresby or Bangkok, take your pick."

"Maybe," Lewis allowed cautiously. "Any problems?"

"About a thousand," Chandler said drily. "We've got three men hurt. Nothing too serious — nothing I couldn't handle." He seemed to preen. "If we'd had a nice day for it, it would have been all kinds of fun, but you know I can't stand the shitty weather, this end of the country, this time of year. The shipment is aboard and safe. The regular crew is running scared. What do you want me to tell them? These dick-heads don't seem to have seen a gun at close proximity before."

"Tell them... the cargo is so valuable, and so confidential, it must be guarded," Lewis said drily. "Classified, company business, none of their concern. If they open their mouths about it after it's offloaded, it's their jobs. Keep silent, and there's a nice bonus in their next pay packet."

"Appeal to basic human avarice — that'll hold them," Chandler agreed. "Where do you want us, Lew?"

Lewis responded at once. "We'll meet you in the morning. You have our position? Over."

"That, I leave to the skipper," Chandler said sourly. "Over-and-out." He shut down the shortwave and appeared in the doorway. He had stripped to the waist, displaying smooth, pale skin and an enviable physique. He was drinking whisky or brandy, and the alcohol brought a rosy flush to his cheeks. His brows arched at Sean and Rob. "You get a reprieve."

"Next stop, Port Moresby, lab rats, property of a drug lord? You call that a reprieve?" Rob demanded.

"The choice is between that and being fish bait, tonight," Chandler told him pleasantly.

Rob's lip curled. Sean had taken a breath to tell him to hold his tongue, but Rob was too fast. "Since we're dead either way, we don't have to listen to your crap. Go fuck yourself, shit-head."

Chandler's flat palm smacked across Rob's cheek, leaving the livid tattoo of his fingers.

"Rob, for chrissakes," Sean hissed.

"Yes, Rob, for chrissakes," Chandler mimicked, with uncanny knack and a creditable accent.

"What's it matter?" Rob licked a fleck of blood from his lip.

"I'll tell you what it matters," Chandler told him blandly. "You're outbound as live cargo. You can either get to Moresby intact, or you can get there with your arms and legs in plaster. Makes no difference to me or anyone else on this ship. Now, do as he says, Rob, and shut your mouth."

"Live cargo?" Sean echoed. "You carry prisoners often?"

"Not as often as you might think. Only when there's someone we want to get rid of, without leaving a body behind us like a signpost. Waste not, want not, Sean, old buddy. That's our motto. To us, you're raw materials. Dead, you'll vector the police in on us. Alive, you'll fetch a few dollars... and knowing where you are will gratify me no end." He cocked his head at Sean. "You'll cooperate, that I promise you."

Sean's blood had cooled by degrees. "Like he said," he whispered, "screw yourself."

"Oh, no." Chandler's handsome head shook. "You'll cooperate." He glanced at Rob. "Or Lewis's boys can have him, while you watch. And then you'll cooperate. Education can be painful."

Sean closed his eyes. A pulse beat hard in his temples and he was vaguely aware as Rob caught him by the arm. Chandler was still talking, but he could not follow the words, and was only half aware as he was hustled down a narrow, ringing stepway.

Out of the wind and rain, it was at least warmer. Some corner of Sean's mind that was still working told him they were well aft of amidships when they were tugged to a halt. Keys jingled, a door opened, and they were propelled inside into dense, uterine darkness. The door slammed and the keys rattled in the lock. Footsteps retreated and were gone.

"Light switch," Sean said hoarsely. "There'll be one by the door somewhere. Ships are dark, cramped little places, there has to be a light."

"I can't find..." Rob stumbled against the wall, and then Sean heard him grunt. "Got it."

The switch was at head height, by the door. Rob flicked it and Sean's protesting eyes saw a store room. Most of the *Lan Tao*'s linen and canned food appeared to be kept here. Sheets and towels, caterer's sizes of cans were stacked on every available inch of shelf space.

At once, Sean grabbed a handful of towels and threw them at Rob. "The least we can do is get dry."

But Rob had sagged down onto a crate, back from the door, and took his head in his hands. "What's the point, Sean, what's the point?"

Sean dropped the towels and knelt beside him. His good hand grasped Rob's chin, made him look up. "Do you want to get out of this mess, or do you want to just quit and let these bastards have it their own way?"

Rob blinked owlishly at him. "What can we do?"

"There's plenty we can do," Sean said emphatically. "But I can't do it alone. And it's going to take some time, so we ought to get dry." He pulled Rob's head down and rested cheek to cheek with him for a long moment. "Help me. Please."

When they moved apart, Rob's eyes were bright with tears. His movements were slow, as if he were wading through molasses. He was pale and smudged, but he stripped Sean to the skin and efficiently scrubbed him until he was dry and gradually growing warm. With the methodical movements of a machine, Rob wrang out the sodden jeans and jerseys, spread them where they could dry a little, and turned his attention to his own clothes.

"Rob?" Sean was worried. That robot-like animation could mean Rob was weary, or that he was about to surrender to shock. The whole day had been an ordeal and a man could not go on forever without paying the price. "Rob!"

As Rob dropped his sodden clothes, Sean caught him by the arms. "I'm all right," he said quietly.

"You're not." Sean reached for a towel and began to scrub him, one handed and clumsy. "You're shocky. Why didn't you get out and run, when you had the chance?"

"And leave you?" Rob stood like a statue, not lifting a finger to help as Sean rubbed him. "You think I'd leave you?"

Sean sighed heavily. "No, I don't suppose I do, at that. You're a fool. And... I'm glad you're with me." He looked around at the store room that had become their prison. "If you weren't, I'd be here alone, and if I tell you the truth, what has to be done, I don't think I can do alone."

"I don't even know what you're talking about," Rob said philosophically. "But..." He lifted his head, blinked repeatedly and took a deep breath. "You've worked on ships like this, haven't you?"

"Several of them. And that, Robbie, is the ace up my sleeve." Sean turned him and rubbed his back and buttocks with short, sharp strokes of the towel that brought Rob's skin up in swathes of scarlet.

For some time Rob was silent, but Sean could almost hear his mind beginning to tick over again. "What sort of speed do these rust buckets make?" he asked at last.

"In good condition, maybe eight or ten knots." Sean knelt and commenced work on Rob's legs. "This ship is not in good condition. Listen to that engine! I can hear it knocking from here! That's a diesel about to take its last gasp. That engine's as old as God. Mind you, these horrible old tubs can go forever, sounding like that. She might have a hundred thousand miles left in her."

"Here, let me do that." Rob took the towel out of his hand and lifted Sean to his feet. "I'll have a look at your hand in a minute." His arms went about the larger, broader body and they clung tight together. "Oh Christ, Sean."

"I know." Sean gripped him until he was sure Rob must protest. "But I can stop this ship, Robbie. I swear it. If we can get through that door, get loose, I can stop this ship dead in its tracks. I know just where to hit it, to hurt it so bad, the engineer'll need two, maybe three hours to get the diesels going again."

Rob licked his lips, digesting what Sean had said, and then his eyes became hollow, his expression bleak. Sean held his face between his palms. "What is it?"

"Those men, Bernie and Jim," Rob said hoarsely.

"I know. It stinks," Sean whispered. He rested his forehead against Rob's and felt him begin to shake. "Come on, Robbie, get a hold of yourself. Not now. Save this till we have the chance to fall apart in peace."

"Fall apart?" Rob cleared his throat and rubbed his eyes. "You don't fall apart. You never do."

"I've been known to, in private," Sean said softly. "I just don't do it in front of a live audience. But not now, not here. Are you dry enough?"

"I think so." Rob seemed to physically take a hold on himself and stood up straight. "Sit down, let me look at your hand... and tell me what you can do to this ship. You're talking heavy duty sabotage, aren't you?"

With a small sound of relief, Sean parked his bare buttocks on the stack of crates and let Rob take his hand. The makeshift bandage unwound, and they both winced as they saw the mess, for the first time in decent lighting. To distract Rob, Sean said,

"That engine noise you're hearing is two geriatric diesels working in tandem. I need a fire axe, a sledge hammer or a pair of bolt cutters. We'll find any or all of those in the tool chests, in the engine room." He sucked in a breath as Rob examined the wound, although Rob was faultlessly gentle. "I'll cripple the injector pumps. What do you know about diesels?"

"Not a hell of a lot," Rob mused. "But I do know that if an injector pump is shot, no fuel is going to get to the engine, and it'll just ... stop." He looked up into Sean's eyes. "The crew will fix it?"

"Not if I've smashed it almost in halves, or buried a fire axe in it," Sean said darkly. "That, you don't fix. It means they'll have to remove both pumps, bring up a couple of spares from their stores, and replace them."

"How long?" Rob let go Sean's hand and cast about for the makings of a fresh bandage.

"Say, ninety minutes, two hours if we're lucky. Three, if I get the chance to do some extra damage, while I'm in there." Sean watched as Rob ripped a bed sheet into strips. "Trust me."

"I always trust you." Rob returned to him with a tangle of ragged bandage. "Give me your hand."

Sean slid both of them around his waist, drew him closer and buried his face in Rob's chest. His mouth fastened there, on soft, furry skin, and his palms slid downward until they had cupped the soft, smooth mounds of Rob's ass. Rob's arms circled Sean's wide shoulders, and for a long time they did not move, as weariness and anxiety enveloped them.

At last, it was Rob who stirred. "Let me fix your hand. Tell me about these ships."

His voice was steady, and Sean knew he had reached some crisis of fear and passed through it. It was called a man's baptism of fire, his blooding. The first battle was the toughest. He kept still as Rob wound the strips of linen around both hand and wrist and tied them off, halfway up to the elbow.

"There'll be a crew of about sixteen aboard. They'll stand three watches. There'll be two in the engine room, that's an engineer and his mate, who work alternate watches. The engineer will do the actual repair work, but his mate can watch the engines under normal running circumstances. The rest of the crew is involved in maintenance and navigation, and then you've got a sea cook, who might have an assistant. The ship's steered from the bridge, which we saw as we came in. They have a nice chartroom. They'll have updated their navigation and radio gear. I'd guess they'll be using a Decca navigator, and they'll have a powerful shortwave. And that's what we need." He stroked Rob's stubbled face as he finished with the bandage. "They may have a medic aboard, maybe not. One of the crew could be trained in first aid."

Rob's mind was working properly now. "When do they eat, when do they change watches?" he asked, and when Sean touched his mouth, kissed his fingers.

"Well, the merchant marine crew will work to their own routine," Sean mused. "All ships have their own peculiar routines, but people generally yell to be fed every three or four hours. They'll gather to eat in the mess at six, maybe seven in the evening. The watch crew on the bridge will have sandwiches and coffee."

"Right." Rob dumped a pile of linen at Sean's feet and sat there. "You can find your way about on this ship, can't you?"

"Was that a joke?" Sean demanded. "The sharp end's called the bow, the blunt end's called the stern, the flat bit's called the deck — "

"Sean."

"What?" Sean let go the attempt at levity and looked down into Rob's eyes. Even smudged and tired, they were beautiful. In that moment, Sean regretted nothing. Not coming to this country, nor getting himself involved with Rob, which ultimately led him into this predicament.

"We have a chance, don't we?" Rob asked softly.

"A damned good one." Sean rested both hands, one bare, one bandaged, on Rob's shoulders, leaned down and kissed his mouth. "The only question we have to work out is how to get through that door. They forgot to leave us a key."

"Then someone else will have to unlock it." Rob leaned over and pressed his face against Sean's middle. Sean stroked his damp hair, and they listened to the steady tom-tom beat of the engines. "So you'll wreck the injector pumps," Rob muffled against him, "and that'll stop her."

"Dead in the water," Sean promised. "Then we'll get up to the bridge and use the shortwave."

"But what —"

"Hush." Sean pressed him down onto the stack of linen. "First, we get some rest. Then we smooth the creases out of the plan. I

146

didn't say it was perfect. But it's workable."

He hugged his hand against him and looked down with a smile as Rob curled at his feet. For the first time since Chandler had appeared, so far away at that farm house on Lightning Ridge, a little warmth had begun to lick through his bones. Foreigners often overlooked the fact that Australia boasted several fine skiing resorts, and the snow was often at its best in August.

Coffee would have been nice, or a large rum, a toddy, a scalding cup of tea, sweet and strong, the way Rob liked to drink it. Sean had grown accustomed to that, begun to like it. He sighed, and instead he stooped down and had Rob's willing mouth.

Eleven

THE DECK heaved constantly under Rob's feet, and while Sean seemed to completely disregard the perpetual motion, Rob found it disturbing. It was luck alone that he never suffered from motion sickness. For an hour he and Sean dozed, propped against one another and growing warmer as they shared body heat. But being naked in this place made it impossible for Rob to relax properly. If Chandler, or any of the others, blundered in and found him and Sean in this state, the consequences could be very bad. The scene of intimacy they imagined would almost certainly invite cruelty.

Investigating their clothes, Rob found them stiff with salt and still very damp. He spread them on the deck, and while Sean watched without comment, used a thick wad of towels to rub and squeeze the denim and wool until it was dry enough to serve. Sean knew what was on his mind, though he made no comment. Most of Lewis's special crew looked and felt like terminal straights who had no sensual interest in their captives. But Chandler was the unknown quantity, who had declared that he found Rob attractive, though he had not been with a man for some time.

That knowledge was more than enough to make Rob fret, and he dressed quickly in his uncomfortable, sticky clothes. They felt like cardboard as he helped Sean to struggle into his own clothes. Sean never even attempted to use that hand now, and Rob knew that as he began to grow warm, he was feeling the injury keenly.

It was entirely possible that they would to die tonight, and Rob was aware of a thin edge of panic in the back of his mind. It lurked there like a wolf, circling his conscious, rational thoughts, ready to snap at his heels, any moment he let his mind wander.

Some people found it necessary to die in a state of grace. What mattered to Rob was that he and Sean had settled their differences completely, and made their peace. It was well and truly made. When Sean tongued across his mouth, frenched him affectionately, Rob sucked him in and then leaned back and looked into the deep blue eyes he had always loved since that first night. It seemed a thousand years ago now.

"You okay, Sean?"

"Not too bad, all things considered," Sean said self-mockingly. "I've had a car accident, been knocked out, doped, almost blown up and half drowned. All in all, I reckon I'm doing pretty good." He hesitated. "The thing that gets me mad enough to yell is that I put on a great show for Chandler. I fucked you, right in front of that voyeur."

Rob made a face. "Look on the bright side."

"There's a bright side?" Sean sounded dubious.

"At the time," Rob said quietly, "we didn't know he was there. Chandler's crazy enough to have held us under the gun and made you fuck me while he watched."

"I did do it to you!"

"But we didn't know we had an audience." Rob gave an animated shudder. "Made a difference. All we did was make love, and it was beautiful, it always is. Doing it for that creep, like a couple of performing mutts, would have been... bloody damned rough."

"You have a gift for understatement," Sean said sourly. "Okay, honey, you win. I'll quit the guilt trip. But I'll make you a promise. If I get my hands on John Chandler —"

"He'll regret it," Rob finished.

"I was going to phrase that in stronger language." Sean touched the tip of Rob's nose with one fingertip. "At least this closet is warm! What we need now, is inspiration."

"What I need," Rob corrected, "is a drink. Not booze — I mean anything wet. Liquid. I could drink a reservoir dry."

"Liquid." Sean pursed his lips, well aware of the dryness of his own mouth, and began to cast around the store room.

They had been immersed in salt water and flood water that was probably toxic, but the last time they had dared drink was many hours ago. Even in such cold weather, Rob was parched. After an hour's rest and acceptable warmth, his legs had ceased to tremble. He was tired and sore, but he was thinking again, aware of his body, and especially of his hunger and thirst.

Every wall was shelved from deck to ceiling, and the shelves were filled. Canned fruit, canned meat, packets and bags, cereals, powdered milk, sugar. Rob tossed a can of leg ham to Sean. "Can you manage that? There's a key on this side. The buggers won't feed us. But if I can puncture some of these cans of peaches, we've got fruit juice by the gallon here."

Carefully, Sean braced the can in his right elbow and coaxed the key around with his left hand, while Rob examined the squeegee which stood propped in the corner. The push-rods that worked to mop end were metal, but where they were mounted into the plastic parts they were also fairly fragile. He waggled one of them back and forth, over and over, until the mounting fatigued, loosened, and broke. In his hand was a thin steel rod, eight inches long, and jagged-sharp on one end.

A can of spaghetti made a good mallet. He sat beside Sean, held a can of peaches between his feet, and hammered the rod through the aluminium top, two holes at opposite sides. The fruit juice was cool and sweet, slaking the thirst of fear. Sean handed him a chunk of ham and they ate in silence.

Their eyes were on the door, and every five minutes Rob found himself looking at his watch, like a nervous tick. It was after midnight when they finished a second can of ham, several cans of sardines and the juice of six cans of peaches and pears. The high energy food began to metabolise, and with his thirst assuaged, his body warm, Rob felt better. Still, no one approached the door.

"They probably figure, come morning, we'll be easier to intimidate if we're half dead of thirst," Sean said cynically. "You can get very thirsty, very fast, if you're deliberately deprived of water. I saw..." A shadow crossed his face and he looked away.

"What?" Rob stopped his restless pacing and sat beside him. "Someone treated you bad? When?"

"No, not me." Sean rubbed his eyes. "I was in Central America, on Jackson's business. I was with a trouble-shooting crew, just trying to get from one place to another, when the airports were shut down in some civil strife. We drove through a village. It was summer. We were having trouble with one of the trucks and we stopped at this village, most of a whole day, to make running repairs. The government army was camped there. They'd caught a rebel soldier, a real tough kid. You know the kind. Beat him, whip him, he'll spit in your face, rape him, he doesn't care. They hadn't laid a finger on him. They just tied him to a tree and walked away. The heat was intense that year. In six hours in the sun the kid was delirious. In ten, he'd be done for." Sean nudged a discarded can of fruit with his foot. "Just that, makes all the difference."

"So Chandler's due a surprise." Rob twisted the steel spike between his hands. "But it won't help us much if they see the evidence. I'd better get the trash out of sight."

The empty and punctured cans were hidden in the back, behind a stack of cartons. When he returned to Sean, Rob brought a folded bed sheet. Sean frowned, and watched as Rob stood beside the door and tossed it into the air. It fell fast. Anyone coming through would have been shrouded. Effectively blind, definitely startled.

"Not bad," Sean decided. "Add to that a crack on the skull with a seven-pound can of ham, and we're in business."

"But, when?" Rob looked at his watch again. "Where the hell are we by now?"

"Heading east." Sean stood, stretched, tried the hand. "That man, Duggan, told Chandler the ship is bound for New Zealand, the French islands, then on to New Guinea, but they'll rendezvous with Lewis first. The *Minuette*."

"That damned cruiser," Rob whispered. "I wish we'd done what you wanted, this morning."

"It was my idea to go aboard and try to help, when we saw the propane tank in the galley rupture," Sean reminded him.

But Rob shook his head. "Go back about three hours before that. We woke up, we took a look out the window at the weather and you said — I'm quoting — why don't we take breakfast to bed, I'd fuck you the way you like it best, then we'd roll over and go to sleep again, maybe stay in bed all day, since the storm was going to break. Unquote." He looked ruefully at Sean. "I wish to God I'd let you persuade me."

"So do I," Sean confessed. "And it would have been nice. But I'm not about to start apportioning blame, Robbie. Things happen the way they happen. We could have stayed in bed, and the storm might have ripped the roof off, smashed the house to driftwood, and us along with it." He held up a hand to silence Rob's protests. "Hush up. We'll be out of this room by about five in the morning."

Rob's brows rose. "How do you know?"

Sean jerked a thumb at the crates and shelves. "Have you ever seen the galley on one of these ships? There isn't enough room to swing a cat — naval variety. So they don't keep much in there, and every time they need stores, the cook has to get in here. It's his pantry. They'll want breakfast by six or seven, so the cook will have to start at five or half past." He pointed at two specific crates. "I see powdered milk, Wheeties, oats, sugar. When you're cooking for sixteen or eighteen ravenous guys, plus half a dozen of Lewis's special crew as guests aboard, you need a lot of everything. Am I right?"

"You usually are." Rob's eyes felt gritty, and he stifled a yawn. "God, I'm tired."

"Then lie down," Sean told him. "You won't sleep long, your mind won't let you, but an hour's rest will put you back on your feet."

"And you?" Rob asked as he threw down a mound of towels and bed linen and curled up on them. "Give me a kick in an hour, and grab some rest yourself. You need it as much as I do. More, maybe... I don't like the look of that hand."

Until the weight was off his spine, he had not realised how much his body was aching. He peered at his watch and closed his eyes, but every second he was listening for sounds in the passage outside that door.

Several times, rubber-soled shoes squeaked by, and once voices shouted, a long way off, but no one approached. Rob knew Sean was not simply guessing. He knew a lot about the way vessels like this one operated. In his odd, checkerboard career he had met more men like John Chandler than Rob cared to imagine.

Chandler would expect them to feast on the ham and sardines, which were easily opened. But they were high in salt, and after eating them the resulting thirst would be fierce. Deprivation of water was the easiest way to break even the strongest man.

Somehow, Rob dozed, and lost track of time until a bell rang on deck to signal a watch change. Was that two o'clock?

Someone giggled in the corridor, rousing Rob with a start. Voices called out, there was more giggling, and a boyish squeal... it sounded like an older man and a youth. Petting and necking? Foreplay. Rob sat up and blinked at Sean, but Sean's dark head shook.

"None of our business. That's just a couple headed for bed."

"Sounds like there are some gays aboard," Rob murmured.

"On ships, there usually are. A lot of guys pair off, it's a way of staying sane and keeping a healthy libido, even if they're mostly straight. But the life attracts gays, for obvious reasons." Sean gave his shoulder a push. "Doze another half hour. Then let me rest."

It was difficult to settle again, and at two-thirty Rob was on his feet, pacing. "I need to piss." The pressure in his bladder had become impossible to ignore. Now it was a real discomfort.

"Makes two of us." Sean stood and looked for inspiration.

"Squeegee bucket?" Rob suggested. "It's not exactly fine porcelain, but —"

"It's either that, or flood the floor," Sean finished. Against the odds, he actually chuckled. "Go on, get it done while I keep an ear to the door. It'd be stupid to botch the only chance we're going to get to make it out of here, because one of us is pissing when opportunity knocks!"

Relief made Rob groan. The bucket was already half full of old floor mopping water and suds. He zipped up again and turned back to find Sean idly watching him. "Cheeky. Your turn."

"You're in better spirits," Sean observed as he fronted up to the bucket.

Rob divided his attention between the sound of distant voices which barely made it through the door, and the sound of splashing water close at hand. With heavy eyes, he studied Sean's broad back, wide shoulders and long legs. "Grab some sleep," he offered. "You need it."

No protests were forthcoming, and with a sigh Sean sank down onto the mound of linen. "Don't let me sleep longer than an hour. Then... will you look at my hand again?"

"I'll look at it now," Rob corrected.

The bandages unwrapped, and as they came aware he swore. The tattered flesh was black, the gashes were yellow with infection, the fingers were scarlet and puffy as sausages, and the whole hand was oven-hot. Sean did not even open his eyes, as if he did not want to look at it.

"Bad?" he asked quietly.

"Yes." Rob wished he could have lied. "Sean, this needs attention, right now. It's gone beyond stitching. You'll need cortisone or something similar to heal this."

"What's it smell like?" Sean licked his lips, a tiny nervous gesture. "Go on, take a sniff."

He raised the hand, and Rob bent over it, nostrils flared. "If you're asking, can I smell rotten fruit," he guessed, "no, I can't. Not yet. That's not gangrene, it's just a lousy infection. Enormous infection, and it's spreading fast."

"Because I'm warm now, maybe. Spilled septic tanks," Sean said philosophically. "There'd have been one in the garden at that house, where they held me under. God knows what bacteria got into this." He looked up at Rob out of dark, slitted eyes, and his voice was slurred. "Wrap it again. I'll get it seen to in the morning."

"Chandler's people won't care —" Rob began as he picked up a sheet and began to rip furiously at the edge, to make several yards of bandaging.

"It's make or break for us," Sean murmured as he sank down into a weary semi-doze. "We either get off this ship, or... we don't, and it'll all be academic, won't it? The cook will need to be in here. We'll be in the engine room five minutes later. I'll cripple the injector pumps feeding the diesels, and then we need to use the shortwave and find a pace to hide."

"And if it doesn't happen that way?" Rob muttered as he padded the wound and wrapped it. The ends of the makeshift bandage tied off around Sean's forearm.

"Then, I don't think there'll be much more for us to worry about," Sean said gently. "Do you?"

Rob knew what he was saying, and his vision blurred. He stooped, mutely kissed Sean's hot forehead, and hoisted himself up onto the crate where Sean had been sitting. At his feet, Sean curled up and his breathing settled into a steady, even pattern. Only his occasional stirrings betrayed the fact that he was not actually sleeping.

Four o'clock.

Rob had never suffered from claustrophobia in his life before, but the walls were feeling close and the air seemed soupy. Still, he was thoroughly warm, almost completely dry now, and he was surprised to find himself hungry again. That must be a healthy sign. Most condemned men would probably be choked by the traditional hearty breakfast.

He stepped over Sean, helped himself to another can of sardines, then pear juice. As he peeled open the fish, Sean's eyes opened, and Rob managed a smile.

"Food'll wake you up a fortnight after the funeral. Here." He held out the can. "They're Norwegian."

"Time?" Sean yawned.

"A quarter after four. And I'm getting twitchy." Rob took a swig of juice, reached for a packet of cornflakes and crunched deliberately on a handful. He had read somewhere that the system needed carbohydrate in order to properly digest protein.

They were quiet, preoccupied for some time, until a buzzer burred quietly, somewhere deep in the ship. Sean's whole body stiffened. "That could be the sound we've been waiting for."

Rob dropped the cans and packets he had been ransacking, patted his lips and kicked the linen out of the way. "Sean?"

"The cook hauls his ass out of bed well before the crew, to get breakfast. Right?"

"And there's his cornies and sugar," Rob jerked a thumb at various shelves. "Even if they keep the ham and eggs in the meat locker, they're going to be in here soon."

Sean held his hand against his chest. "I'm guessing, that buzzer rouses either the cook or his assistant."

Rob's heart thumped. "How long do we have?"

"Give the guy a few minutes to get his pants on, get a coffee and a wake-up cigarette. Then, he remembers he can't just walk in here, he has to dig a guard out of bed. That won't be so easy. They're not merchant seamen, they're Lewis's pampered pet goons, used to mansions, limousines and yachts, not this kind of grind."

"Ten minutes?" Rob guessed.

"Or fifteen." Sean rubbed his face. "Then, remember, they think we've been without anything to drink for maybe fourteen, fifteen hours... and they'll know we helped ourselves to the ham and sardines."

"So Chandler's men will be complacent," Rob mused.

"Complacent enough to deserve what they have coming," Sean agreed. He selected a large can from the nearest shelf, hefted it to judge the weight, and nodded. "This should do nicely."

Rob had moved to the door, pressed against the wall beside it and was listening intently to the passage outside. An eternity passed, nothing moved, and he had begun to wonder if Sean was wrong, despite his knowledge of this kind of vessel, this kind of merchant marine crew.

But a glance at Sean assured Rob otherwise. Sean was up on the balls of his feet, his eyes fever-bright, alert and waiting, eager for the chance to strike back. As if a clock were tricking away inside him, Rob thought, and he knew to the second what the crew on this ship would be doing.

The wild card was Chandler's men. The actual crew were professional merchant seamen, and ships were the same the world over. Every vessel worked to a basic routine that had evolved over the span of centuries to accommodate the safe running of a ship. Sean's knowledge of this was their most precious advantage, because Chandler could not possibly know that Sean had the experience.

It was impossible to calculate how many miles the old freighter had made. Every hour the *Lan Tao* chugged east took her further from the populous area of the state. The city of Adelaide sprawled north and south along the Gulf Saint Vincent, but this was a very

155

large state with a very small population, thinly spread. Soon, the ship would be beyond Encounter Bay and off the Coorong, which was a wilderness area, a protected bird sanctuary, where there were no towns at all, few villages and no local state services on easy call.

Geoffrey Lewis had chosen one of the most ideal places to do his business, make his shipments. How much of the state's drug supply came into South Australia by this route? Once it was ashore, who was there to notice how it was trans-shipped? Most of the drugs which hit the street in Victoria, New South Wales and Tasmania could be imported by the same route.

Against all of that planning, geography and strategy, there was the dumb luck of a couple of weekend fishermen on a stormy morning, who tried to stand by a vessel which they imagined was in distress. The fall of the cards might have almost amused Rob, but Sean lifted his good hand and hissed sharply,

"Shh, listen! Hear that?"

With an ear pressed to the door, Rob heard footsteps. It was not easy at first to make them out from the background throb and drum of the engines, but Sean was much more accustomed to that bass sound of diesels. Rob picked it up a moment later: two or three pairs of feet, coming closer. A voice grumbled... keys tinkled.

"That's it!" Sean whispered. "Rob!"

"Okay." Rob's palms prickled with sweat as he held the sheet ready. Opposite him, Sean was poised with a large, heavy can in his good hand. He had plastered himself against the wall, far enough back from the door to render him invisible from outside. Rob lifted the sheet, checked its folds, and held his breath.

The lock rattled as a key was inserted. They shared a look, and Sean nodded: get it right first time — you got one chance, make it good!

With a faint squeal of an unoiled hinge, the door swung inward toward Rob. His pulse hammered in his ears as he lifted the sheet. He waited until he had caught a glimpse of a dark blond head, and then flung the linen up and out. It caught the man about the shoulders — he yelped, cursed, and the weapon in his right fist jerked wildly. Involuntarily, Rob grabbed for it and wrenched, and in the same instant Sean smashed the can down on the bowed, shrouded head.

The man went down like a poleaxed ox, leaving Rob panting and vaguely surprised. The whole manoeuvre had taken less than a second. A pace behind the fallen guard, the hapless cook had no chance even to cry out before Sean shot out his good hand, caught him around the neck and dragged him into the room. A single blow dropped him, and he sprawled over the legs of the guard.

"Keys!" Sean hissed.

"Still in the lock." Rob jiggled until they came out. In his hand was a small weapon, block shaped, with a skeletal stock and a ludicrously short barrel. After far too many movies, he recognised it at once. The Ingram machine pistol was ridiculously small, even in Rob's unaccustomed hands. It was less than a foot long, if he ignored the stock. He turned it quickly, examining it, and Sean's voice startled him.

"Careful! The damned thing's charged."

"Ready to shoot?" Rob handled it gingerly. "How can you tell?"

"Look on the side — the ejector port's open. And it'll fire a thousand rounds a minute!" Sean held out his good hand. "You'd better let me have it."

"You're bloody welcome to it," Rob said fervently as he passed it over and stooped over the cook and his guard.

A quick body search turned up a knife in the guard's hip pocket, not quite Swiss Army, but very serviceable. Rob appropriated it, and at once used it to slash the sheet into strips. With all speed, he bound and gagged both the men, as ruthlessly as he knew how.

At the door, Sean had the Ingram braced against his left shoulder. "You finished?"

"Done and done." Palms sweating on the carved ivory hilt of the knife, Rob joined him. "You hear anything?"

"Not yet." Sean leaned out to make sure. "If this tub is anything like the *Rosie Malone*, we're not going to meet anyone but the watch crew at this time of the morning. The rest are sound asleep. Bet your life Chandler and Winkler and their people are snoring their lungs out. It probably took the cook all his time to drag one of those guys out of bed — and that dick-head was still half asleep!" On the threshold, he paused and looked back at Rob with a wry expression. "If they'd tied us up before they tossed us in there, we'd be dog meat."

"But we don't draw that much respect," Rob said bitterly as he closed up the store room, locked it and pocketed the keys. "We're just a couple of good looking gay boys, worth a few bucks to a dope lab needing batch-test guineapigs, so Chandler said."

"Good looking?" Sean echoed as he stepped out into the passageway.

"Damned right." Rob licked his dry lips and followed. "We want the engine room. Which way?"

"Aft, and down." Sean whispered. "Stay close to me."

Rob dropped his voice to a murmur as they moved off from the comparative security of their cell. "How many in the watch crew?"

"Three or four." Sean glanced back at him. "There'll be one man baby-minding the engines. Not the chief engineer. He'll be getting his beauty sleep, but his mate'll be minding the store. The others'll be on the bridge. There'll be the quartermaster — that's the ship's pilot, in the merchant navy, incidentally. The purser organises the ship's stores. Then, the navigator will be monitoring the Decca. There may be a radio man, though the navigator can handle the shortwave if they're running short-staffed."

They had reached the top of a stepway, and the steady chug-chug of the diesels was much louder now. The beat reverberated through the deck, and struck up through Rob's feet and legs. His grip shifted on the knife. "What happens when you sabotage the engines?"

"They stop," Sean said acidly. "Instantly."

"The crew'll hear," Rob whispered. "They'll be so used to hearing that sound, feeling that vibration, the second it stops, they'll know."

"Sure they will," Sean agreed. He cocked an ear to the deck and the stairwell. "You hear that? That heavy metallic thunking sound at the end of every piston stroke."

"They're losing a bearing," Rob guessed.

Sean grinned mirthlessly, like a snake. "And they know that. You can bet this old lady breaks down seven times a day. When the diesels quit on them, they'll figure they're on the fritz again. They'll just roll over in bed, pull the covers over their heads and wait for the engineer to get down there and hammer something till it works again." Cautiously, he moved down onto the stepway. "We've got time, Robbie."

Time to get into and out of the engine room, leaving chaos behind them, get up to the bridge, account for the two or three men on watch there, and use the shortwave. Rob swallowed hard on a throat that was abruptly dry as a dune.

"We'll have to transmit fast," Sean whispered as he went down. "About five minutes after the crew wake up to what we're doing, they're going to take a pair of bolt cutters to the radio mast up top, and disconnect us."

"Jesus." Rob licked his lips. He would never have thought of that. He hurried to catch up as Sean approached the bottom of the stepway. "How long will we have to make the call?"

"As long as it takes the engineer to get out of bed, get down here, see the mess, realise they've been sabotaged, and hit the alarm." Sean looked back at him. "Maybe fifteen minutes. We can transmit until they actually cut the wire and turn us off."

Trusting him was instinctive. Rob's heart beat hard at his ribs and sang in his head, almost like a rush of speed. If he had popped a pill, he would be loving the artificial adrenalin high. Like riding his bike, flat over the tank, watching the speed climb up over a hundred miles per hour, while the 1100cc motor snarled like a wild animal under him. Adrenalin was addictive.

But here, now, Rob felt none of that craving for more. After a day of being so cold that he could barely feel his fingers, sweat was prickling his ribs as followed Sean into a cavern of dimness and noise that made him think of nothing so much as hell.

The reek of old oil hit his nostrils. The din of twin diesels that stood ten feet tall was stunning. The crank cases and sumps were beneath deck level, and still the size and bulk of the engines was overwhelming. The vibration was like being physically shaken, while the diesels bellowed and thumped. A mess of pipes, tanks, pumps and old-fashioned mechanical gauges loomed through the reeking dimness, and behind the engines were the twin gearboxes, housing the massive reduction gearing.

Sean was pacing like a cat, his eyes everywhere. Lights burned here and there, yielding enough illumination for them to pick out the engineer's mate, who would be finishing his watch, looking forward to a breakfast he was not going to get. He was a young man, Rob saw, clad in filthy coveralls, dozing on his arms at a littered table, as far from the engines as he could manage. Around him was a clutter of stale food, dirty crockery, and some of the most lurid European pornography Rob had ever seen. In his ears, wisely, were shooter's earplugs, wads of moulded white wax which offered a little protection against the incessant clamour of the engines.

The boy could never have known what hit him. The Ingram thudded into the back of his skull, one sharp rap, and he slithered to the floor. Sean looked up at Rob over the table.

"Will I tie him?" Rob shouted. "What with?"

"Rags in the bin." Sean pointed. "Gag him, too. Just shove him under the table, the engineer'll find him as soon as he gets down here. The minute we're finished, it won't make any difference who finds him or what he says."

The deck was bare metal, stamped with a non-skid pattern. Rob could not hear his own footsteps as he hurried to the plastic garbage bin that stood beside a series of tool lockers. He dragged out a handful of rags. They were none too clean, but he could not afford to be choosy.

"You recognise this engine?" he bawled as he began to tie the boy.

"Not this model," Sean shouted, "but they're all pretty much alike." He stabbed a finger at the pocket-sized, straight twelve-cylinder engine, head high, on the right side of the main cylinder bank of the nearest diesel. A line fed into it from a fuel header tank; a dozen more lines fed out of it to the main engine itself. "That is one of the injector pumps. And that's where this whole system starts — and stops."

Rob was panting as he manoeuvred the engineer's mate under the table, tucked his legs in and pulled the chair up to conceal him. Nervous, cautious, he leaned out through the open door, but he saw no one.

When he turned back, Sean was standing in a puddle of yellow light, a muscle twitching in his jaw as he studied his right hand. He was trying to clench it, trying to move those fingers. They twitched, they made a fist, but Rob did not have to touch it to know Sean was in trouble. Pain twisted his face, sweat broke out across his forehead and upper lip and his cheeks flushed brightly. He had a feverish look, and Rob knew that a hand on his forehead would discover him hot enough to cook an egg.

"I've got no grip," he said, almost too quietly for Rob to hear him over the continuous roar of engine noise. He looked up, and his eyes were wide, the pupils contracting only a little in the dim light. "I can't grip, Rob."

"I know. Don't fret." Moments before, Rob had seen the fire axe alongside the extinguisher, bracketed on the wall by the door. He fetched the axe, tried the weight between his own hands and found it oddly familiar. "Let me understand this. I hit the injector, smash the cylinder block, it stops — everything stops?"

"Two diesels, two injectors, two blows." Sean backed up against the table, held his right hand cradled against his middle and the machine pistol in his left. "And then we get out of here, fast. I know the way upstairs, and this —" he gestured with the Ingram. "This will get us to the shortwave."

Rob swallowed hard. The beat of the engines was making his ears ache. How did the engineers tolerate it, hours on end? Or did they simply become deaf?

"Do it!" Sean shouted.

Without thinking, reacting on pure instinct, Rob paced to the nearest of the massive, beating engines, took a grip on the axe and swung it into the injector pump with every erg of strength he could produce.

The axe bit deeply, smashing everything in its path. Oil gushed, spattered the deck at Rob's feet, and in seconds the diesel fed by this pump missed a beat. It seemed to gargle as it slowed, slowed... and quit.

"The other one!" Sean yelled, but Rob was already moving. He wrenched the axe out of the smashed machinery and walked around the steel railing which guarded the edge of the pit that cradled the massive crank cases and sumps.

One solid, well placed blow destroyed the second injector. Again oil gushed, the main engine skipped a beat, slowed, and that too died.

The silence was as overwhelming as the noise had been, and Rob's ears protested with a sudden sharp pain. He dropped the axe, spun toward Sean and gave him a shove toward the door.

A clock in his mind seemed to be counting, marking every beat of his heart, but the ship remained quiet as they climbed back up to deck level, and then on, high up into the towering forecastle. The absence of engine noise and vibration was peculiar — it would wake the crew as surely as a sudden cacophony.

Already, the engineer must be stirring, getting out of bed. But he would have to dress, and he would surely try to call the engine room, to ask his mate what was wrong. The mate would not answer. Would the engineer assume the boy was absent? He would be annoyed, he would get dressed and make his way down there. Ten minutes?

The deck rolled under Rob's feet. The sea was still rough, and as they came up he saw that the sky was still dark as pitch. Dawn was not so long away, but the overcast was miles thick and the sun would be near the horizon before it began to grow light.

"This way," Sean whispered, leading him upward again, and left, or forward, toward the bow.

Almost unexpectedly, Rob recognised the lie of the land. This was where they had come in. There was the bridge, where Chandler had used the shortwave to call Lewis aboard the *Minuette*. A pulse quickened in his throat.

The lights were low, so as to minimise the glare in the instruments. Directly ahead were immense glass plates, overlooking the foredeck, the derricks, the bow and the violent sea. Aft of the bridge was the chart room, and to left and right were the lookout wings, vast windows affording unimpeded views amidships.

Three men were standing watch, as Sean had predicted: one stood at the wheel — the quartermaster, or ship's pilot; another was looking into the green screen of the Decca navigator, and a third was drinking coffee, gazing into the pre-dawn north. A surface-search radar screen flickered to his left, and behind the man Rob glimpsed the alcove which would once have housed the enormous, clumsy radio gear of the 1950s. Now it accommodated a much smaller but far more powerful modern shortwave, and a tall stack of crates, painted in some shade of brown or khaki.

None of the crew wore any kind of uniform, but the man drinking coffee looked twenty-five years older than the others, and it was a safe bet that he was the officer of the watch. None of the three noticed as Rob and Sean stepped into the chart room, closed the door quietly and padded on, into the bridge itself. Sean gave Rob a nod.

On cat-silent feet, Rob crept up behind the older man. The side of his fist struck home hard on the back of his skull, and the jarring impact sent the officer sprawling. The grunt and thud as he hit the deck at Rob's feet announced their presence, and the younger men spun toward them.

"Don't!" Sean rasped, and gestured with the Ingram. "Just get over there, sit on the deck, hands on your heads. Move!" For a moment they were too stunned to respond physically or verbally, but a sharp gesture with the weapon seemed to galvanise them. They scrambled to the door, sat against it and gaped up at Sean with faces filled with disbelief. "Rob, block the door. Drag a couple of those crates over here. Quickly!"

Rob reacted instinctively to that tone of command. The crates were astonishingly heavy and he grunted with effort under the weight as he manhandled them into place.

"What the hell is in these? Feels like lead bricks!" He heaved a third crate out of the radio shack and in front of the door, lifted it up onto the others, and was satisfied that it was securely blocked.

"Take this," Sean said tersely, and held out the Ingram. His face was running with sweat, his cheeks brilliant with heat.

The fever was rising fast, with stress, excitement and exertion. It was what Rob had been afraid of. With one hand he took the weapon, with the other he felt Sean's face. "You're burning up."

"Tell me about it." Sean wet his lips. He propped himself on the side of the wide, littered chart table until he had regained his wits and balance, and then gazed into the flickering green screen of the Decca navigator.

"Can you read that thing?" Rob asked quietly. "Where are we? If we're going to call for help, we have to have some coordinates."

"Yes, I can read it." Sean scrubbed his eyes. "This is all in kilometres. We're about twenty klicks off the coast, just east of Encounter Bay. Robbie, you know what you're doing with that shortwave?"

"I have half an idea," Rob confessed. "I'll work it out. It's Channel 88 we want."

The international mayday frequency. The set was brand new, Japanese technology, and it was turned on, probably monitoring Lewis's frequency. Rob leaned over the bench and spun the tuner over. Several pairs of earphones lay on the desk beside it, but he switched the set to speakers and picked up the small, white plastic mic.

He shot a glance at Sean and cleared his throat. The pressure of his thumb held down the transmit button and he called,

"Mayday, mayday. Freighter *Lan Tao* to anyone on this frequency. Mayday, mayday, this is the *Lan Tao* in distress. Anyone on this frequency, respond."

He let go the key and held his breath. Nothing. Sean took a step closer and peered at the machine. Red LED lights were on, indicating that it was working. "Again."

Once more, Rob repeated the message, and then again. The thin edge of panic had just begun to slide between his ribs when a woman's voice responded, and he sucked in a breath.

"Reading you, *Lan Tao*. This is the Volunteer Coast Guard, what is your position?"

"Twenty kilometres offshore, just east of Encounter Bay," Rob reported hoarsely.

"What kind of vessel are you?" Reception was reasonably good this morning. The storm had raced on, leaving clear air behind.

"She's an old freighter." Rob licked his lips. "And we're in trouble."

"What is your emergency?" The woman was brisk, efficient.

Rob took a breath and plunged in. "Two men, prisoners on this ship, will be killed unless you get us off. Helicopter, another ship, doesn't matter, but make it fast. The engines are shut down, she's drifting east with the current. Get us the police, Sea Rescue, anything. Over."

Several seconds' stunned pause answered him, and then the woman asked, "Who is this?"

By her suspicious tone, she had every reason to believe the call was a hoax. Rob groaned. "My name is Markham, my mate is Sean Brodie. We stood by the motor cruiser *Minuette*, in distress, went aboard and saw about a million bucks worth of drugs and guns. Repeat — drugs and guns. We've been trying to get away from them ever since. There's no place left to run! Call the police, ask them if they know the names of Geoffrey Lewis, or John Chandler. There's a bunch of goons on this ship, heavily armed. This is not a joke. Please!"

Once again, she was brisk. Perhaps she had answered enough genuine calls to recognise the razor's edge of fear in a man's voice when she heard it. "You say your engines are shut down?"

"Yes," Rob said breathlessly. "She's drifting, she might even beach herself. The sea's still pretty heavy out here."

"What is the cargo?"

Rob gaped at the radio, and then at Sean. He held down the transmit key. "The manifested cargo — we don't know. But she could be carrying more drugs and guns. She belongs to Geoffrey Lewis. They're heading for New Caledonia, and New Guinea. Hurry! We don't have much time."

She was taking him seriously now. "Stand by, *Lan Tao*, I'll see what I can do."

Sean leaned against the radio and pulled his sleeve over his sweated face. "She'll see what she can do?"

"Give them a chance," Rob murmured. "This isn't like the States. We don't have a military-type Coast Guard. There's no towns on the coast here, no army bases, no airforce base between here and Edinburgh, the navy's small and strung out all the way around a massive continental coastline, and the nearest police are country coppers, miles away."

"Christ." Sean closed his eyes. "Then, who are you talking to?

Coast Guard, she said."

"Volunteer Coast Guard," Rob corrected. "A bunch of civilian boaties and trailer-sailors who donate their time and expertise, monitor the radio, and pull idiot fishermen off sandbanks. And we're lucky they were monitoring us!"

"Great." Sean rested his bandaged hand on top of the radio. "Any chance they can get us a chopper?"

But Rob shook his head. "There's only State Rescue."

"What the hell is that?"

"A Bell Big Lifter, operates out of Adelaide."

"A Big Lifter?" Sean's eyes widened.

Rob nodded. "I told you, this isn't like what you're used to in the States. We do the best we can, but we're twice the size of Texas, with the population of a couple of Los Angeles suburbs. I'm ... sorry." Absurdly, he felt he must apologise.

"Why? It's hardly your fault." Sean touched his face. "Give the lady a buzz, see what they're doing."

"*Lan Tao* to Coast Guard," Rob called as the transmit button depressed. "It's getting tight, what's happening?"

The radio crackled, and then the woman's voice returned. "I've marked your position using your radio signal. Leave your radio open so I can keep track of you. I called the police in Victor. They don't know the names you quoted, but they recommend we treat your emergency as genuine —"

"It is bloody genuine!" Rob exploded. "Lady, we're dead if you don't get us off this ship!"

She skipped a beat. "Understood. The local police can't help you. They don't have a large enough vessel, or the firepower to take on the opposition you describe. They can call in a special tactical squad from Adelaide, but it would be a couple of hours before —"

"A couple of hours?" Sean rasped. He swiped the mic out of Rob's hand and managed it clumsily. "This is Sean Brodie. Lady, in a couple of hours, we'll be dead. Just what do you suggest we do?"

A burst of static punctuated the transmission, and then the woman said stridently, "Try and stay out of their way. I called the Navy two minutes ago. I'm sure there's a patrol boat in your area. It can't be far away."

"A what?" Sean looked blankly at Rob.

A rush of premature relief had raced through Rob. He felt the flush of heat in his cheeks as he turned to Sean. "A Royal Australian Navy Fremantle class patrol boat. Pocket-sized warship. Small crew, but all professionals. Armed." He gave the mic a smacking kiss. "You beauty!"

"Coast Guard to *Lan Tao*, are you still receiving?"

Rob's thumb hit the button. "We got that. A patrol boat in our area, you called them. They responded?"

"Coming in now, *Lan Tao*. Stand by."

As he let go the button, Rob looked at his watch. It was a quarter after five, and the engines had stopped nine minutes ago. He looked up at Sean, whose brow was creased in a deep frown. "Sean, how are we doing?"

"I... don't know," Sean whispered. "Depends where this patrol boat is, how long it takes them to get here. There's only so many places on a ship this size that you can hide. And," he added bleakly, "we have to get off this bridge and find a safe place. The other element we have to consider is Geoffrey Lewis. The *Minuette* is supposed to be rendezvousing with us. If we don't show, they'll come find us. We don't have long. What's keeping that Coast Guard woman?"

Beyond the wide glass windows, the sky was showing a glimmer of steel-blue in the east. Dawn. The sea had begun to smooth and the deck beneath Rob's feet was not rolling with the vigour it had demonstrated a half hour before. Rob hit the button once more.

"*Lan Tao* to Coast Guard, come in." No response. "*Lan Tao* to Coast Guard, we're just about out of time. Please!"

"Coast Guard," the woman responded. "I just spoke to the Navy. Lieutenant Commander Rodgers, commanding the HMAS *Newcastle* is sixty kilometres from your position."

"Thirty-seven miles," Sean whispered. "How long?"

"How long?" Rob called urgently. "We're out of time."

"She'll be with you in about fifty minutes, an hour at longest," she told him. "It's the best we can do. Can you hold on?"

"Oh, Jesus. An hour." Rob leaned heavily against the shortwave set and pulled in a deep breath. His mind swirled, but he was aware of Sean's hand on his shoulder. He hit the transmit button again and cleared his throat. "*Lan Tao* to Coast Guard, can I talk to Captain Rodgers? Over."

"He's standing by to talk to you right now. I'm patching you through."

The shortwave crackled, hissed, and Sean's fingers clenched deep into Rob's arm. "Make it fast, Rob. We can't stay here for much longer. If they corner us in this enclosed space, they've got us. I —"

166

"*Newcastle* to *Lan Tao*, this is Captain James Rodgers. To whom am I speaking?" The voice was strong, bold, with that unmistakable Sydney accent.

"My name is Markham," Rob said quickly. "I don't have time to talk. Are you tracking this ship?"

"You're on radar, *Lan Tao*. What is your emergency?"

A red mist veiled Rob's eyes. "I described it the Coast Guard! Two men, prisoners aboard, didn't she tell you?"

A short pause, and then Rodgers said smoothly, "She gave us enough, Mr Markham. Please be calm."

"Rob," Sean said urgently. "Rob, come on!"

"Mr Markham, is the crew armed?" Rodgers called.

"Yes, they're armed," Rob said breathlessly. "Be careful. And for the love of God, be quick! I can't talk any longer. We're on the bridge, we have to get out before we're trapped."

He dropped the mic, and though Rodgers's voice called once more, both he and Sean ignored the man. The officer of the watch was still unconscious, and the two boys sat against the crates blocking the door, pale with fear. With difficulty, his eyes glittering with the savage onset of fever, Sean gestured with the machine pistol.

"Move it, you two, get away from there!"

They scrambled to obey, and Rob hurried to unblock the door. As he cracked it open he heard voices, shouting, furious, deeper in the ship. "Sean —"

"I hear them." Sean was right on his heels. "Out! If they corner us in here, we're fish in a barrel."

Rob pulled open the door, and he had taken a half step through before he glimpsed faces in the dimness of the passageway, not fifteen feet from him. Three men, big and brawny, swung toward him and began to run.

"Out of the way!" Sean's voice cracked like a whip, with such a tone of command that Rob had flung himself out of the doorway before he had time to realise what he was doing.

On full automatic, the Ingram cycled a thousand rounds a minute, but the magazine held just thirty .45 calibre rounds. Sean had locked it on single shot to make the ammunition last. He could get off a round as fast as he could squeeze the trigger, which was still fast enough. The difficulty was that accuracy was not the Ingram's strong point. When the target was more than three or four yards away, hitting anything specific was down to luck. Working left-handed increased the odds again.

Still, for the ten rounds Sean squeezed off, he made contact with two, and two out of three of the men in the corridor went down, cursing and groaning, clutching wounds that would incapacitate them.

The door slammed shut once more, and Rob dove for the piles of khaki-painted crates which cluttered the radio shack and the rear of the chart room. They were heavy, dense. He was sweating, panting and swearing as dragged them through and stacked them in front of the door, more thoroughly than before. When he was finished the pile was higher, wider, heavier.

Hands propped on his thighs as he caught his breath, he blinked up at Sean. "Now, what?"

"Now?" Sean licked his dry lips as he leaned back against the Decca for support or balance. He cuffed his face and raked his fingers through his short cropped hair. "Now, we wait."

Twelve

SEAN SLIPPED his left arm about Rob's shoulders and urged him over to the side of the bridge, away from the barricade. "They might be able to shoot through that," he said quietly. "The door doesn't look too sound. It's only wood laminate. The whole chart room has been customised, years ago, probably by the previous owner or crew. You wouldn't spend money to give a facelift to a barge this old."

"Chandler's people know they've been sabotaged." Rob was looking out through the wide glass windows. The sky had lightened visibly.

"Oh, they know. But the radio shack here is well protected." Intent on his hand, Sean flexed the fingers.

"Let me look at that." Rob stepped closer, reaching for it.

But Sean fended him off. "It's okay."

"Bullshit," Rob said flatly. "You're running a fever. There'll be a medic on the *Newcastle*."

If we're still alive when she gets here. The thought took Sean unawares. He shook his head to clear it of the fog which had begun to settle about his senses, and fended Rob off more determinedly. "There's nothing more you can do for it. Let it be." He gestured at the shortwave. "Call Rodgers. Tell him we're trapped. He needs all the details he can get before he engages these bastards, or someone could get hurt."

Rob nodded slowly, but was looking at the two boys, who sat on the floor, against the radar unit, listening to every word, mute and pale. "What about them?"

"I'll watch them." Sean gave him a push. "Call the situation in."

But Rob hesitated, and took Sean's face between his hands. "You're burning."

"Surprising." Sean summoned a faint, reluctant smile. "And I'm still damned proud of you, Robbie. You're something special."

"Me?" The compliment seemed to fluster Rob. "I'm just trying to stay alive."

He turned away to the shortwave, and as he called Rodgers's name, Sean transferred his attention to the two boys. One was dark, with regular features and shaggy hair, not particularly handsome but not disagreeable. The other was very fair, his hair almost curly and cut short to control it. He had Swedish good looks, rosy cheeks, blue eyes. Both were in jeans and jerseys, and the dark-haired boy wore a black wool 'beanie' on the back of his head. They could be no older than twenty or twenty-two, and they were scared rigid.

"You two," Sean began. They looked up at him, wide eyes darting between his face and the machine pistol. "Oh, for Christ's sake," he groaned, "I'm not going to hurt you. You're regular crew on this ship, are you? Who do you work for?"

The blond kid discovered his voice with an effort. "The skipper. Captain Anderson."

"Then, you're regular merchant marine crew," Sean concluded. "What do you know about John Chandler?"

The boys glanced at each other; the dark one shrugged. "Not even the name. We were told to divert and stop here and pick up some people and a small cargo, right off the coast. The owner's special orders."

"The owner?" Did they know Geoffrey Lewis? It was doubtful. Sean glanced into the radio shack, where Rob was talking in sporadic undertones with the commander of the patrol boat. "You kids have names?"

"I'm Tim Craig." The blond boy clasped both hands about his knees.

"Mick Tanner." The dark kid's brown eyes flickered to Rob and the shortwave. "Look, I don't know who the fuck you guys are, but — do you know what's going on on this ship?" He gestured at the door. "I mean, we take our orders from the skipper. Who the Christ owns this bucket of rust, we never knew. Then, suddenly there's an English guy on the radio, the skipper says it's the owner and we have to detour. A boat comes alongside, and a bunch of goons come aboard, with guns! They bring a pile of boxes in here and tell us, if we touch them, if we look in them, they'll chop us up. Then, about twenty klicks further east, they brought you on board." His mouth twitched nervously, and he gestured at Rob. "He just told the Navy you sabotaged our engines."

Sean gave the boy a lopsided smile devoid of humour. "We did.

And there's a Navy patrol boat coming. So if you're as innocent as you claim to be —"

"Sweet Jesus Christ!" Tim erupted. "We haven't done nothing! Captain Anderson is pissed as hell, taking orders from the goon squad, but he says he has to. Owner's instructions. The way they're guarding that cargo, it must be a billion bucks' worth of diamonds! We just do as we're told and try to stay out of the way of that bloody maniac."

"Chandler?" Sean guessed.

"Don't know his name," Mick growled. "The good looking one."

"John Chandler," Sean affirmed. "And you're right to stay out of his way." He worked his neck to and fro and promptly wished he had not as dizziness assaulted him. He was more feverish than Rob knew, and his hand felt like a balloon, on fire. "What's your legitimate cargo?"

The boys shared a nervous look, and Tim coughed. "It's supposed to be auto spare parts, canned food and hardware. But I'm sure that's not all. I mean, there's plenty of legit gear in the holds, but there's other stuff."

"Stuff?" Sean's brows rose.

"Crates," Mick added, "that don't show on the manifest."

The implications were rich. Sean cocked his head at the boys. "When all this began for us, almost a day ago, we caught a glimpse of a cache of drugs and guns. Heroin and assault rifles. Is that what you're hinting at?"

They seemed relieved that he had been the one to say it. "It's what we've been suspecting," Tim admitted, "but we haven't been allowed anywhere near the cargo on this voyage. Captain Anderson was fucking furious when he found out the load doesn't match the manifest. We've got all this extra gear we shouldn't have, and we could get in trouble. He was saying to the engineer, if we get searched in New Zealand, he's going to be wading in shit up to his arm pits."

"The man has a picturesque turn of phrase," Sean said drily. He relaxed his left arm, let the Ingram drop. "Okay, I believe you. Get in the radio shack. You know Chandler is going to try coming through that door. You don't want to be in the firing line."

Sudden panic seemed to galvanise them, and they scrambled through into the cramped space. Rob stood aside to make room, and as Sean joined him, he was just shutting down the radio. Sean handed him the Ingram and leaned heavily on the bench which held the powerful shortwave.

"You look rough." Rob set aside the machine pistol.

"I feel it." Sean bowed his head and made some quiet sound as Rob's hands closed gently about his skull and rubbed his scalp with soothing fingertips. "Christ, Robbie, I'm tired."

"I know." Rob's voice seemed to come from a long way off. "It's all been wonderful Sean. Everything. Even when we had our differences and began to drift for a while, and even when we got into this mess."

Sean lifted his head and blinked his vision clear. "What's this, the 'goodbye, it's been great knowing you' speech?"

"Maybe." Rob's eyes glistened. "Rodgers just told me he's making the best speed the *Newcastle* can manage. They've got us on radar, they'll sight us visually in about fifty minutes, maybe a tad less." He shook his head slowly. "We're not going to make it." He glanced at the blocked doorway. "That's all that stands between us and them, and it's not enough."

"But Chandler's people know they're in trouble." Sean forced his tongue around the words. "They'll know we've used the shortwave, and they can expect company. Any fool can dial up Channel 88 and yell for help, it doesn't take any special talent."

"But..." Rob gestured vaguely. "They're going to come for us, and it won't be long."

"And the first ones through that door will get hurt," Sean said raspingly. He reached for the Ingram and put it into Rob's hands. "Nobody wants to risk getting injured or killed, Robbie, so they won't be eager to rush us. That'll make them slow. They could have been here by now — why are they waiting? They're thinking about it, coming up with fifty different reasons not to rush us. They'll use the standby shortwave, or even a mobile phone, to call the *Minuette*. They'll do anything before they put themselves in harm's way. It's basic survival instinct. People are not crazy."

"That makes sense," Rob said slowly. "Hey!" As Sean began to slide sideways he slipped his arm around him and dumped him onto the radio operator's swivel chair.

"Damn." Sean pressed his burning face into Rob's middle. "I won't do that again." His arms circled Rob's narrow hips and held on.

A quiet cough, and Tim Craig said cautiously, "You're lovers, aren't you?"

Over Sean's lowered head, Rob said levelly, "Yes. If that offends you, I'm sorry."

"Doesn't offend us," Mick scoffed. "What d'you think we are? Not that the skipper knows. He'd go ape shit, man. He likes his Bible a bit too much, if you know what I mean."

"I can imagine." Rob's hands stroked and kneaded Sean's tense neck and shoulders. "It's a small world. Are you gay, or is it just convenient between you while you're aboard?"

"Started off being a convenience, when we first signed on," Tim admitted. "The more we did it together, we got to like it better than straight sex. You?"

"I was born gay," Rob said easily. "Sean?"

"Mmm." Sean stirred resolutely before he could slither down into the sleep for which he was yearning. "I knew I was homosexual by the time I was about seven years old. What is this, a show and tell session?" He looked up at Rob, and smiled tiredly until he saw a red LED light winking nearby. "What's that?"

Rob had not even noticed it, and Tim answered. "It's the intercom. They'll be trying to get through to the officer of the watch... that's my Uncle George. He got us these jobs. We'd been out of work since we got out of school."

"Your uncle?" Rob echoed. He shared a glance with Sean. "How well do you know him?"

"He means, does Uncle George work for your skipper, or for the owner, Lewis?" Sean added.

"George Craig, work for that mob?" Tim demanded. "You have to be kidding. He's so straight, man, when I told him I was gay, he thought I meant I was having a good time!"

"And I've given him a concussion," Rob said ruefully. "He's still out cold. You'd better drag him in here. That goon squad won't take much longer to screw up its courage, and your uncle could get hurt."

Grabbed by the feet and hauled across the deck, the older man's body tucked neatly into the radio shack, and Tim propped him up against a crate. "He has this dream about working on cruise liners in the Pacific. Where does he wind up? On an antique rust bucket, running illegal cargo to nothing places."

"New Caledonia and New Guinea," Sean argued. "Hardly nothing places. There'll be rebel gun traffickers in both places, feeding two different miniature war zones."

"Oh, sure," Tim said bitterly. "It's real exciting, looking down the wrong end of a gun." He glared up at Sean. "This is not what we signed on for."

"How long?" Mick asked sharply. "How long before they can fix the engines? What did you do to them?" He looked from Rob to Sean and back again.

Rob held Sean's head against his shoulder. "I smashed both the injector pumps with the fire axe. They can't fix them. They'll carry spares, but it'll take time to clean up the mess and install the replacements. Is your engineer any good?"

"When he's sober, he is," Mick snorted. "Last night, he was good and pissed. That South African arsehole — Winkler, is that the name? — had been giving him a hard time, handing out orders like he owns this ship himself. Old Fred Webber doesn't even take Captain Anderson's orders with a grin. He swung one at the South African, tried to knock his head off. Ended up flat on his own ass for his trouble. He grabbed a bottle and locked his cabin door... and when he does that, he usually drinks the bottle dry."

"So he's more or less hungover this morning." Sean looked up into Rob's face. "He'll be slow, Robbie. He won't get those engines started before the *Newcastle* gets here." He paused. "Time?"

Only seconds before, Rob had looked at his watch. "Forty-five minutes."

He might have said, a year. Sean closed his eyes and summoned his wits. "Check with Rodgers."

The shortwave was still on Channel 88, and Rob had only to hit the button and call to reach the captain of the patrol boat. "*Lan Tao* to *Newcastle*, are you receiving? Over."

"*Newcastle*," Rodgers responded at once. "What is your situation?"

"The same," Rob told him. "We're barricaded into the bridge, they haven't moved on us yet. Where are you?"

"Heading your way as fast as we know how," Rodgers assured him. "Just sit tight, stay calm. Don't do anything to provoke them. You said you have a gun? Threaten them with it, but don't use it unless you have absolutely no other option. When your ammunition is spent, you lose your ability to intimidate. If they try to talk you out of there, negotiate. Keep them talking. Waste their time."

"Give you a chance to get here," Rob finished. The sky beyond the enormous windows was brightening steadily toward a steel-blue twilight hue. "Time," he murmured. "Time." Then he shook himself and said crisply, "Understood, *Newcastle*. We'll do what we can." He set down the mic and rubbed his palms together. "Clammy," he muttered disgustedly.

Sean snaked his good arm around him. "You heard the man. We're doing the right thing."

"You really think they'll try to talk us out?" Rob demanded.

"Chandler?" Sean's mouth compressed. "Not a chance. It'll be Winkler who's holding him back right now. Chandler would have been in here minutes ago, guns blazing, like a remake of Iwo Jima."

The red light was still winking on the intercom, and Sean considered using it. If he could somehow convince Chandler or Winkler to talk, discussion could eat up valuable minutes. He was about to suggest this when Rob lifted his head, listening intently, and a moment later Sean heard the sounds too.

Footsteps clattering on a steel deck.

"They're coming," Tim whispered. "Oh, Jesus Christ, they're coming." He crossed himself, a reflex gesture that must have sprung out of his childhood, and crammed himself in against the wall with Mick.

Heart in his mouth, Sean glanced at Rob, and then at the machine pistol. "That's on single shot. Stroke the trigger very gently. It's sensitive." Rob's face was bloodless, but he nodded. Sean swallowed on a dust-dry throat and looked back toward the door.

A weight fell against it, pushing, heaving, but the stack of crates held it firmly shut with an even greater force. Sean expected to hear a barrage of gunfire, but instead it was a voice that came through to them.

"You're wasting your time." Chandler. "We know you used the shortwave. Who did you call?"

Rob shifted his grip on the Ingram. "We put out a mayday, what do you expect?"

"And it was picked up," Chandler added. "By whom?"

"The Coast Guard," Rob told him tersely.

A pause, and then Chandler gave a bark of laughter. "The Volunteer Coast Guard? My God, and Winkler was worried." His voice was sharp as a knife. "Come out of there. Come out right now, and you'll live. Make a fight of it, and I promise you, you'll be feeding the fish an hour from now. You want to live?"

The threat was no overstatement, but Sean was feverish enough for it to seem almost humorous. "Why don't you go to hell, Chandler," he rasped.

For a moment there was silence, and then a muddle of half-heard voices over which only Chandler's cut clearly: "How you two idiots ever convinced Lewis to hire you is beyond me. Just give that thing to me, will you, and get away from that damned door. Thank you very much!"

"Rob —" Sean sucked in a breath.

Before he could go on, the bray of an assault rifle on full automatic drowned out his voice, and he crammed his hands over his ears to save them. Within moments, a second rifle joined the first, then another, and by Sean's calculations they expended several magazines. At the cycling speed of those weapons, a clip was spent in under five seconds.

The crates Rob had stacked in front of the door were shoulder high. Shots ripped through the door itself, but the boxes stopped the rounds dead. Only a few stray rounds got through, over the top of the crates, and angled into the ceiling. Two ricochets punched into the bridge electronics, and several small electrical fires ignited, forward of the chart room.

The fumes would be toxic, but two extinguishers were to hand, and as the braying din from outside the door stopped, Sean gave Tim a nudge. "Get those fires out before we choke. No — stay down low, under the line of the crates!" His ears were aching, ringing, but he looked grimly at Rob. "They didn't cut through."

"Those boxes," Rob said breathlessly. "They must be filled with metal. No wonder they were so heavy, I could hardly move them." He licked his lips. "You thinking what I'm thinking?"

"Guns?" Sean nodded. The fires were swiftly out, in a billow of retardant vapour. Tim and Mick hurried back, eager just to be told what to do. "You got any tools?" Sean asked. "Something to get these crates open." He gestured at the many boxes still in the radio shack, Lewis's special, guarded cargo.

"Just this." Mick leaned out of the alcove which had been customised to house the shortwave, and produced a fire axe similar to the one which had crippled the pumps. "The skipper makes a big thing out of fire precautions. She's an old ship, stuffed with new electronics, you know."

"Bless Captain Anderson," Rob said drily. "Give me a hand here, kid."

All Sean could do was stand back, watch them and listen to the door. Chandler and Winkler were bellowing at each other, and Winkler sounded not simply furious, but afraid.

"You maniac!" He roared. "You want to blow us the hell out of here? They've blocked the door with the crates!"

Blow —? Sean's pulse began to speed. Explosives?

The lids wrenched easily off several crates, and while Rob and Tim attacked another Mick began to scrabble among the shredded paper which had been used to pack and insulate the contents.

In the first box, Sean glimpsed the barrel of a rifle, instantly familiar to anyone who often watched the television news. The Russian Kalashnikov was the weapon of choice of so many guerrilla armies. It was manufactured, sold and traded by the tens of million and had become common the world over.

But when Mick lifted the mess of shredded paper out of the second crate he froze, and all at once Winkler's furious shouting made sense.

"Robbie." Beckoning him, Sean took a step closer. "They're shipping grenades."

Colour flushed Rob's cheeks as he reached gingerly into the box and lifted one out. He gave a glance to the crates he had stacked in front of the door. "Those must be filled with the guns. If they'd been full of grenades or ammunition..."

"Our worries would have been over. Permanently." Sean rubbed his face hard. "Talk about dumb luck. They won't dare try to shoot their way in again."

"Then, all we have to do is wait for the *Newcastle*," Rob said hoarsely.

Some sixth sense made Sean's skin crawl, but he could not put his finger on the cause. "I... don't know," he whispered. "I just don't trust them. Time?"

Rob looked at his watch. "Forty minutes." He knuckled his eyes and glared at the crates of weapons strewn around them. "There's enough to equip an army here!"

"But none of us is a soldier," Sean warned. "Sure, I've been in places, mostly Central America, where I've seen this stuff prepped and used, but if we try to use gear like this, we'll be the first ones who get hurt."

They were silent, mute and seething in frustration, and the voice Sean might least have expected almost made him jump out of his skin.

"I was a platoon sergeant in Vietnam, 1969 to '71. You blokes would have been little kids at the time. What the hell is this about? Jesus Christ, a bunch of bloody kids on the rampage."

Tim spun toward his uncle. "You're awake!"

"That's a brilliant observation, that is." George Craig was sitting up, holding his head in both hands. "What hit me?"

"I did," Rob said apologetically. "At the time, it seemed the best thing to do." He extended his hand to pull Craig up to his feet. "I'm sorry."

Sean took a step nearer to the door. The voices had receded but a steady buzz of furious conversation half reached him. They were talking, arguing amongst themselves. Anger and ambition were powerful catalysts to action.

"Have you been awake for long?" Rob asked with a gesture at the shortwave. "How much have you heard?"

"Not a lot." Craig seemed to have regained his wits and his balance. He was not tall, stocky and muscular, in his late forties, dressed in the same jeans and jersey as the boys. He smoothed his silvering, sandy coloured hair and fixed Tim with a hard look. His eyes were blue, his face jowly, like a bulldog, his eyes nested in deep creases. "I suggest you tell me what this is all about."

"Tell him." Rob shoved Tim toward his uncle, and joined Sean in the chart room. "Sean, what is it?"

The voices were too soft for Sean to make them out. "I wish I knew. I can't hear the words, but from the sound of them, they're planning something. They won't shoot, and they must know we will, but that won't stop them for long."

The door was in tatters. Three magazines had been emptied into it, and little of the woodwork was hanging together. Only the barricade of heavy, steel-filled — potentially explosive — crates blocked off that door. Sean gave Rob an anxious glance.

"Sean, think. Think of something," Rob whispered. "You're the one with the brains and all the experience." He laced his fingers at Sean's nape. "You tell me what to do, and I'll do it."

"We have to get out," Sean murmured. "In here, we're easy pickings. Out there, we at least have a chance."

Rob took a deep, audible breath. "I know that. Tell me how."

"Grenades." Sean nodded at the crates. "You don't know one end of a grenade from the other... I don't know a hell of a lot about them myself, although I've seen a few. Guerrilla troops sometimes show off with them, like tossing firecrackers around. It scares shit out of travellers, gives everybody a big laugh." He looked at the older man, who was still listening intently to Tim. "Platoon Sergeant Craig, however, has the experience. I think maybe we lucked out. And it's about time."

The lines of Craig's face were etched so deeply, they might

have been scars. When Tim fell silent he turned toward Sean and Rob, thrust his hands into the pockets of his baggy blue jeans, and looked them up and down critically.

"American tourists?" he asked dubiously.

"Sean Brodie. I work in this country," Sean corrected.

"And I was born here." Rob rubbed his palms together, and held out his hand. "Rob Markham." Craig shook his hand readily. "You know what you're doing with those?" Rob gestured at the grenades. "Sean reckons they're the only chance we have left."

The lines about Craig's mouth deepened as he grinned, and his eyes glittered with genuine humour. "Sean would probably be right. And yes, I can handle them." He arched his brows at Sean. "You got a plan?"

Dizziness and heat filled Sean's head, and he held his right hand against his chest. "I just know we have to get out of this closed space. Those men will find a way to get through that door... unless we exercise the only advantage we have."

"Advantage?" Mick demanded sharply.

"Surprise," Sean told him. "It'll be closer to shock." He nodded at the ripped, torn door. "They're aft of us, I think they're clustered at the head of the stairway. Lob one grenade among that lot, and they'll be down those stairs like jackrabbits before it can go off. Can do, Sergeant?"

"That's no problem," Craig mused. "Let me check the way these things are set up. I need to know how the fuses are timed. They could be anything between three seconds and ten."

Ten seconds was long enough for Chandler to pick up a grenade and lob it right back. By now, he had probably concluded that the crates behind that door did not hold grenades, since he had not triggered an eruption. That argument was sound, and Winkler would not be able to hold him on a leash much longer.

As Craig fiddled with a grenade, fresh out of the box, Sean continued to listen at the door. He heard Winkler, heard Chandler, and a quiet, intermittent blast of static. Rob was close enough for Sean to feel his body heat, and he murmured, "You hear that? A radio. They're talking to the boss."

"The *Minuette* must be close," Sean guessed. He closed his eyes, the better to listen. "If I was on the outside, I'd rush that door with a battering ram. Just break it away, shove it open, physically push the crates away with something heavier than they are, and then shoot anything in here that moves."

"That sounds like Chandler's style," Rob said bitterly. He looked at his watch. "Thirty-five minutes."

"Too long." Sean leaned heavily into Rob's side. "We're not going to make it."

"We are," Rob hissed. "Have a little faith."

Faith? Sean blinked at him. Wearing a full day's stubble, tousled and dishevelled, Rob might have been a gypsy. No virgin was safe, Sean thought, and they would surrender with a sound of bliss. Rob grasped his good hand tightly, and then released him as George Craig turned away from the open box with a grenade in each hand.

"They're set up on seven-second fuses," he said grimly, "and they're armed. These babies are going to war."

"New Caledonia and Bougainville," Rob guessed. "This ship is bound for the waters around Port Moresby. That means a midnight rendezvous with traders before you make port. What the Kanak gunrunners don't take from you, the Bougainville traders will."

The older man's face was bleak. "How many of those assholes are we up against?"

Sean and Rob shared a glance, and Sean guessed, "Maybe a dozen. Most of them seem to be clustered at the top of those stairs. My guess is they'll try to beat their way in here with a battering ram. Shove those crates aside, and then..." He looked away.

The two boys were panicky. Tim was white as a sheet. "Whatever you're planning," Rob said quietly, "you'd better make it fast."

"Planning?" Craig echoed. "There's shit-all to plan, son." He gestured at the door. "If you want to get out and have somewhere to run, you clear the stairwell. You keep the mongrels running in front of you, and then you get up into the bow and take cover." He pause. "Of course, they're going to shoot at you. And I suggest you grab a couple of those. Kalashnikov AK-47s. There's about five dozen of them, and all the 7.62mm ammunition you could pray for. Spray enough of it around now and then, and even if you don't hit anything, the least you'll do is make them keep their heads down." He gave Sean and Rob a hard look. "Call the *Newcastle,* tell the skipper what we're doing. His lads could be walking into a hornets' nest."

With a start, Rob seemed to jerk back into gear, but when he tried the radio it was dead. Its lights were out. He checked the power and leads, and swore. "Either we lost power when those fires started, or they've pulled a fuse on us. There's no juice getting through here."

"Then, the *Newcastle* will have to look after herself," Sean said sourly. "Time, Robbie?" His own sense of time was weirdly distorted. A minute could seem like an hour, or his mind might wander and it could flash by unnoticed.

"Thirty minutes." Rob forced in a deep breath. "And you'd better show me how to use one of these."

Determined, resolute, he lifted an AK-47 out of the nearest box. He tried it for weight and fit, tucked it into his shoulder.

Craig was at his side, his manner crisp as an instructor. "You've used rifles before?"

"Just an air rifle and a .22, a few years ago." Rob felt the weight and found it acceptable. The old-fashioned wooden stock was almost familiar.

"That's the fire selector," Craig said brusquely, pointing out the long bar right above the trigger mechanism. "Middle position is safety. Push it up for full automatic, down for single shot. Got it? Magazine. Thirty rounds. Slide it in like this. Smoothly, don't jam it." The curved magazine inserted with a sharp metallic sound, and locked. "The rest, you know. Point and shoot." Craig stood back. "Stuff your pockets with ammunition. Drop that magazine out, load it and slap it back in. Take a spare clip, you'll need to reload. One magazine will never go the distance." He frowned into his nephew's pale face. "You want to play cowboys too?"

The boys had been following every word he told Rob, and without a sound they followed Rob's lead. Sean leaned against the chart table as his senses grew thicker than molasses. He knew Rob was beside him, he was half aware of the sound of 7.62mm cartridges rolling around on the table, and he struggled to focus. The fever was spiralling upward rapidly, fanned by stress and exertion. He seemed to be standing in an oven and his mouth was as dry as sand. He forced himself to listen as Craig said very quietly to Rob, "He's hurt, isn't he?"

"His hand. It's a mess, badly infected. You're looking at the beginning of blood poisoning, and he needs a doctor, fast." Rob was loading the magazine, slipping the rounds in one by one. "There'll be a medic on the *Newcastle*." He slapped the loaded magazine into the weapon and began to fill his pockets. "Sean?"

"Yo," Sean said wearily. "Still with you." He pulled his shoulders back and forced air to the bottom of his lungs to clear his head.

Rob took him up the upper arms. "You'll have to move fast, honey," he whispered. "Can you do it?"

"I have a choice? Watch me," Sean rasped. Craig had appropriated his own rifle, attended to the magazine, and was now scooping grenades out of the crate. Sean dropped his voice to a murmur. "You reckon he knows what he's doing?"

"He seems to." Rob's teeth worried his lip. "These weapons are not exactly new. They might have fought in the Vietnam war with him! It'd be ironic, wouldn't it? The Kalashnikov that tried to kill you in '69 might save your life today." He gave Sean an anxious look, and Sean summoned the ghost of a smile. "Stay behind me," Rob said quietly. "I don't want to brag, but I used to be a good shot with an air rifle when I was nine. Shooting cans and bottles in the back yard. Like he said, it's just point and shoot."

Several deep breaths fetched Sean's senses into line, and he blinked his eyes to focus. George Craig was at the door, listening absorbedly, and his face was a bleak mask as he looked back over his shoulder.

"The buggers are getting excited," he said tersely. "Tim, Mick, get these crates moved. We're just about out of time. Move your asses!"

"Time," Sean echoed soundlessly as he lifted the Ingram machine pistol in his left hand. The small weapon was all he could manage. He moved in behind Rob, like his shadow.

Time was the one thing they did not have.

Thirteen

THE ROAR of a grenade in an enclosed space made the eardrums overload. Pain stabbed through Sean's head, jerked him back to full awareness and left him more alert than he had been since they had scuttled out of the engine room. The adrenalin that pumped into his bloodstream was better than a shot of speed. It would not last, but in the short term it was magic.

The battered door was open wide, George Craig's stocky figure was framed in it, and he had another grenade in his hand. He had held the first until four of the fuse's seven seconds were spent, and then bowled it hard and fast, into the midst of the knot of men at the top of the stairway.

They went down so fast, most of them must have made a headlong dive. Some would not reach the bottom alive. A shrill scream and semiconscious groans echoed up as Rob took Sean's arm to urge him out of the chart room. Tim and Mick were a pace behind, panting so heavily with stress that Sean could hear every breath.

Up ahead, Craig was already at the top of the stairwell, and this time Sean clamped his hands over his ears with a moment to spare as a second grenade was bowled. The roar and shockwave rolled over him, and he peeled himself off the wall.

Move! As he forced his body into gear, got it moving, kept it moving, he felt better. Adrenalin was a powerful drug. His right hand was stiff as a piece of wood, hot as cinders, and his head was singing.

Fever. Strange, how fever sharpened some senses while it dulled others. Colours seemed lurid, sounds reverberated, and he noticed the oddest details he had not seen before. Tim wore a gold plug in his left ear. Mick had stitched a Harley Davidson patch onto the shoulder of his jacket. Rob's hands were scratched and ruddy with abuse, and he cradled the rifle almost like a lover. He had beautiful hands, Sean thought abstractly. When they held him, caressed him, they could drive him past the brink of sanity, into a sublime madness.

"Clear!" Craig's voice bellowed.

There was no need for subtlety now. Craig was hurrying down toward the deck level as he shouted, not even bothering to look back. He could not be responsible for the others — survival was an individual endeavour. Craig was not a soldier now, he was just a man who remembered how to safely handle weapons. That kind of education, one never forgot.

Pain dragged a cry out of Sean's throat as he supported himself on his right hand and clambered after Craig as fast as he could. Two bodies lay underfoot, sprawled haphazardly and spattered with blood. Without a glance, Sean knew they were dead. Damage wreaked by the grenade was everywhere. Fragments of twisted shrapnel studded the walls.

Steely daylight spilled through the glass on the port side, northwards. How far had the ship drifted? The tide would carry her east, but the *Newcastle* had her on radar and would not lose her.

Twenty-five minutes, Sean thought with a weird, skewed rationale. He slammed his hands over his ears as Craig bowled another grenade with all the gracelessness and raw animal power of big Merv Hughes... Rob was fond of cricket. Living with him, Sean quickly grew accustomed to the sport, the five-day tests and limited-overs matches, the strange language that described in-swingers, slip catches and cover drives —

"Sean, move!" Rob's voice exploded in his ear.

His mind had been drifting, but as Rob shouted he adrenalin surged again, and Sean flung himself in the wake of George Craig. They were almost at deck level now, going down the ringing steel stairs at reckless, dangerous speed. One slip, and they would be tangled at the bottom. Sean's breath rasped in his throat, and he turned his head away as Craig let loose a fourth grenade.

The stunning burst stabbed through his ears, made his chest shake and left his legs trembling, but when he looked back he saw Craig at the door. Big, brown hands wrenched it open and a wave of cold, salt air broke over Sean's face.

Of Chandler and his men, there was no sign. They had fled, taken cover. Rob's arm was around Sean, hustling him, but the adrenalin sang through his veins like a priceless, forbidden drug. He was through the door not a pace behind Craig, and paused only to let Rob catch him up. Tim and Mick were somewhere behind, sticking close.

The dawn twilight provided just enough light to see. Craig was diving forward toward the bow as if the devil were on his heels, and Sean plunged after him. The devil or John Chandler — there was not much difference.

The foredeck was a tangle of cranes and lashed-down cargo. Vast containers were roped to the deck, headed for New Zealand. Parked on two pallets, to port and starboard, were a pair of scarlet Holden Commodores under transparent plastic sheets.

Three sets of handling gear arched and reared like the legs of immense steel spiders between the forecastle and the bow. They and the deck cargo provided cover aplenty. George Craig was already safe, down behind the foremost crane, just twenty feet back from the pinnacle of the bow itself.

Sean was two yards from safety when shots cracked out from behind them. A dozen rounds ripped off on full automatic, and fear sent him lunging into the cover of the crane. He hit the steel hard with his right shoulder, and fire raced through him from his fingertips to the pain centre in his brain. Sweat broke from every pore as the agony winded him. His head reeled and he wondered absurdly, how do masochists enjoy pain? Was it something they learned or a trait born in them? If he was a masochist, would he be enjoying this?

"Sean! Sean!" Rob caught him before he could fall, supported his weight and helped him down, so that he was sitting against the monstrous root of the crane. "Sean, are you all right?" His voice was sharp with dread.

"I'm okay," Sean panted. Rob's face loomed closer. Those brown eyes were wide and anxious. "Time, Robbie?"

"Just over twenty minutes," Rob told him bleakly. "We're safe here. They've got no line of sight."

"Won't stop them," Sean warned. He bent his neck back to look up into the ship's towering superstructure of cranes and forecastle. "All they need is some elevation, and they've got us."

"Bullshit," Craig said acidly. "If they shin up there, monkey up a stick, it'll be like shooting pigeons for supper. I used to be good."

From somewhere, Rob produced a feral grin. "Damn it, you're enjoying this."

"No way," Craig argued. "But I'm not going to let a pack of mongrels put a bullet in me. Not when there's a patrol boat almost on top of us." He settled back against the rusted machinery, cradled the rifle in his arms and looked Rob and Sean up and down with a deep frown. "Who in hell are you, anyway?"

Rob puffed out his cheeks and shrugged. "We came down here to get away from it all and do some fishing. We took the boat out to catch a few. You know the way they swear the fish bite best when there's a storm coming in."

"That's freshwater fish," Craig said scornfully. "Old fly-fishermen's lore."

"Freshwater?" Rob echoed blankly.

"Air pressure forces the insects down close to the surface of a lake or a pond," Craig said patiently. "Just before it starts to rain, the fish'll rise to any bait to get a good meal on board before the bugs they prey on can't fly till the rain stops. But not at sea, you don't get the bugs at sea."

"Ah... shit." Rob subsided against Sean. "We should have stayed in bed."

"Like I told you." Sean leaned his head back against the oxidising, paint-peeled steelwork. "Next time, we will."

"Next time," Rob began, but he was not really listening to Sean. "Do you hear that?"

"Hear what?" Craig leaned forward, head cocked in the direction of Rob's pointing finger.

But it was Mick Tanner who said, "There's another boat coming in."

"That's got to be the *Minuette*," Sean guessed as Craig bobbed up to look over the side, off the port bow. "You see a big, dove grey motor cruiser, looks like ten million bucks?"

"That's the one." Craig watched it wallow alongside, in the lee of the freighter, and then returned to his knees at Sean's side. "You know it?"

"We were aboard, yesterday morning. It belongs to the man who pulls your strings," Rob said sourly. "An English guy, name of Geoffrey Lewis. You know you've probably been running his cargoes of drugs and guns for years?"

"Not a chance," Craig said emphatically. "The *Lan Tao* changed hands in a straight sale, maybe six months ago. This is only our second run on this route." His brows knitted. "Drugs and guns. Jesus bloody Christ. Captain Harry Anderson wouldn't touch dope with a ten foot pole, and he sure as hell wouldn't get involved in gun running."

"Speaking of whom," Rob said tersely, "where is your skipper?"

186

Craig's seamed brown face set into granite lines. "I haven't seen Harry since Chandler and Winkler boarded with their special cargo."

"That means he's probably under cabin arrest." Sean coaxed his legs under him and looked over the side.

The sea was dark, the chop still around three or four feet, and the *Minuette* was tossing as she cut speed. Her engines shut back to idling. White light spilled from the bridge windows, and Sean glimpsed shapes inside. He recognised Geoffrey Lewis himself, and the bodyguards, Meredith and Parker. Those names and faces, Sean would never forget.

For interminable, precious minutes, the two vessels lay idle and there was no sign of movement aboard the *Lan Tao*. They would be talking via radio, Sean knew. Lewis would want a full report of the situation, and Chandler could give him only the equivalent of a Chinese puzzle. Even if the engineer patched her up, the *Lan Tao* was not going anywhere until this predicament was resolved, and her regular crew was being difficult.

The sky brightened by slow degrees as they waited. The wind was cold, and Sean held his right hand open to it, letting it strip away a little of the heat. Craig was watching the superstructure and Rob looked at his watch every thirty seconds. He held the Kalashnikov over his knees and settled back against Sean.

"I make it fifteen minutes," Sean said quietly. A clock seemed to be ticking in the basement of his mind. Craig's back was turned to them and the wind was high enough to whip away every word they said, if they spoke softly. Sean rested his left hand on Rob's knee and summoned a smile. "I love you, Rob. Part of our problem before was that I never told you often enough. If we get out of this mess, I won't make that mistake in future."

Colour flushed Rob's cheeks. "I always knew you loved me. I think I knew a few days after we met. But sometimes I just didn't know how to reach you. When I took that job, we had so little time for each other. And then, when we were together at last you'd look at me accusingly."

"Accusingly?" Sean was surprised. "I never accused you of anything!"

"That's not what it seemed like," Rob said ruefully. "The way it looked to me, you were accusing me of being the one who wasted our time, never tried to meet you halfway."

"That's crap!" Sean's voice rose. "What was I going to do, ask you to stay home, clean house and cook, be a good little housewife, because I'm the one with the brilliant job, and I want you available twenty-four hours a day?" Exasperation exhausted him. "Do you have any idea how many straight marriages have been driven on the rocks by that big-he-bull attitude? You think I'd jeopardise us for — "

"Cover!" George Craig bellowed, and out of the corner of his eye Sean saw the ex-soldier bob up, bringing the Kalashnikov to shoulder height.

Before Sean could get a grip on the Ingram, half a clip had ripped out of Craig's magazine. He was shooting high, and the first dozen rounds were wild. He was way out of practise, and he'd had no opportunity to check the alignment of the weapon. Correcting on the fly, he jinked the Kalashnikov over a little, and gave a grunt of satisfaction.

The dark shape of a man was silhouetted against the body of the crane just forward of the bridge. It was not a good perch from which to shoot, what with the roll of the ship, and he got off only a single burst of fire before Craig made contact. The body fell heavily, Sean heard it smack into the deck with a sickening sound. Craig ducked down behind the crane once more and sucked in a breath.

"They won't try that again," he panted. "Shinning up a mast? Christ, how dumb can you get?"

"Not dumb, desperate," Rob corrected. He gestured at the *Minuette*, which was standing by the freighter, riding just off the bow. "Geoffrey Lewis will have told them to winkle us out of here, no matter how they have to do it." He looked from Sean to Craig and back again. "They have options, haven't they?"

"More options than we do," Sean said acidly.

Tim shuffled forward. "They're not going to start throwing grenades around?"

"They might," Craig mused. "But if they do, they'll rip the legitimate deck cargo to tatters, and that'll cost. I'm looking at sixty grand's worth of General Motors product, for a start. So grenades will be their last resort, not their first. No, they'll try for elevation and a better sniper's nest." He jerked a thumb at the forecastle. "Up above the bridge."

The sky was like bright twilight now. Sean looked up at the towering steel cliff, amidships, outlined against the cloudscape. "Just how good are you, Sergeant?"

"The bad news is, I'm out of practise," Craig growled. "and that means I'll waste a lot of rounds. The good news is, I grabbed plenty of reloads." He positioned himself beside the crane, just forward of a stack of containers, and peered up at the forecastle. "Damn, I wish the light was better. Shooting in twilight is bad."

"Then again, Chandler's men have the same problem," Rob added pointedly.

"But then again," Craig added sourly, "Chandler's men will be shooting down, not up. It makes a difference."

Right now, Sean thought as he pulled up his collar and huddled deeply into his jacket, out of the wind, Chandler's men would be disputing over who would go up and place himself in the firing line. Every one of them had the expertise, but none had the death wish. They were not soldiers, they were highly paid professional bodyguards who expected to live long on rich fees. They had lost three men already, and several more injured, and while Lewis might be quick to issue orders, the people who carried them out would be less eager.

Minutes slithered by like warm oil. Sean counted them off silently, and at last it was Rob who murmured, "I make it ten minutes before the patrol boat finds us, Sean."

"So do I." Sean levered himself up and gazed around at the wide horizon. The world was brightening in the east, still dark in the west. "Jesus. You don't realise how big the sea is, till you're lost in the middle of it. I don't see the ship yet."

"She must still be miles away, you'd never spot her without binoculars. Grey hull against grey sea. Give them a chance." Rob looked along at Tim and Mick. "You two okay?"

"Yes," Mick began shakily, all too obviously a lie.

"No," Tim said curtly. He thrust out his chin. "It just occurred to me, there's no way out of this for us. If those goons capture you or kill you, Mick and me know about the illegal cargo now. What the fuck happens to us?"

The question had haunted Sean also, and the answer was painfully obvious. He glanced at Rob, and Rob nodded. "They can't let you walk away," Sean said quietly, under the sough of the sea and the steady growl of the *Minuette*'s idling engines. "You know that."

"We managed to work that out," Mick said bitterly.

"Are you wishing you'd jumped us, when we were using the shortwave?" Rob arched a brow at the boys. "You could have handed us to Chandler, maybe bought yourself some credit with him."

Perhaps they were thinking along those lines, but neither Tim nor Mick could answer before George Craig shouted across their voices. "Get down, stay down — they're up on top of the bridge!"

Heart thudding wildly, Sean shuffled sideways, hugging the ice-cold forward surface of the root of the crane. Rob pressed against him at his left side, Tim was a trembling huddle on his right. A gull wheeled overhead against the silver-grey dawn sky, and a dozen rounds coughed out of Craig's weapon.

Answering shots peppered down from the forecastle, spitting and whanging off the steelwork around them. Sean pulled his arms and legs in tight and held his breath as he remembered what he knew about ricochets.

When a bullet bounced off something solid, although a lot of its potential energy was spent it was also chewed up, twisted, by its first impact. It hit its next target and scythed through like a 'hollow nose' round, infinitely more dangerous than a fresh ammunition.

Fever swirled around in his head. Sean's heart was racing, his body sweating while every extremity but his hand was painfully cold.

Rob knew. He dragged Sean down, pulled his face into the curve of his shoulder and threw an arm across Sean's head. There was no real protection he could offer, but the strength of his gesture was its emotional support, and Sean clung tight to him.

Shots smacked into the deck cargo, others slammed into the aft side of the crane and made the steel chime, like mallet blows. Craig was firing intermittently, but this time around Chandler's men were taking no senseless risks.

"Five minutes, Sean," Rob shouted over the noise. "The *Newcastle* must be able to get a visual sighting on us by now! She'll only be a few miles away. Sean!"

The adrenalin surge of fear hit the fever head-on, and Sean's whole body was suddenly quivering. He cursed himself but it was difficult even to think clearly. He was half aware of the shots that continued to pelt down from the forecastle, and of the lull when Craig ducked down into concealment to change magazines. Tim was trying to reload for him, a clumsy novice who spilled a handful of ammunition onto the deck, earning himself a furious bellow.

"Here, for chrissakes, use this!" Rob yelled, and Sean glimpsed the Kalashnikov as Rob passed it over to him, butt-first.

Craig locked it onto single shot to make the magazine last, and the weapon cracked repeatedly, hurting Sean's eardrums. Rob was shouting, but the words were blurred, and Sean twisted, trying to make sense of the scene.

Two, possibly three men were firing from the superstructure above the bridge. In the half light they were difficult to see, and Craig's frustration began to get the better of him. Cursing, he shuffled forward, perhaps to get a clearer or easier shot.

"Get back here!" Rob yelled. "Craig! No!"

One split second of rashness was all it took. With a hoarse cry, more of surprise than pain, Craig spun and flung himself onto the deck. His arms and legs straggled untidily. The weapon Rob had given him only moments ago clattered away out of reach. Tim screamed, lunged after his uncle, but Rob caught him by the sleeves and dragged him back.

"No, Tim, no!" Rob dumped the blond boy into Mick Tanner's lap. "Hold onto him, for God's sake."

All this, Sean saw in a flurry of lurid colours and echoing sounds while his heart raced as if it could escape from his chest. The hail of shots from up above was now unchallenged, and they could only cram themselves into the scant cover afforded by the crane. George Craig's eyes were wide open, staring vacantly at the morning sky. Blood oozed from his shoulder and the side of his chest, startlingly red. Sean looked into the dead face and felt only numbness. Shock would assault him later, but for the moment he felt nothing. The complete absence of feeling was surreal.

And then silence descended as the gunfire ceased all at once. Rob's panting was a warm, moist draft against the side of Sean's neck. Sean's left fingers searched for the Ingram and pulled it closer. What an absurdly insubstantial weapon it seemed. It was useless in these circumstances, but he needed to feel it against his palm.

"Where's the Navy ship?" Tim whispered. "Where the fuck are they? They said they'd be here!"

Rob gathered himself, pushed up against the steel, shoulders rasping against the rusted metal, and his wide eyes searched the dawn twilight sea. Sean looked up at him, mutely entreating, but Rob shook his head. Not yet.

The voice whipping down from the forecastle took none of them by surprise. "You want to come out of there now?" Chandler bawled. "You're just wasting my time. If you want to live, you have five minutes. I have a whole crate of grenades up here, but one is all it's going to take to root you out of there. Do you hear me?"

"We hear you," Rob shouted, though he did not move a muscle. "Go to hell, Chandler."

"Me? Maybe I will," Chandler admitted. "But you bastards will be there before me. You have five minutes!"

"Five minutes," Sean echoed. He dragged his good hand over his face. "Take another look, Rob. Careful!"

With exaggerated caution, Rob pushed his legs straight and searched the grey, heaving sea. Sean saw his lips compress, saw the tiny shake of his head. A sound of anguish issued from Tim's throat, and the boy pounded the crane with the sides of both fists.

"The *Minuette* is coming around," Rob said. "Can you hear their engines? I think she's moving alongside. Lewis could put more men aboard."

Sean leaned back against the crane and closed his eyes. His good arm snaked around Rob's waist, pulled him closer, and when Rob turned toward him Sean hunted for his mouth. The kiss was cold and brief, but for a moment Rob's tongue was warm in Sean's mouth, and while Sean watched, Rob calmed visibly. The hard lines of his face softened.

"We don't have much time left," Sean murmured. "Tell me you love me. I want to hear it."

"You know I do." Rob's fingertips traced his brow, his lips. "I always did."

Always will? Sean smiled. It would not be long now, come what may. Knowing that the nightmare was almost over brought a sense of relief which lapped his feverish mind.

Until they heard a bellow from the superstructure behind them, a heavy but discreet thud on the deck cargo, and then the unmistakable metallic clatter as a small steel object hit the deck and rolled. Sean's vision and hearing seemed to shatter into a kaleidoscope of images.

"Get down!" Rob shouted, and flung himself over Sean's half-prone body. Tim and Mick went down flat, arms over their heads, an instant before thunder seemed to peal out of the air, so close that Sean felt the wave of heat from the eruption.

His ears were still ringing when he heard another metal impact, another sound of some small steel object rolling. Rob was panting against his face, and Sean held his breath, waiting for the blast.

It was closer this time, close enough for his ears to fill with pain and his brains to rattle in his skull. One more like that, and all Chandler would have to do was come down here and pick up the pieces.

And then Rob was moving. "Sean, come on — Sean!"

A thud hit the tarpaulin covers on the deck cargo not ten feet behind them.

Tim and Mick were up and moving, too fast for Sean to grasp what they were doing. And then he knew. Rob's right hand clenched into his left arm, pulling him to his feet, shoving and heaving, and Sean bunched the muscles in his thighs for effort. He hurled himself out and over.

The deck was on the down-roll as they went over the side. Twenty feet below, the sea was a heaving crucible of molten lead. Above, the grenade burst like a thunderclap, but Sean barely noticed it.

Down — down, falling for less than a second — why did it feel like minutes? Rob was almost close enough for Sean to reach him, his arms windmilling as he steadied himself in mid-fall. Sean held his legs together, flailed his own arms in a desperate attempt to hit the water cleanly.

A rattle of shots pelted toward them, not from the old ship but from the gorgeous, graceful shape of the *Minuette*. She was no more than thirty yards away, engines running to bring her about in a tight arc as Sean sucked in a breath and the water rushed up fast.

And then, a wail of sound, a piercing siren, from where, Sean did not know. A voice boomed over a loudhailer, but he caught only the first words before he went under.

"Cease fire! Lay down your weapons, or we —"

The water forced into Sean's nose and swirled over his head as he plunged deep, driven down by the energy of the fall. The cold was shocking, the sense of suffocation immediate, and he threshed, kicked, fighting back to the surface.

His first thought was for Rob, but he need not have worried. Like most Australians, Rob had swum like a fish since he was a child. He was splashing furiously toward his lover as Sean broke surface, and the next he knew, strong arms had circled him, helping to buoy him up.

"Sean! You all right?" Rob rasped urgently. "Sean!"

"I'm okay. Where are the others?" The sense of responsibility for Tim and Mick was burdensome.

"There." Rob pointed. "They hit the water okay, they're safe. Jesus — look at that!"

Treading water with regular, measured kicks, Sean turned to follow the line of his arm. Exhaustion was not far away, but the sight before him banished his weariness.

Seen from the water, the patrol boat was a leviathan. As warships went, she was a minnow, but from this vantage point she seemed immense and terrible, sharp-bowed and predatory.

The *Minuette* was manoeuvring, showing her tail to the *Newcastle*. The patrol boat had cut back speed as she approached the freighter, and on the deck Sean glimpsed figures. Three men wearing white flash hoods stood by the Bofors gun on the foredeck. The gun traversed, swinging around to follow Lewis's cruiser.

It might have been an absurd display of strength, but then Sean looked back at the *Minuette* and his heart skipped. On the transom, over the fancy lettering spelling out the craft's name, were Meredith and Parker. The two men were struggling against the roll and pitch of the deck, fighting to align a weapon.

Sean knew a rocket launcher when he saw one. So did the lookout aboard the *Newcastle*. A LAWS rocket, impacting at the waterline, would hurt the patrol boat badly. How many of these skirmishes had Lewis fought against police and coastal patrol craft, up in the islands? If he was here today, he had won them all. Sean shook water out of his eyes and twisted his neck to look up and back at the deck of the *Newcastle*.

As she approached, he began to lose sight of figures on the foredeck, but he did not have to see them to know what they were doing.

On the transom of the *Minuette*, Meredith and Parker were shouting urgently. Sean could not make out the words, but as he blinked the salt from his eyes he heard the rushing whoosh of a launching rocket.

Wide — it was wide by a few yards. The flaretail raced by the bow of the *Newcastle* and on, out over the sea. Sean spun in the water, kicking to keep his head above the choppy surface, and mouthed a mute obscenity as he focused on the transom of the *Minuette*.

Meredith and Parker were reloading.

As she came closer, the drum of the warship's engines began to fill Sean's head. Did he hear, or did he imagine the voice from the deck high above them, that shouted piercingly, "Four rounds, rapid fire, engage!"

The 40mm Bofors gun had a deep, dull report. Like someone using a baseball bat to hit a box full of carpets, Sean thought feverishly. But there was no mistaking its firepower. Each clip held only four rounds. Four were enough.

The first scythed through the bridge of the *Minuette*. The second ripped into the deck and exploded through the side of the hull. The third smashed into the engines, silencing them forever. The final round discovered Geoffrey Lewis's precious cargo.

Grenades, ammunition and explosives erupted like a volcano come suddenly to life in the middle of the ocean. Heat and blazing debris hurled in every direction, pounded into the side of the freighter and into the bow of the patrol boat. Orange-yellow flame blossomed briefly as the *Minuette* ripped itself to blazing shreds.

The shock wave knocked the breath out of Sean's lungs. Rob's hands clawed for him, almost caught him, but the churning sea teased them apart. Water swirled over Sean's head, dark, grey-green. His lungs burned and his senses dimmed. The weariness that had dragged at him like a weight of iron manacles for hours seized him now, and he felt the strength drain from his body.

The last he knew was a sense of peace, before a warm darkness closed over his head.

Fourteen

WARMTH AND muted lighting wreathed him, and he stretched right down to the joints of his toes before he cracked open his eyelids. For a moment he could not focus, and his ears were filled with an odd, off-key singing, but Sean was immediately aware of the presence beside him, and turned readily toward it.

"You're awake," Rob said quietly. "I was starting to wonder if I should buzz for the medic. You've been out for hours."

Sean's left hand was held between both of Rob's. He was lying on a soft surface, swathed in linen, one blanket over him. As he coaxed his eyes to focus he saw pale coloured walls, a locker and chair, which seemed to fill the tiny space. Rob's face was close beside him, looking large against the background of the tiny, closet-sized compartment. Rob was dressed in a pair of white slacks, a little too large for him, otherwise bare-chested in the warmth of the cabin.

"What happened?" Sean's throat produced a peculiar bullfrog croak.

"You passed out after the *Minuette* blew itself into the middle of next week." Rob sat on the side of the bed, leaned over him and kissed his throat. "The crew pulled us, and Tim and Mick, out of the water. They boarded the *Lan Tao* and searched every square foot of it — with the gleeful assistance of the freighter's crew and skipper." He kissed the planes of Sean's breast. "There were no survivors from the *Minuette*. She went up like a bomb. She must have been loaded with munitions for the rebels."

Recollection barrelled into Sean, and he took a deep breath. "Tim and Mick are okay?"

"More or less. They're shocky after what they've been through, and they can't quite make themselves believe George Craig is dead. The doc gave them some pills." Rob lifted up his legs and lay precariously on the side of the narrow bunk, warm along Sean's body.

"So how do you feel?"

"I don't know. Hot, and woozy," Sean admitted.

"Not surprising." Rob's flat palm stroked Sean's breast, mid-riff and belly, dipping down into the bedding. "They did your hand as soon as we were brought on board. It's been cleaned, stitched and packed with cortisone. You're full of antibiotics, so you should start to feel better soon. The cold of the sea stripped the fever out of you. Trying to keep your body temperature up was the hardest part, for an hour. Your problem now is what the doc referred to as a mild case of blood poisoning, but you've had enough antibiotics to kill a horse, so you'll feel better soon."

"I think I already do." Sean stretched again, shuffled over to make a little more space, and turned his face to Rob's. His face was smooth, he smelt of soap and cologne. Their lips met, and Sean tasted coffee, chocolate.

"The sickbay's full," Rob told him softly, speaking against Sean's hair. "Last night they pulled the crew off a trawler that was break-ing up in the storm. The injuries are pretty bad. So they told me to keep an eye on you and put us in here for the trip home."

"Home?" Sean lifted his right hand and blinked in a little sur-prise at the professional dressing and splinting. Beneath it, his hand was still fiercely painful, but his head was clearing little by little.

"Adelaide," Rob added. "The doc said that hand will mend. You'll have a beauty of a scar, but they've stopped the infection."

"Saved my fingers," Sean added. "I... was worried." He looked up into Rob's dark eyes. "What about Chandler?"

Rob jerked a thumb at the ship around them. "I'd like to tell you I heroically ran him down and beat crap out of him, but the truth is he and Winkler are in custody. Most of their merry men, too. Captain Rodgers took a statement from them an hour ago, and they're falling over themselves to rat on the late Geoffrey Lewis. If they share the blame around, implicate everyone in sight, they can probably shorten their own sentences." He paused and drew his lips over Sean's nose. "Captain Rodgers wants to talk to us, too. Tim and Mike are too punchy to make much sense."

"And Captain Anderson?" Sean heaved a deep yawn and rubbed his back against the sheet.

"Was found in his cabin, stoned out of his skull," Rob said drily. When Sean's eyes widened, he nodded. "It seems he argued with Chandler, and Chandler shot him up, same as he doped you. It certainly keeps a guy quiet for a while." One fingertip circled Sean's nipples. "I told the doc you'd been drugged yesterday, and he was careful with what else he gave you."

"Thanks." Sean arched his head into the pillow, buried his face in Rob's bare chest. "You smell wonderful."

"They let me use the crew facilities. I had a shower, shave, large meal, and they treated me to a small medicinal brandy," Rob told him. "I'm supposed to call the medic as soon as you wake. They want to check you over again."

He had leaned over to touch the intercom, but Sean caught his hand. "Not yet. As soon as they know I'm awake, the skipper'll be in here asking a million questions."

So Rob settled against him once more, and covered his mouth languidly. Sean opened to it, surrendered to it, and emerged flushed and breathless.

"There's a reward," Rob told him huskily.

"For what?" Sean groaned pleasantly as Rob's tongue explored the sensitive folds and creases of his ear.

"Australia, New Zealand, France and New Guinea have posted rewards for information leading to the closure of Lewis's operation. He's been a flea in the ear of four countries for years. The governments couldn't figure out how the drugs and guns were moving around, or where they were coming from." Rob sat up with a smile, teased down the bedding and surveyed Sean's well-muscled torso. "They should pay out enough to cover the damage."

His hands were magic. Sean's thoughts shattered apart as Rob stroked him, and he asked, "Damage?"

Rob pinched his nipples, returning Sean to the present with a start. "My Toyota, and the *Fancy Dancer*! The car is on its side in a ditch on Lightning Ridge, and the boat will be a total write-off. We didn't secure her, we just got out and ran. The storm would have picked her up and dashed her on the rocks."

"Oh." Sean blinked up at him. "Yes, of course." With his good hand he reached up and touched Rob's face. "You were great."

"Just trying to stay alive," Rob said dismissively. "I'd have been dead a dozen times over if it hadn't been for you."

"Mutual admiration society?" Sean wrinkled his nose and urged Rob down to kiss again. When they parted, he licked his lips and summoned a faint, tired smile. "Maybe you'd better ring for the medic. I won't get anything to eat until they've taken a look at me."

"You hungry?" Rob touched the intercom. "You are better!"

A voice crackled out of the little speaker, and Rob turned away to inform someone called Gary that the patient had rejoined the living. Sean was not listening. He stroked Rob's chest and back as he spoke to the medic, but when Rob had turned off the intercom he stepped away from the bed and gave Sean a slightly reproving look.

"You be good till we're off this ship."

"What do you mean, be good?" Sean struggled to sit up, felt the spin of his head, the weakness of his muscles. Heat rushed through him, and he sagged back down again. "Rob, my love, I don't think I have the option of being bad."

Rob laughed quietly as he pulled a crew jersey over his head and shoved his feet into deck shoes. "We'll be in Adelaide by tonight. They don't think it's necessary for you to go to hospital, so we can go home. The police will take Chandler and Winkler into custody, and I guess that's where the real fun will start. We're major witnesses, but I'll try to get them to put off the interviews for a day or two, till you're over this."

A knock at the narrow door announced the medic, and Rob fell silent as he admitted a young seaman. Sean lay submissively, let himself be poked and prodded, his temperature and heartbeat measured and recorded. Dark, crop-haired little Gary Provine promised him another shot of antibiotics in four hours, plus a card of tablets to follow the shots, and repacked his bag.

"Food," Sean muttered as he sat up once more and swung his legs off the bed. He was wearing someone else's underwear, a pair of boxer shorts that felt peculiar. "I'm starved."

"I'll fetch you something to eat," Rob told him. "I know my way around by now. You want to tell the skipper he's awake, Gary? He's about as lucid as he ever gets." Sean gave him a glare as Provine withdrew to the door.

"And clothes," Sean insisted. "I'm not a bloody invalid!" He gestured with the wrapped, splinted hand and fixed Provine with a hard look. "Will it heal properly? I'll use the fingers, won't I?"

The medic grinned impishly. "You'll have to skip your violin practise for a couple of weeks... and use your left hand for the other thing. But if you keep it clean and let it rest, it'll be fine."

"I'll be good. Scouts' honour," Sean promised, saluting left-handed. As Provine stepped out, he pointed Rob at the door. "Clothes and food, not necessarily in that order!"

The door closed behind Rob, leaving Sean alone in a cabin the size of a broom closet. He gave the walls a distrustful look, got his feet on the floor and stood carefully. His senses spun, his legs trembled, but he was already aware of tendrils of strength returning. In a day or two, he might feel as if he had suffered a bout of 'flu. He knew how lucky he had been.

The engines were drumming, driving the patrol boat southwest. She would round the southernmost tip of the Fleurieu Peninsula and turn north, into the storm-battered Gulf Saint Vincent, where Adelaide sprawled along the east coast. Rob called it home.

Since the moment he arrived, Sean had been undecided what to make of it, and lately he had been aware of a growing restlessness. The months he and Rob had spent drifting apart were almost enough to make Sean move on. The job with Aurora Petroleum was up in eight more months. They would ask him to stay, offer him extended working visas and the opportunity to apply for permanent resident status, if not actual citizenship.

Still, Sean was not sure if he wanted to go that far, and tie himself down to what he thought of as a small town in a remote state, in a part of the world that was considered obscure in the places where the lights shone brightest.

But of one thing he was certain. Wherever he went next, he wanted Rob with him. Nothing else mattered so much as that.

The door swung open without a warning knock, which told him it was Rob. Juggling an armful of clothes and a tray of food, Rob stepped inside, but before Sean could embrace him he glimpsed another man, right on Rob's heels.

Lieutenant-Commander James Rodgers was forty, just on the threshold of middle age. He was not good looking, but his face was strong, his features powerful beneath a receding hairline. His uniform was crisp, his whole manner poised and proper. He gave Sean a smile in lieu of a handshake, and stood in a corner of the cramped cabin as Rob helped Sean into the pair of uniform slacks and crew jersey.

"You wanted a statement from us?" Sean asked as Rob zipped him up. Damn, but it would be awkward, managing one-handed.

"More of a report." Rodgers gestured with a clipboard, and uncapped a pen. "We'll dock in Port Adelaide and you'll be met by a detective from the police. They'll address the legal aspect of all this. What I need from you is a report for my own superiors... how the hell did you come to be aboard that ship? Where did Mr Chandler come from, and where was that vessel, the *Minuette*, until it appeared here?" He gestured aft. "We interviewed Chandler and his

South African friend separately and heard two entirely different stories. I'm hoping you might be able to shed some light."

"We only know part of Lewis's business," Rob said cautiously as Sean began to eat. "We only know what we saw, and that wasn't much. You'd probably learn more from Captain Anderson."

"I talked to him, too, before we got underway, while his engineers were repairing the damage." Rodgers leaned against the bulkhead and gave them a rueful look. "Apparently you gentlemen wreaked a great deal of chaos. It took over two hours to restart the engines. We stood by the *Lan Tao* while she was adrift, of course. She was only two kilometres off the shore when the diesels restarted. Captain Anderson said the damage was... extensive, and expensive."

"It was," Sean said through a mouthful of steak and onion pie. "I know where to hit a ship to hurt it."

"You have experience on merchant marine vessels?" Rodgers was making notes.

"Some. I worked for a oil company in the States before I came here. I'm with Aurora now." He looked at Rob, who had seated himself on the side of the bunk beside him. "Lewis owned the *Lan Tao*, so there shouldn't be any come-backs about the damage we did."

Rodgers looked up at them over the clipboard. "That ship is headed for a wrecking yard just north of Bombay! She's uninsured, registered in Laos, and she looks like a death trap to me."

"You got that right." Sean propped his hand on his shoulder to ease its throb. "Did Chandler or Winkler say where Lewis was getting his guns?"

"Yes." Rodgers's brows arched. "Winkler was the source, acting as agent for an enterprising entrepreneur based in Johannesburg. It seems that sometimes a shipment of weapons intended for some war in Africa is diverted to New Caledonia or Bougainville, and they're shipped via Australia out of geographic necessity. Private enterprise." He made a note on his clipboard. "Now, tell me about the *Minuette*."

The story consumed most of an hour. Rob told most of it while Sean ate and then stretched out on the bunk and rested. Fatigue was a constant companion, and the effort of dressing, eating and talking quickly tired him. Rodgers meticulously took down the details. His brow creased and his face set in bitter lines as he heard them out. This patrol boat might be reassigned to the Coral Sea on her next duty cruise. His men could be facing many weapons which found their way into those waters by this route.

At last Rob fell silent, and Rodgers recapped his pen. "There's not much more we can tell you," Sean said tiredly. "It was just dumb luck that we were on the *Minuette*. We... just don't know enough about fishing." He and Rob shared a wry smile. "It was only chance that brought us to this part of the country at all."

"And ignorance that sent us out on the water when Lewis's boat was in the area," Rob added. "If we'd known more about the feeding habits of fish..." his face darkened and he looked away.

He was thinking about George Craig, Sean guessed. "You brought Mr Craig's body aboard?" he asked Rodgers.

"Yes, we have him. His family in Perth will be notified, and his nephew and Mr Tanner will be going home for the funeral." Rodgers stirred and opened the door. "Why don't you get some rest, Mr Brodie? You look like you need it. Don't hesitate to call for help if you feel ill."

Simple weariness had overhauled Sean, and he was pleased to sag, flat on the bunk. But he held out his good hand to Rob. "Don't go, Robbie."

Rob took his hand, sat on the side of the bed and stroked Sean's face. "I'm not going anywhere. Not ever."

Sean looked up at him. "You might be going plenty of places. But not without me. You ever wanted to take a look at the States?"

"Often," Rob admitted, "especially after I came to know you. I haven't done much travelling — I haven't even seen most of this country." He studied Sean with a frown. "When your time's up with Aurora, you're leaving, aren't you? I thought you would be. That's what worried me the most, all the time we were drifting apart. I knew I was really losing you."

"Maybe," Sean admitted. He brought Rob's hand to his lips and kissed the palm. "But I'm not leaving not without you." He summoned a smile. "I want you to come home with me."

"San Francisco, New Orleans, New York?" Rob teased.

"That's one hell of a grip of geography," Sean observed as he settled into the mattress. "Come home with me, Robbie."

Rob's fingers slipped through his as Rob moved away to let him rest. "Count on it."

"That's settled then," Sean murmured lucidly as sleep stole over his mind.

More action-packed adventure by Mel Keegan:

Mel Keegan
DEATH'S HEAD

On the high-tech designer worlds of the 23rd century, the lethal designer drug Angel has become an epidemic disease. Kevin Jarrat and Jerry Stone are joint captains in the paramilitary NARC force sent in to combat the Death's Head drug syndicate that controls the vast spaceport of Chell. Under the NARC code of non-involvement, each of the two friends hides his deeper desire for the other. When Stone is kidnapped and forced onto Angel, Jarrat's love for him is his only chance of survival, but the price is that their minds remain permanently linked.

"Unputdownable. Keegan has taken the two-dimensional Marvel/ DC comic strip and made it flesh, and what flesh" — *HIM*

"A powerful futuristic thriller" — *Capital Gay*

ISBN 0 85449 162 7
UK £6.95/US $10.95/AUS $19.95

Mel Keegan
EQUINOX

Angel — a lethal synthetic drug so pervasive and deadly that it has built empires and torn down worlds. Equinox Industries is a commercial monopoly mining the gas giant Zeus, challenged by a growing faction for its environmental record, and suspected of manufacturing Angel. Enter Kevin Jarratt and Jerry Stone, joint captains in the paramilitary NARC force at war with the Angel syndicates, and lovers whose minds have been bonded together. In their second action-packed adventure, the heroes of *Death's Head* need their empathic powers as well as the 23rd century's technological wizardry to outwit their corporate enemies.

ISBN 0 85449 200 3
UK £6.95/US $10.95/AUS $17.95

Mel Keegan
FORTUNES OF WAR

Seven years ago, in the spring of 1588, two young men fell in love: an Irish mercenary serving the Spanish ambassador in London, and the son of an English earl. After Dermot had to leave England, Robin eventually despaired of hearing from him again. But when Sir Francis Drake leads a fleet bound for Panama, Robin sails with him to ransom a kidnapped brother. His ship is attached by privateers, commanded by Dermot Channon. The couple's adventures on the Spanish Main make a swashbuckling romance in the best gay pirate tradition.

"With more historical detail than you would expect, *Fortunes of War* is a fine example of this genre" — *Gay Times*, London

ISBN 0 85449 211 9
UK £7.95/US $10.95/AUS $17.95

Mike Seabrook
FULL CIRCLE

An RAF bomb-aimer in the Second World War, shot down over the Bay of Biscay, Brian Hales has already had to overcome a crisis of conscience when his lover ended their relationship and went to prison as a pacifict. The risks of attempted escape are his next hurdle, bringing him into conflict with his superior officers in the prisoner-of-war camp where he is eventually taken. But his most disturbing experience is still to come, when he finds himself falling in love with a young German guard.

This author's novels on contemporary themes have won wide acclaim. "I loved the book" wrote Jilly Cooper on *Unnatural Relations.* "A spot-on psychological narrative," London's *Gay Times* called *Conduct Unbecoming.* In a new departure, Mike Seabrook has tackled a historical theme and brought his keen insight for personal relations in an all-male world to bear on the complexities of friendship with the enemy.

ISBN 0 85449 242 9
UK £9.95/US $14.95/AUS $19.95

Gay Men's Press books can be ordered from any bookshop in the UK, North America and Australia, and from specialised bookshops elsewhere.

If you prefer to order by mail, please send cheque or postal order payable to *Book Works* for the full retail price plus £2.00 postage and packing to:

Book Works (Dept. B), PO Box 3821, London N5 1UY
phone/fax: (0171) 609 3427

For payment by Access/Eurocard/Mastercard/American Express/ Visa, please give number, expiry date and signature.

Name and address in block letters please:

Name
—————————————————————————————————

Address
—————————————————————————————————

—————————————————————————————————

—————————————————————————————————